**"YOU ARE TOO COMMON TO TOUCH ME. . . ."**

Eva's eyes blazed at him. She could still hurt him, too, and she wanted to.

"I hate your dirty hands," she hissed, "and your ugly, common face."

Rall flushed dark-red, panting, then buried his face in her flesh, scratching her with his dark beard. He unpinned her long, soft, reddish-brown hair and combed it roughly with his fingers, bringing tears to her eyes, but she did not cry out. She could not stop him, after that . . .

She had never known passion or even imagined it, never suspected its strong ties between men and women she knew, and, in the end, it was his passion that awakened her. His passion, not her own. His was sufficient.

"Oh, yes! Eva! Oh!" he cried, and her eyes opened wide with pain and astonishment and she was lost in the feeling even as she feared it, and clung to him. . . .

# FAREWELL, MY SOUTH

Cynthia Van Hazinga

*Produced by R. Smith Kiliper*
*Based upon original historical research*
*by Gary J. Neeleman*

BANTAM BOOKS
TORONTO · NEW YORK · LONDON · SYDNEY

FAREWELL, MY SOUTH
*A Bantam Book / May 1984*



ISBN 0-553-23988-0

*Published simultaneously in the United States and Canada*

---

*Bantam Books are published by Bantam Books, Inc. Its trademark, consisting of the words "Bantam Books" and the portrayal of a rooster, is Registered in U.S. Patent and Trademark Office and in other countries. Marca Registrada. Bantam Books, Inc., 666 Fifth Avenue, New York, New York 10103.*

---

PRINTED IN THE UNITED STATES OF AMERICA

H 0 9 8 7 6 5 4 3 2 1

# FAREWELL, MY SOUTH

# Prologue

Texas. A warm spring night. The black sky cupped close over the clear river and the sweet, rich bottomlands reeling with rank growth and tangled into a tropical thicket, dense and dark and full of secrets.

It was a world where weeds and broad-leaved trees shot up six feet in two months to choke the stagnant swamps along the river. It was a watery world alive with frogs and mud turtles, bottom-feeding fish and stick-legged blue cranes. Alligators sank out of sight and fat water moccasins slid off moss-green logs.

The night was noisy with crickets, cicadas, hoarse frogs. A hunting owl rustled leaves, found his perch, closed his talons around a branch.

On the riverbank, in the clearing below the owl's tree, on the moist grass pressed into a sticky, spicy-smelling carpet they lay, two young bodies locked together.

"Will you, Miss Elinor?" he begged. "May I? I want to so much! I waited so long." His thin fingers fumbled at the layers of cotton and white lace that swathed her like a Muslim.

"Yes, yes . . ." she whispered, her mouth on his, drinking his need and quenching it, feeding him first love. Her hands fluttered over his thin shoulders, square under the faded threadbare gray of his uniform, touched his long, smooth hair, his neck dry and dark with sunburn. I will! Why not? We have waited long enough. We have come into a new age. None of the old rules matter. Everything is changed and this is my duty. After giving everything else, I am giving myself to the Cause . . . the Cause, lost now although some will never say so. Others say there is nothing left, but they are the old people, not us. Not I. I cannot die when I have not yet lived—I will not, I will go on.

His body quivered, his long bare legs shuddering; the toes of his cracked boots dug into the soft earth. She gasped, choking on the wet night air, and mosquitoes whined in her ears.

His breath was harsh, rasping; he kissed her greedily. She smelled of soap and sunshine; he was still rank from four years of war, gamy with the smell of wet tents and marching in filthy boots, of countless ghastly moments of overwhelming fear in the wilderness of death.

Surprise drowned her thoughts, and then, the wildness of her beating heart washed her into a new place, carried there by his passion, swept past pain into an elemental rapture, a blind, full-tilt pleasure, a never-expected feeling that filled her eyes with stars. She called out for more.

"Oh! Oh, yes!" She would take his last strength, take all she needed to go on. She loved him! She loved all of life, everything, and only wanted more.

He groaned and trembled violently, then collapsed into her softness and inhaled her dark hair. Their breathing hushed, settled down to the shared clamor of heartbeats, their ears opened to the world expanding beyond their own skin. Everything stopped.

The silence held, swelled, then was gradually eaten away at its edges by the insects, the birds, the rustling leaves, the river itself, the dark heavy river moving past the clearing still singing its own song. Neither of them could move.

And then, gunshots.

To him, it was yesterday, the warning reports of an attacking Yankee patrol, a moment of breathless panic relived. He jumped to his feet, his body gaunt from war, from bad food and constant marching, knife-hard and wiry, alert as a wolf.

"What is it?" Her conscience stabbed her. Was it God's immediate punishment for their sin?

She lifted herself from the drift of white petticoats. She blinked at the starlight, reached out for him, but he stumbled, unmoored by his memories of other gunshots, launched into hopeless confusion. He began to run.

"Wait!"

"Come on!"

But he was gone and he had left her alone. She reached for one petticoat and a camisole. Her feet were bare. The gunshots were very near, and now she could hear the men yelling above the thud of hooves and the snorting of the horses. She stumbled and began to run, but where?

She was alone in the blind labyrinth of the river-bank thicket. She didn't know which way to run, but she must. Desperately, she turned back and flung herself at the owl's tree, gasping, branches scratching her bare arms and catching at her petticoat.

Leaves closed around her. She found the highest steady branch and clung to the tree's trunk, pressed her cheek against its cool smoothness and struggled to catch her breath. The mosquitoes settled in on her face and neck. She looked up, surprised to see the same old yellow moon hanging like a lantern in the west.

Dear Lord, she prayed, believing as never before, save me now and I will never do it again. She choked back sobs and clung to the tree, fighting nausea and panic, feeling her thigh muscles aching, shivering with fear. Who was riding here by the river? Why?

When the riders entered the clearing she recognized two of them. One was Jesse Rall, formerly the overseer on Buck Wilson's plantation, a massive black-haired man with a sweeping handlebar mustache and a florid complexion. The other was her own fourteen-year-old brother, Laray Holt Richler.

She leaned forward in surprise, called, "Laray!" Papa wouldn't allow Laray Holt to be out riding at night. What was he doing here? Her voice was lost in the volley of shots and then she did not cry out again, but bore silent witness to the scene below.

"Here they come!" Jesse Rall yelled, and she saw all the men and her brother pull hoods and white sheets down over themselves so that they looked like ghosts. She saw five more hooded white-swaddled men ride into the clearing, driving two Negroes ahead of them like cattle, whipping them so that they jumped like frogs to stay on their feet.

Elinor recognized the Negroes. Everybody knew them; they were the Ruffins who had bought the old Gleason place. They were fancy niggers, very young and very light-skinned.

Both Ruffins were already hurt. The man was half naked and his back and shoulders were bleeding. Blood ran from the woman's mouth and her eyes were swollen shut. Elinor stared without understanding, too frightened to move. What was Laray Holt doing with this ugly gang? Why did they pretend to be ghosts?

The men passed a stoneware jug. "Haven't had a drink since Shiloh," one of them said. "Damn, I'm thirsty!"

Some of the men carried wood and torches made of poles wrapped with oil-soaked rags. Choking black smoke spiraled up from the torches and they cast a horrible red light. The Ruffins clung together like frightened children.

Jesse Rall grabbed the woman away from her husband. "Shall I give it to you one more time? Have you had enough?" He laughed as she twisted away.

"Stop, in God's name! Spare her, for Christ's sake," Ruffin begged.

Rall cut at him with his horsewhip, slitting the skin across his face from ear to ear. Blood leapt to the cut, tracing a grotesque grin.

"Tie 'em back to back," Rall ordered, and Laray Holt helped another man bind the Ruffins with rawhide strips back to back to a beechwood cross.

"Have mercy on her!" Ruffin shrieked, spitting blood.

The white men laughed. One of them heaped branches around the Ruffins and splashed them with oil. Elinor hid her face, but she heard the fire catch and the woman scream, heard the horses shifting restlessly around the clearing, smelled the acrid smoke.

When she looked again, the flames were burning spears and the masked men stood in a circle, passing the jug. The smell was sickening and the woman had begun to howl.

Elinor looked down on the scene from hell. Then there was a clear snap and the cross fell forward onto

Ruffin. The fire raced over his wife, covered her, but he scrambled out from underneath. He was free. He began to run toward the river.

The dense black smoke hid him from the men's view, but Elinor saw him from above, saw him trailing flames, saw him hit the water, saw Laray Holt running after him, heard the volley of shots, saw her brother stop, jerk backward, fall.

"No! No!" she screamed. Her voice was lost in the yells and gunshots.

"Get that nigger! Catch him!" Jesse Rall ordered, and they were all running, the horses splashing and whinnying, only the woman's burning body left in the empty clearing.

Elinor let go of the branch. She dropped from the tree like a white moth, found her feet and ran for home.

# Chapter One

Everything looked the same, or if not quite the same, it was the most unchanged place Tyler Ashby had seen in four years. He paused, tall and erect, a rail-thin man in a faded, patched gray uniform, his head bent so that a lock of bleached hair crossed his scarred forehead. Intense, he looked everywhere, listening greedily, sensing with all his faculties, savoring the sights and sounds and smells of home.

Home. How often he had dreamed of it, remembering it and all it represented—a world once perfect in itself, then challenged, conquered, destroyed. How completely he had despaired of being here again, of standing here at the tall white wooden gate, looking over the dense hedge of sweet-smelling honeysuckle toward the huge white clapboard house with its enormous porches and the wide flight of stairs that led up to the front door.

Open. The door stood open in the warm July twilight and a shaft of yellow lamplight spilled out onto the porch. He still paused, his heart pounding, in no hurry to end this moment, for who knew what surprises the next hour held? He heard family voices, but how many—who might be missing among them? Few Alabama families, few Southern families could have endured the war undiminished, and he had received no word from home since before the Battle of Gettysburg, that fatal wheatfield, now a memory of flashing bayonets, magnificent, unwavering columns of men in gray, closing up the gaps with banners, with steady step, sweeping on in an irresistible wave of fate, men falling all around, cannon and rifles dealing death. . . .

In four years he had faced fire in forty-four battles and skirmishes, he had been wounded five times, and had been incarcerated in the Fort Delaware prison for six months. He had nearly starved there. He had endured all this, and he had survived. He had stood witness to an enormity of human experience—ten lifetimes' worth, much of it terrible, some degrading—drunken men scouring the hideous debris of a battlefield, risking their own lives to plunder the dead; some hideous— corpses swollen to twice their size after three days of summer sun, puffed out and bursting with foul gases; some pathetic—the intense gaze and heartful voice of a dying man repeating the words, "God have mercy on me, a sinner, for Jesus' sake."

He had seen all this, and worse. Perhaps the worst of all had been a morning in the Tennessee hills when he had surprised a young woman washing at an outdoor sink. He had caught her off guard. She had looked up from her toilet, her dark eyes wide, her dark hair falling in damp ringlets. Then she had coolly pulled a pistol and shot at him. How could a woman shoot at him? How could he be so hated at sight? What soulless monsters did war create? The incident haunted him.

He would never be the same for it, could never be the same. He was not the same fastidious young man who had studied law to please his father, then turned to his real love—the study of medicine—then put down his books to join the Fifteenth Alabama. He, the oldest child of seven, now twenty-eight, always the favorite, the tallest, handsomest, best educated, the link between generations, would never be the same. How could he? How could any of them? They could not, and that was what was so amazing about standing here again, looking across the fragrant thickets of honeysuckle at his family's Alabama home and waiting for the moment that felt right to go in.

The twilight thickened as he waited. It was warm, or no warmer than it ought to be on the fifth of July in southern Alabama, in a small town called Mount Pleasant. He felt the close, hot tightness of his collar band, almost like a noose around his neck. He had escaped that, too, though he had seen fellow officers swing, chosen by lot to fill quotas in the Yankee prison. He was glad to be warm; he had been cold enough at Fredericksburg to last a lifetime, sleeping in the snow without a blanket.

He would never forget all he had seen and suffered. He would never forget, nor could he, that Tennessee woman's face, so guilelessly pretty, so wide-eyed, so surprised. With extreme luck or terrible skill, she had hit him directly in the collarbone, damning him with her screams. He had been badly hurt. At first he had not only wanted to die, he had tried to die, refusing food and water in the crazed chaos of the field hospital where he lay, sleepless, heartless, useless, deserving death.

But death, though omnipresent, would not take him, as if he were too guilty to leave this life. Death collected the souls of the others, the feverish man to his left, the legless wreck of a man to his right, even the plump rosy-cheeked boy with only a shard of rusted metal in his foot who limped between the cots urging all of them to take water. Death would not have him, not then or in the years of the war that followed, one upon the other, determined to risk himself, to win the punishment he deserved in his own eyes, although not in the eyes of the others. By them he was praised and promoted.

His Colonel, William C. Oates, a man he came to love and trust—as a soldier must love the man who leads him open-eyed toward extinction, that is, desperately, with an agonized pride and a mutual fear of dying together—had called him one of the best soldiers in the regiment.

And so he had gone on fighting, hating himself and driven by guilt, but hating the Yankees as well, for it was their greed and despotism that had begun all this, had created a world where women shot at men and men shot at them and at each other, deliberately, again and again. He had not yet been able to stop hating, or fighting the war. For him it was not over. It was too strong a habit, now, more than a habit but ingrained like one, carved deep into his soul after so many battles. He had kept a record, of course, he, the man of science, had kept careful records, and though he had lost them as he lost everything else—his watch, his Bible, his mother's letters—at Hatcher's Run on February 7, 1865, when he had been captured and stripped of everything but his boots and marched to prison, by then it was too late to matter. That was his last engagement, anyway, and by then he knew the total of them was forty-four.

The figure had amazed him, at first. Later he was proud, in a weary way, for he had done it, he the most nonviolent of men, born and raised to be a doctor. He had steeled himself with hatred forty-four times and gone forward to meet the enemy under fire. He had been present for duty every time his regiment was called on to fight, and he had discharged his duties faithfully.

Under Colonel Oates, and under the great and gallant Stonewall Jackson, he had learned hatred and cultivated it to full fruit. At first it was a vague hatred, for the Yankees' having made the war necessary, for forcing this outrageous challenge on an honorable and Christian people, for disrupting lives and turning the world upside down, which was what war was. Later, battle by battle, month by month, death by death, the hatred fed on itself and multiplied, a Hydra born of so much suffering, so much misery, so many terrible days and nights of agonized waiting and indescribable confusion and inconceivable horror. And for the murders, one by one, of so many men he had marched with and lived with and fought with, for all of them.

How could those who had stayed at home understand? In four years he had grown closer to the men he fought with than to his family, but now he was parted from all of them, parted of course from many by death, and from the others by time and distance. Now that the war was over, perhaps none of them would ever meet again, each one of them shaken roughly off the bough to roll in different directions, homeward, if there were still any homes left.

With all this in his mind Tyler Ashby called upon all his remaining strength and proceeded with determination, almost marching, toward the house. The lush greenness of grass and gardens surrounded him, so sweet, almost cloying, pure as perfume and also dew-soaked so that the air had taken on the odor of the earth itself—strong, black and fetid with primeval fertility—and another odor, the teasing, breath-catching pungency of new-mown grass.

He could hear the clear voices of his sisters and the soft tinkle of a piano being played, then stopping, and the voices starting up again in easy turn, in mannerly conversation. He crossed the porch, every white-painted board familiar to him, recognized his mother's voice just as he stepped into the light of the open doorway and saw them all, clearly, as in a tableau, arranged in chairs around the parlor.

He paused. "A shadow in rags," his sister Amelia said, later. "A ghost from the grave," his mother said. "Son? Son?" his father asked in a tremulous, unbelieving voice, staring. "Son, is it you?" and then all the women screamed.

It was shocking to see them all in black, his white-haired mother thin and erect in stiff black silk, all three of his pretty sisters surrounded by yards of black, ankle to wrist to chin, his father and brothers in black. It confused him.

Who has died? he wondered. He looked around the parlor again, from face to face, scanning them, trying to see who was missing. Amelia's husband, of course, the General, had been killed, but that was early in the war. Who else? Only later when it was explained to him did he come to understand what might have been immediately obvious. The mourning was for him.

"Pa?" he asked. "Are you well?"

"Tyler? Son?" the Colonel repeated with rising joy in his voice.

"Yes I've come home," Tyler said.

Finally, the women's screaming turned to crying

and Amelia, always the first one to do anything, ran forward to him and took him into a warm, womanly hug the likes of which he had not felt in years. Her sweet softness made him believe he was home as nothing else had. Amelia clung fiercely, her face shining with tears. Finally she pulled back a little and said, as women will, "Let me look at you! Oh, Tyler!"

His mother was next, and then they passed him around, each one taking a turn, each of his sisters, Margaret, Amelia, Amanda Ann, each of them with stories to tell that would come out later, each crying with happiness. He was dazed to be here among them, so close to so many kin all at once, and through the wondering why they were all wearing black, through the constant searching of the faces—yes, there were his three brothers, Yancey and John Bradlaw and Charley Owen—to see who was missing, he gathered that he had arrived just at the moment of a family conference to decide their mutual fate.

During all the women's hugging and crying and his enduring it his father stood there, "Colonel" Clifford Ashby, Colonel long before this war, lordly and white-headed, awe-inspiring, still erect and characteristically proud in bearing, swaying only a little. He waited, restraining himself as long as he could.

"Son," Colonel Ashby said, "I reckon we waited just long enough for you to come home, although I admit we despaired of it and we didn't despair fast."

"I came as soon as I could."

"I reckon you did, God bless you, and I look forward to you telling me quite a story," the Colonel said, "but not just now. We are gathered here, all the Ashbys on earth, to decide something and you have come right on time to take your part in the decision."

"I'm glad for that," Tyler Ashby said.

"This country," the Colonel said very simply, "is not fit for us to live in anymore. If you don't know it yet, you'll see it soon enough. We're plannin' on movin' out, goin' to a better place. Son, will you go with us to the Brazils? We're planning to relocate there, as soon as we can."

How could he hesitate? Wasn't it clear that he had walked in at the right time to make the decision that was waiting for him to make, one that would turn his whole life in a direction that he had never thought of two hours before, perhaps one that would save him?

He spoke simply, too, and his voice was as calm and courteous as his father's. "Pa, I'd follow you to hell."

Terrill Ruffin had left Gonzales, Texas, the day after his wife was murdered. He had buried her himself, digging her grave six feet down through layers of clay and sand. His wife's maid, a former slave who spoke little English and had attended Marie-Anne for her lifetime, mixed the camphor water, bathed her, and dressed her for the last time, for eternity. Strangely, it was only the back of her body that had been badly burned and when she was dressed in white lace and her face had been treated with the camphor water, she looked beautiful.

When Ruffin fled the farm that he had bought from the Gleasons, he took the old woman, leaving everything else—all the horses and cows and chickens, all the new furnishings he had ordered from Galveston and all the absurdly fancy clothes his wife had brought from New Orleans. He left silently in the last hour before dawn, ignoring the old woman's soft and ceaseless sobbing, knowing that it was the only thing he could do.

Of course he was right, for by noon of that day a posse of vigilantes had scourged his farm and ransacked his house, killing the cows and swine and smashing dishes and furniture. Ruffin had not known that he would be blamed for Laray Holt Richler's death, but he knew that he would be connected with it in people's minds, and that would be enough.

Ruffin was misunderstood by the ignorant and angry Texans who had tortured him and killed his wife but he understood them as well as he understood himself. Proud but not vain, Ruffin knew himself to be in every way an unusual man, superior to his attackers and his neighbors—more intelligent and better educated, for he had been raised and spent most of his life in a Jesuit monastery school in Louisiana, richer, by the legacy from his unknown white father that had enabled him to buy the Texas farm—and he knew that none of it mattered, nothing could protect him from the random violence of fate.

Ruffin was a young man when he rode out of Gonzales County, but he had the courage and confidence and particularly the faith of a man twice his age. Behind him lay years of training in discipline, self-control and hard work. He had been in the world but apart from it, had seen life from behind the walls of the Sanctuary, a Jesuit monastery where he had lived since the age of five. In the past four years he had seen the scourge of war and the occupation of the city of New Orleans, death by pestilence and fire, death by starvation—seen it all from behind the shield of a monk's brown robes.

It had made him what he was—in every way an

unusual man, let alone an unusual Negro man. The brothers who taught him said that he was the best student they had ever had, and surely he was, devouring the Latin Bible and the rules of Euclid with equal appetite. The brothers had chosen him to be one of them, a scholar and teacher. He had been raised with this ambition and then had lost it, all at once, on the day he had met Marie-Anne Bienville, herself the child of a heritage as secret and mixed as his own, sent by her last relative to the Sanctuary for hiding during the worst days of the Yankee occupation.

Their love had been born in the monastery, burst into bloom and blossomed there into full, radiant flower, and it had been blessed—in the end—by the Jesuits, who could not deny that God had intended it and had made the two young people for each other.

Sharing a dream of an agricultural Eden, Ruffin and his bride had left Louisiana for Texas soon after the war ended. "We want only to be left alone," Ruffin had told his neighbors, but the Ruffins had represented a future some of them could not bear. From the start they had been shunned by the community's decent folk and hated by the elements intent on maintaining the superiority of the white race.

"Why we ever come here? Why you bring her to this place?" the old woman cried as the small carriage that held the two of them passed through a grove of eucalyptus trees.

"You hush, *Gran'mère*," Ruffin said without listening. He was, above all, shocked . . . still too shocked to do more than bend to the reins, his body curled in pain, blood dried along the cut across his face, his shirt stuck tight to his burned and beaten back, covered, to deflect attention, with two cotton shirts and a black frock coat. His own pain meant nothing to him. He offered it to his God and plunged on, his mind entirely absorbed by a horrible cycle of remembering the night before, each of its elements clear but unconnected, each seizing his memory in turn, each seared on it: the riders, the faceless men foolishly dressed in white—most of them not really strangers, their saddle horses familiar, their ignorant voices familiar—hunted and driven by them, whipped out of their home with the old woman hiding under the front porch steps, Marie-Anne violated in front of his eyes . . .

"My baby gone . . . daid . . ." the old woman wailed, beating her wrinkled gray fists in her lap.

"Hush up, you hush up or I'll leave you here!"

The clearing . . . the river, the fire, the cross. To use the sacred cross as an instrument of torture! His mind reeled. Seeing her on fire, feeling himself at the moment of death, and then the shots, feeling the cold clear water close safely around him . . .

"I remember his face. I will never forget his face, old woman," he said, his own face dark with rage, shaking the buggy whip over the horses' backs, every stiff gesture an agony.

"So you do? So you do?" she answered, lifting her head with surprising vehemence. "What're you gon' do?"

"I don't know," he shouted, howled, all his pain and rage and frustration coming together in this one cry.

# Chapter Two

There is no beginning without an ending. On the bleak October morning in 1865 that the Richler family left home forever, piled "like gypsies" as Zaidee Richler complained, into a vulnerable and creaky wagon drawn by two undersized and undernourished mules, it felt so much like an ending of the most cataclysmic sort that it was hard to remember that it was an important beginning.

A keen westerly wind, bitter cold for late October, snapped the oiled cloth drawn tight over their boxes and baggage, nudged the three Richler women deeper into their shawls and bonnets, and whirled a sticky red dust up into their faces. The air was full of moisture. Dense clouds, cold and clustered, all one blank, even gray, hung low over the flat prairies, threatening something worse than rain, and vultures ranged themselves along the nearly leafless branches of the post-oak trees, for it had been a disastrously dry summer and the weakened rabbits and groundhogs made easy prey.

Devastated by drought while still reeling from the aftermath of war, the bottomlands of the Guadalupe River Valley had succumbed early this year to the damp, gray monotony of winter. The summer's drought had shrunk the vegetation, the sun had seared the earth and baked it into bare, hard cakes eager enough to take up the rain and become mud. The grass had turned dry and brown back in July and the cotton crop had been the worst in memory. Now, the road they traveled was rutted and dusty; when it rained, it would be a sink of viscous mud.

"Do you think it's goin' to rain?" Zaidee Richler asked, speaking for the first time since they had left the sight of home behind and rolled slowly down the dirt driveway to the larger artery that would take them first to Hallettsville, then on to Houston.

"Of course it's goin' to rain, Zaidee," Elinor Richler declared impatiently. She wished it would pour. It was a nervous moment, everyone knew it; it had good reason for being so, and perhaps a deluge would ease it.

Elinor sat up very straight beside her younger sister, high on the wagon's hard wooden seat. There were no new wagons to be had. Before the war this one had served to cart their people to prayer meetings on the far side of Gonzales; it was so rickety that even Sheridan's Raiders, overrunning central Texas on their way to the Mexican border last May, had passed it by.

On the seat ahead, Franklin Richler held the reins and drove the mules. Next to him sat his wife Daphne, a tiny, brown-haired woman in a black dress and black bonnet who cried silently as the wagon moved along the rutted dirt road, its worn hubs grating and straining against the worn axletrees and tossing the Richlers from side to side in a jolting rhythm that forced the girls to cling together, arms entwined, as if they were sitting for a portrait.

Strangers always knew them to be sisters, and would until their dying days. At first glance, they were very much alike, although Zaidee's ample, silky hair was reddish-gold and Elinor's was as dark as a ripe chestnut, it glinted with the same sort of reddish highlights. Their faces were like: even oddly like. The same large bright blue eyes looked out of each with the same forceful and curious intelligence, and their full-lipped mouths and pert determined chins were as like as could be.

Zaidee, christened Sarah Daphne, was just eighteen, but she was exactly as tall as Elinor, who was two years older. Both girls were beauties, and in a society that prized feminine beauty they had been shaped by their comeliness, but beyond their physical similarities, they were as different as Cain and Abel in ways that went far beyond being blond and brunette. They were so different they agreed on scarcely a thing and had always struggled to maintain the appearance of sisterly compatibility their parents and convention demanded.

Like their mother, the girls wore black, but this was nothing unusual in the South, in 1865, for what family did not have a father or a brother to mourn, or both? So much had died, and so many, a quarter of all the young men who had marched off to war, a republic conceived in hope and dedicated to honor, glory and dreams, a class of people who had made living an art, a whole world, an era, a way of life. All these were dead, and more, and a puzzling new world had been born, one delivered in violence and retribution to a people who stood devastated in silent and submissive apprehension.

The Richlers and thousands of families like them had all this to mourn, and if the Richlers had lost their young son to the unrest and turmoil of the new era and not at First Manassas or Antietam or the Wilderness or Chickamauga or Shiloh, it was only so much sadder for them to face the future in a land exploding with retribution and revenge, a land crossed and recrossed by night riders in white and smug-faced Yankees in blue, a land losing value every day, a land burned and beaten down and being taxed deaf, dumb and blind.

"Trouble with pride is you can't eat it," Franklin Richler had said, coming home from the war in western Virginia and Tennessee and Mississippi with little else, walking home in cracked, half-shod boots all the way from Memphis when the war ended, lucky to be alive. It took him thirty-three days. All his family, the women and suddenly tall Laray Holt, ran to meet him, collecting by the front gate with those of the colored people who hadn't yet run away. More of them had left since, but not all of them. Some would not go, for where could they go? And to whom?

The Richler plantation, that familiar tract of land running between the bottomlands and the post-oak forest, five hundred acres in all, planted in good years in two hundred acres of cotton, had been home to fifty slaves plus the white family. The Richlers had lived there for nearly twenty years.

"Can't afford to stay," Franklin Richler had said, even before the tragedy of Laray Holt. The Yankees had put such taxes on land that it was not possible to pay them, and at the same time they had contrived to lower the price of cotton, the government taxes taking one-quarter of what was already a poor price. The taxes made Franklin Richler so angry he went red, then white, and they were just part of the program the Yankees were trying to shove down the throats of the Southern people.

But when he had just come home from the war, all he wanted was food and to be alone with his family. "I dreamed of your molasses bread, Mrs. Richler," he whispered, and his weak, scratchy voice was as frightening to his family as the sight of the Yankees riding past the gate, every day, so many of them, so big and healthy looking while all the Texans were half starved and didn't know where they'd get their next sacks of cornmeal.

"There is no wheat, Mr. Richler," Daphne Richler had to tell him, hating to tell him, but happy and relieved to see him alive (and shocked to see him gone completely gray), feeling both blessed and guilty for all the women whose men hadn't come home. When she killed the last chicken to make him a pie, she sent half the breast meat down the road to their neighbor, Mrs. Webb, who had not heard one word from her husband since a letter written to her the night before he went out to fight at Chattanooga.

"We have potatoes, Mr. Richler," she had said to him, and cooked the first of them, no bigger than walnuts, boiling them up with salt and sending Elinor and Laray Holt on the mule into Gonzales with Lucas, one of those who hadn't run off at the passed-along word of Mr. Lincoln's Emancipation, to trade twenty pounds of new potatoes for butter. "Delicious," he called the mashed potatoes and the chicken pie and he didn't notice that he ate the whole pie by himself, and then he had fallen asleep and slept for two days, so long that she began to worry.

Franklin Richler had not been himself after coming home, not for a long time, although there was nothing to show wrong with his body—all his limbs were intact, at a time when every second man getting off the train in Clarksville was missing one arm or leg and Joseph Tarpley, who had been the best rider in Fayette County, the next county over, was delivered home without either his right or his left leg. Franklin Richler had been injured in spirit, so it seemed, for he wasn't himself—for some days he couldn't find a single word to say, for some weeks he just lay in his bed, not taking the slightest interest in what might be going on outside the door of his bedroom, just eating every meal his wife brought in to him on a tray, every crumb of cornbread, every bit of the fried eggs and salt pork, every morsel of the mustang grape pie without asking where on earth she had managed to find sugar and eggs in Gonzales County.

"I have walked home from Tennessee," he said at last, and they could only imagine how he had managed to do that, what he had seen along the way, and what he had thought of.

Just how and why Laray Holt had died was one thing Daphne Richler still could not understand and perhaps never would. "It's broken her," her neighbor Mrs. Webb said, meaning her spirit, or her will. Her boy, her son, had been her favorite (and the girls knew it and thought it was only right) and losing him was more than she should have been asked to bear.

Just what Elinor had been doing there, alone by the riverbank, was a question that never got asked and was forgotten. It was plain to see that Elinor had been shocked and was still troubled by what she had seen and since her family loved her, why would they trouble her with questions? It was something they all needed to forget.

Hot as the day was, it was cool beneath the immense, spreading elms that shaded the sloping west lawn at Spring Bank plantation. At the foot of the lawn was the river, its green-blue currents tamed by dams and channels, its grassy banks scalloped with water-lily saucers holding pink and white blossoms like teacups, the green-and-white boat house miraculously untouched by war or any other trouble. At the top of the lawn was the big house, west-facing verandas all along it bristling with settees and rocking chairs and a long swinging couch, full of little girls in white dresses.

And in between the house and the river was a party. All the rugs and carpets in the house had been carried out and spread on the grass. All the pillows from all the upholstered chairs and couches in the house had been heaped on the carpets, nearly every one of them supporting a lady dressed in white, a gentleman lounging in an open-collared shirt, or the lady's cousin and the gentleman's aunt.

Every single member of the Ashby clan had gathered for this party, and all their dearest friends from all over the county and as far away as Georgia. It was a family reunion, of sorts. It was a farewell party, of sorts, for the Ashbys of Spring Bank would give up this house and move to Brazil in the fall. And it was a party in the very latest Southern vogue, a "starvation party," a party where no food would be served, "to show the Yankees and everyone else that we can have just as much fun as in the old days without spending a penny." However, at the last minute, Colonel Ashby, who never touched hard liquor himself, had determined to clear out the cellars of old brandies and Jamaican rum that his Uncle Clarence Ashby had built under the kitchen-house.

So there was plenty of liquor for the gentlemen, and spring water and lemonade for the ladies and children, but there was not one platter of food to be seen.

"I have never heard of such a thing, really I haven't," Cousin IdaSue Hollister murmured to her husband, Herbert, who was Lusina Ashby's brother.

The two guests from Middleton County picked their way between their relations on the pillows and carpets and strolled toward the riverbank where their grandsons were taking out a tiny white rowboat.

"What's that, dear?" her husband asked. "It makes me laugh to think of those Yankees comin' here and tryin' to tear the place up while the cellar was full of this old brandy!" Hollister had already drunk liberally of the fine French liquor and was willing to swear that it had aged well. "Per'aps if the colonel'd try a drop he'd talk sense."

"I see that Lusina's rose gentians are as fine as ever this year," Cousin IdaSue said. "And her summer roses! It's a shame to think of Lusina leavin' her gardens."

"Not a particle of sense in movin' to some outlandish, half-civilized country," Hollister said. "Tyler, tell me, are you set in this plan?"

How thin he looks, IdaSue Hollister thought. There was something about the expression in his blue eyes that made her shiver. He looked wounded. Of course, Tyler had always been aloof and somewhat cerebral—he got that from the Ashby side of the family. What was the use of bein' so smart, she wondered, if your intelligence cut you off from other people?

"Yes, I believe Papa's decision is right," Tyler said. What relief there was in following his father's lead, just as if he were a boy again. He believed that the best this life could offer was a chance to fall again, safely, into the bosom of his family. Let them save him if they could.

"Have you exhausted your patriotism, then, Tyler? Do you owe your country no further duty?" Hollister asked, thumping the grass ineffectively with his silver-headed walking stick.

"I no longer have a country, Uncle Herbert. I have

no flag, no emblems, no public spirit. I live now simply to live, and for my family."

"God calls us to higher loyalties," Hollister sputtered.

Tyler shrugged. What was the use of arguing? Many Southerners felt as Uncle Herbert did, that emigration was desertion. "God will find us in Brazil," he said, smiling to soften the remark as his father bore down on the conversation to take up the argument with Herbert Hollister.

"Come with us, Hollister," Colonel Ashby said. "Leave treachery, perfidy and persecution behind!"

Tyler slipped away and wandered up the lawn to join a group of five or six young people sipping ice water from long-stemmed crystal goblets. His sister Amelia's laugh floated out to greet him.

"Oh, there you are, Tyler!" Amelia called out. "I was just telling Merinda the story of my great sale!"

Tyler smiled. Amelia was his favorite sister. Although she had suffered from the war as much as any woman, her spirit and courage were undiminished.

"Perhaps I shall make a fortune from my sketching yet," Amelia joked. "I have made a fair start!"

"Tell me what happened, please!" Merinda Ragsdale asked, looking sideways at Tyler, who was, she thought, handsomer than ever. She had endured a secret crush on her friend Amelia's brother since she was a girl in braids. And now he was to go off to Brazil, still unmarried. It was terrible to think of, but perhaps it was not too late. She gave Tyler a dazzling smile, lowering her lashes to hide the hope and longing, and turned back to Amelia.

"I had set up my easel just outside our front gate," Amelia explained, "as I had in mind to do a portrait of Spring Bank. As a remembrance, you know, to carry to

Brazil. To my astonishment, a blue-coat offered me twenty dollars for it!"

"Twenty dollars!" Merinda exclaimed. "Why, whatever for?"

"To send home to his mama in Wisconsin, apparently." Amelia giggled. "Just think, he wants to remember Mount Pleasant as a typical Southern town."

"Did you sell it to him?"

"Not for twenty dollars!"

"You refused him?" Merinda asked with wonder.

"I told him I could not take a penny less than twenty-five!" Amelia laughed and the others joined her.

"Oh, Amelia," Merinda said admiringly. How she would miss the Ashby family! Every one of them was handsome and talented. Life would never be the same once they had gone.... Of course life could never be the same.

It was all over. The Cause they had fought for and been so sure was just was lost. The ease and happiness of their former lives seemed a dream. All we have left is ourselves, she realized, and because she was young the thought buoyed her and the sound of Tyler's fiddle tuning up on "Soldier's Joy" filled her with a wild happiness and she took Amelia's arm and pulled her close in a hug.

# Chapter Three

Two months later, Terrill Ruffin had fixed on what it was he wanted to do, even if he didn't know how he would do it. He wanted revenge, wanted it not the weak way he wanted to go on living, but intensely, unambivalently, above all else. His own strength had returned, his scarred back had healed, and his mind, ever his strongest and supplest asset, had settled on revenge.

He returned to Texas in search of the man whose face he had seen, the man he blamed for his wife's murder. He entered the county disguised as a French émigré, using the name Jacques Marin. Easily passing for white, he took a room in the only boardinghouse in Gonzales, and began to make inquiries. He found that what was unattainable through honest good will was easily attained through deceit. One of the other boarders befriended him and took him to meet his friends. The white community of Gonzales was not large and the war had left them poor and embittered. Despairing of progress, they were committed to hatred of Yankees, carpetbaggers and Negroes. The incident with the Richler boy seemed to confirm this hatred.

Ruffin waited. He told his new acquaintances that he was on his way to California. One night in the tavern, his fellow boarder drank nearly a quart of raw whiskey and told him about the men's secret society that had been formed in Gonzales to protect white people and administer justice. Ruffin listened with his heart pounding and learned that its founder and titular head had been a big, florid, black-mustached man, a former overseer and Cavalry hero named Jesse Rall who hated Negroes.

From everything he heard, Jesse Rall was the man he sought, but he could not find him. The Yankee police sought him, also, in what was generally considered to be an unjust prosecution. Everyone knew that Rall had led a raid against a pair of outrageously bold Negroes in which a young boy had been accidentally killed. Popular opinion was that the niggers had asked for it. It was a damn shame about the kid, but wasn't that somehow the fault of the niggers, too? Rall wasn't the best type of man, but he was a white man, and he'd only been trying to take care of his own.

So they said. But where was Rall? Ruffin asked quietly. He was told Rall had left Texas to escape the law. The rumor was that he had emigrated to Brazil. A good number of county folks were off to Brazil. Brazil was a country that still put white men first.

Ruffin was incredulous and frustrated. He made further inquiries. The rumor seemed to be true. Without any further clear intentions, Ruffin left Texas and returned to New Orleans.

Tyler Ashby had agreed at once to his father's plan to emigrate to Brazil. Behind his acceptance lay a deep and reckless despair about the rest of his life. To his friends and family it was not evident how profoundly Tyler had been changed by the war—to them he was still the handsome, courteous, soft-spoken, Southern gentleman.

All the easy optimism of a rich planter's son had been blasted out of him. It was hard to say exactly where or when—so many times and places might have done it, but his nightmares were trained on the incident with the dark-haired woman in Tennessee. He had gasped in shock and pain when her bullet hit him, and then, instinctively—that is, with a soldier's instincts and in violation of a lifetime pledged to the protection of women—he had fired back at her.

He had stood so near her that his shot exploded in her face, baring bloody teeth, stripping her rose-pale skin off like a mask. The shot had pitched her backward into a stand of hollyhocks, as red as her blood sprayed over his uniform.

"The man who strikes a woman is not fit to live," his father had taught him, and since that Tennessee morning he had remembered it every day. He could never forget her face. God could not forgive him and he would not forgive himself. He found civilian life so strange, so irreconcilably unlike the four years just past, that the idea of leaving Alabama, of booking passage in a decrepit old schooner and sailing south to the other side of the world was not one whit stranger.

The situation that Colonel Ashby had called unbearable on the night Tyler came home was no better. There was no government of any kind throughout the state. Raids by Yankees, freed Negroes and rabble dressed as Yankees went on every night; by day packs of starving Negroes and their children roamed the dusty roads crying for food, for help, for anyone to take them in and feed them and tell them where they could sleep that night.

"We cannot help them all, not a fraction of them," Amelia mourned. She was overcome by the sight of the bands of ragamuffins who came to the house, who hung over the gate and slept on the grass between the gate and the road. "It's utterly hopeless, Tyler, isn't it?" she asked.

Tyler's sympathy went out to Amelia. Of his sisters, she had suffered particularly. Amelia had been married to their neighbor, Huntington Beauregard Scott, a Major. He had left at once for war and had been promoted to General by the end of '62, but their marriage had lasted for only two desperate, tear-soaked reunions. Scott had died at Vicksburg, and his little daughter, Susan Jane, could not remember him at all.

"Of course not, Amelia," Tyler said to her, although in his heart he felt it was so.

His other sisters, and many other Southern women, were surprisingly capable of unbounded rage. He marveled at their energy. They felt personally insulted by the presence of Yankee soldiers. When Margaret saw a Yankee soldier coming along the street, she crossed to the other side, lifting her hoopskirts neatly, righteously angry and vitalized by her desire to snub the bored, confused sons of Missouri who had been posted to their town.

Resentfully, the soldiers enforced their rules, even breaking into the Ashbys' parlor one night to stop Amanda Ann playing "Dixie" on the piano. When their cousin, Lucien Ashby Stearne, returned home to Florence, Alabama, wearing the only suit he owned, his Confederate uniform, Yankee soldiers stripped him and forced him to walk two miles in his underdrawers. In Mount Pleasant, the soldiers hung bright new Union flags over the main street and laughed to see the ladies duck under them.

Tyler Ashby made an effort to ignore the soldiers, although he hated them instinctively and profoundly. By day he helped stand guard over his mother and sisters, believing every Southern woman in danger among the soldiers. He drove his sister to the cemetery and his mother to the shops. Then he worked with his father and brothers to prepare for their emigration. There was land and property to sell, accounts to settle, purchases and innumerable arrangements to be made. Chartering a ship to sail to Rio de Janeiro was next to impossible. There were countless restrictions on travel, countless documents to complete, countless Yankee officials to placate and pay off. These arrangements occupied his days and helped him to avoid considering the state of his soul.

By night he could not avoid it. When he left his family and closed his bedroom door, he stopped being son and brother and once again was soldier. By night he belonged to the ordeal just ended; he had not yet been able to sleep through a whole night without dreams as powerful as reality that he was in the midst of raw warfare, preparing for a battle or just leaving one, stumbling over the bodies of comrades with heart-stopping recognition, feeling the guilt that he had once more been spared and the exhausted resignation that he must go on.

How long would it last? As the months passed, he began to suspect it would last forever. He felt very alone, painfully estranged from the family life he left downstairs every evening, after playing his violin in the parlor with his sisters and their friends, always one or two wide-eyed and admiring young ladies, their pretty faces turned to him in longing and love.

"Tyler, dear son, perhaps you should marry," his mother whispered to him as part of her goodnight, her sweet voice as soft as the rustling of her black silk gown. Lusina Ashby knew better than the rest of the family that Tyler's silences among them covered a discomfort whose nature she could not understand but instinctively sensed. "There are so many lovely young ladies . . ." she said persuasively, thinking of Merinda Ragsdale, of Celeste Sanders.

But Tyler Ashby knew that he could not choose one. As strong as a wall between himself and all these young ladies with imploring eyes was the image of the dark-haired, dark-eyed woman in Tennessee who had died by his hand. She was there as powerfully as she had ever been and he still did not know if she would ever leave him alone, and until she did he was not free to look at a living woman.

"No, Mother, I cannot marry yet. I am not ready. But we will soon be in Brazil," he said, as if that explained everything, including why he was so indefinably not himself, any more than any of them were.

"Thank God for that," his mother said.

Galveston, the Queen City, Texas's major seaport for twenty-five years, was the biggest city that Elinor Richler had ever seen. There is always excitement, sometimes even the anticipation of deliverance, in the approach to a new city, all the more so in this instance, as it followed the long trek from Gonzales across the drought-wasted prairies, swept by dusty winds and swarming with packs of homeless, helpless former slaves foraging for food and trying to reconcile the new idea of freedom with the old realities of hunger and despair.

Already, Elinor thought, it seems as if we have come very far. The journey from Gonzales had taken two weeks, the first part of it by wagon and the latter part, after they had been joined by four other families also bound for Brazil, by railway in specially hired freight cars piled high with all their baggage.

Elinor's first view of Galveston was just at daybreak, from the railroad station, and as soon as she looked down at the glittering blue bay with its tall-masted ships at anchor, the first she had ever seen, she felt her spirits soar. The world is opening up, she thought, the world is large—almost infinitely large—and I am to go out into it.

Behind her, the train's steam engine puffed and bells rang. She stood on the tiny ironwork deck, alone for a minute while the rest of the family still slept. The thought of going out into the world, of leaving the only country she or any of them had ever known, was undeniably exciting, but it was also frightening.

She shivered.

"Good morning, Miss Elinor. Ah? Are you chilled?" a man's voice inquired from just behind her.

It was Darius Yates, a widower from Georgia who had joined their party at Houston, and was also bound for Brazil. Yates seemed old to Elinor, for he was a man in his early thirties, but it was character more than age that gave Yates dignity. His expression was proud, even aristocratic. He was handsome, to that Elinor would have testified, but his handsome features and deep-set hazel eyes were outweighed by his air of aloofness, of fine breeding and worldly experience.

Although she was not at all ashamed of herself or

her own family, Yates intimidated Elinor. Shyly, she could not meet his eyes, but instead let her own rest on his black silk cravat and the pin that secured it. Surely, it was pure gold. Surely, the stone set in it was either a sapphire or an aquamarine. She had never seen either sort of stone before, and as she studied its blue-green fire, she blushed.

How little we know ourselves, especially at twenty! Elinor did not know that she could cause some men to fall helplessly in love with her at first sight and never forget her. She sensed only that something about her interested this older man. She could not guess that he found her entrancing, so guilelessly beautiful that he was quite ill at ease in her presence. Instead, she felt foolish. Instead, she felt her pulse race in anxiety. Whatever I say, she thought, I shall sound naïve.

Her bosom trembled in confusion. He stared.

"May I fetch you a shawl?" he offered.

"Oh, no! Please don't trouble," she protested. "I shall be fine. See, the sun is rising and it's warmer already."

Together they turned to face the sun, ascending in a glorious blaze of pink and purple that striped the pastel sky from edge to edge.

"So it is, Miss Elinor," Yates admitted. Her eyes, he thought, are delightful. I have never seen prettier eyes. He could not stop himself from glancing toward her bosom. For months he had counted himself as good as dead and had forgotten that such beauty and innocence could survive in the world that had come. She is the sort, he thought, who could raise the dead to life.

Studying without comprehending the emotions playing across Yates's face, Elinor took a deep breath and drew herself deliberately to her full height. He *will* laugh at me, she thought, if I stand here like a silent ninny.

"Mr. Yates," she asked calmly, "do you intend to buy land in Brazil?"

"Perhaps..." he said seriously, flattering Elinor with his grave attention. "My plans are uncertain. My father and grandfather were cotton planters, and I suppose plantin' is in my blood, but I should like to see a bit of Brazil, first, before I settle down. I have much to forget.... Ah, Miss Elinor, we all face this future with some uncertainty, do we not?"

"Yes, sir, we do," Elinor said softly, surprised and stirred to sympathy by the tremor in his voice. How much he must have suffered. How much all our soldiers suffered.

"So this is Galveston," Yates said, when a minute or two had passed.

"If all goes well, we shall not be here long," Elinor said.

They both turned at the scraping sound of a door opening behind them. It was Franklin Richler with Zaidee. Zaidee yawned and blinked at the clear morning light, but Franklin Richler frowned.

"Good morning, daughter. Good morning, Mr. Yates. Ah..."

"Good morning, Papa," Elinor answered, and dipped in the graceful curtsy that had been her habit since childhood. "Is something wrong, Papa?"

"Mrs. Richler is unwell," he admitted. "I must go at once to find a doctor. Elinor, I ask you and Zaidee to remain with your mother. Mr. Yates, may I ask you to take my place in the committee of gentlemen who depart at once to see the captain of the brig *Victoria*?"

"Of course," Yates answered, glad for something

specific to do. He liked Franklin Richler. The man was a gentleman and smelled only faintly of defeat. Besides, Richler was the father of the two lovely young women who adorned their party, and as he walked with him across the muddy station yard, Yates glanced back.

Miss Zaidee is beautiful also, he decided, but although she is even more . . . he searched for a word to describe the exact difference between them and settled on striking . . . with that gorgeous red-gold hair, I believe I am more attracted to the older sister. Nonetheless, it was a study he did not want to conclude prematurely.

"I hope Mrs. Richler is not seriously ill," he said to Franklin Richler, feeling a slight embarrassment at his thoughts.

"I don't believe she is, merely nervous," Richler answered. "Yet perhaps a good doctor can prescribe a tonic before we sail."

"Poor Mama," Elinor said softly, leaving the wrought-iron platform and disappearing into the airless railway car where they had all slept.

But Zaidee lingered and looked out over Galveston and the group of men who had caught up with her father and Yates. That man, she thought with characteristic intuition, is falling in love with Elinor. Well, we shall see about that!

# Chapter Four

It was a sultry late October day that threatened rain. The steel-gray sky glowered and inky clouds scudded over the harbor at Mobile, once the second cotton port of America, now a battered, half-deserted ghost of itself. Five months ago twenty tons of captured Confederate ammunition had exploded in a warehouse being used as an arsenal and most of the city known as the Gem of the Gulf had trembled, erupted, and burst into flames. Warehouses, docks, shops, public buildings and stately homes stood in ruins, and only a pitiful few steamships and schooners lay in at the charred landings.

One of them was the *Talisman*, a low-slung schooner that had seen brighter days and had crept past the harbor's sandbars on many dark nights. This undecorated war veteran had served as a blockade runner using those dark nights and gusty Gulf storms for cover, slipping secretly in and out of Mobile Bay through the schools of sharks and fever-ridden swamps.

At the beginning of the war, she had carried essential goods under the orders of the Confederate War Department. Her priorities had been first, arms and ammunition, usually from Europe through Cuba; second, clothing, boots, shoes, hats; third, much-needed drugs and chemicals, including quinine, chloroform, ether, opium, and morphine. By the end of the war, after Admiral David Farragut had captured the forts defending the harbor's entrance, the nature of essential goods had changed. Then the *Talisman* carried jets and cameos, silks and satins, French brandy and Haitian rum, fancy slippers and Paris hats, risking herself and her crew for them, commanding fabulous prices and exchanging everything for cotton.

And now she rested, creaking at dockside as the Ashbys' carriage approached along the levee. It was a day long planned and anticipated.

"She is small," Tyler Ashby said, studying the *Talisman* as she bobbed next to the ruined docks.

"I should think she's fast," Colonel Ashby answered. The two men were seated in the buggy which had carried them from Mount Pleasant with only three other members of the family, Amelia and Yancey and Amelia's tow-headed daughter Susan Jane. Behind them were piled their trunks and boxes and under the seat were the five strong new carpetbags into which Colonel Ashby had packed hundreds of gold coins.

"Dear Papa, are you sure she's big enough?" Amelia asked anxiously. "Are you sure she's seaworthy?"

"Of course, Amelia," Yancey said. He, the oldest remaining brother, would head the family while Tyler and the Colonel explored Brazil. During the months of planning and preparing, the Ashby clan had enlarged itself. Tyler's younger brother John Bradlaw had married Lucinda Rose Marshall and his sister Margaret married Dalton Hilliard. John Bradlaw and his bride would come with the rest of the family, following Tyler and the Colonel as soon as they found land in Brazil, but Margaret and Dalton had decided to stay in Alabama. They would live on Dalton's father's plantation, Rosehill. The news had been disturbing to the family, particularly to Lusina Ashby. What if she should never see her daughter again? Would she be denied forever the wonderful sight of Margaret's children? Pain stirred in her heart, but she consoled herself with the hope that the Hilliards might join them later in the new land.

Brazil lay ahead of them, glittered in imagination, a tropical paradise across a blue sea. From everything they had heard and read, it seemed a wonderful land, governed by a wise and cultured emperor who personally sought them as emigrants. Colonel Ashby had received a letter from his agent in New York; he encouraged them to come, to visit Brazil and judge it worthy. To him they were not a conquered people, but a misunderstood aristocracy. He sought their expertise in growing cotton; he sought their contribution to a prosperous future for Brazil.

"It is a great moment," Colonel Ashby declared, looking out over the gray harbor, over the crowded confusion of the levee, swarming with horse-drawn cabs, heaped with bales and boxes, to the cloudy sky where gulls swooped and circled.

Tyler fumbled in his side pocket for a cigar. The moment of departure had moved all his anxieties to a crisis point. All the months of planning and preparing were over—the voyage lay ahead. But did it matter? How could it matter, any of it? He squinted at the *Talisman* and tried not to imagine the thirty or forty sleepless nights stretching out between him and the other shore.

But they were as hard to imagine as not to imagine. He had never before traveled anywhere by sea, nor had his father. They had never willingly left home, let alone entrusted their lives to the ropes and sails and keel of a schooner. Ten years ago, none of this would have been imaginable, but in the years they had just lived through, the unimaginable had become commonplace.

Tyler jumped out of the carriage. He stretched his long legs nervously and reached up to embrace his sister and pretty little Susan Jane. "Kiss Mother for me . . . again," he told her, "and all the others."

A swarm of porters and stevedores descended on the carriage as the Colonel climbed out stiffly, taking two carpetbags from Yancey's hands. Tyler took the others.

"We will write as soon as we arrive," his father promised. "And expect all the rest of you—perhaps by the beginning of the new year."

"God willing," Yancey promised.

"God go with you," Amelia whispered, kissing her father goodbye.

"Goodbye, Grandpapa. Goodbye, Uncle Tyler," Amelia's child shouted.

Surrounded by the rest of their luggage, Tyler and the Colonel moved slowly along the dock toward the *Talisman*. Tyler felt the wet salty air soak into his clothes. His father's breath was labored and he was close to tears.

"We are the vanguard," the Colonel said, raising his voice so that heads turned all along the dock.

Hope rose in Tyler's heart. He was leaving behind—likely forever—the only home he knew, innumerable dangers lay ahead, and yet he felt very strongly the immense beauty of the sea world around them and the possibilities of the challenge that lay ahead.

We have all changed, he thought, but we must change more. The South can never go back to its past. We must change again, endure more suffering, go on.

Brazil will give us a chance. Perhaps in Brazil we will break free of our bonds and traditions, shed the past—perhaps *I* will, even I!

He looked at his father with a mixture of love and embarrassment. The Colonel had pulled from his pocket a handkerchief embroidered with the bonny blue flag and was waving it above his head.

"The voyage begins," Tyler said, and the *Talisman* slipped sedately past the ruins of Fort Morgan. Two of the passengers—passing between them a bottle of rum—broke into a spine-tingling, spirit-rousing Rebel yell and the Ashbys added their voices to the cheering.

Terrill Ruffin, who had lived all his life within sight of the city of New Orleans, came back into that city after his brief visit to Gonzales as if he had never been there before. His first stop, after leaving the train that brought him from Lake Pontchartrain, was at a tailor's in Poydras Street which he had heard was the finest in town. Speaking his least colloquial Creole French, he ordered two complete suits, submitted to the tape measure, and gave the tailor, M. Leroy Piché, his address as the St. Charles Hotel.

Leaving the tailor, he went to the hotel and registered as Jacques Marin of Lyon, France. His hand was trembling as he signed the hotel register and his throat was so dry that he could not speak as he followed the black porter to his second floor room. Wordlessly he tipped the porter one dollar and turned away from the old man's bow.

"Thank *you*, sir, Mons'er Marin, sir. Now I hope you be comf'able, sir, thank you kindly, sir."

In his eyes I am a white man, Ruffin realized. Alone, he shrugged his shoulders to release some of the tension that had gathered there and faced himself in the mirror. He could do it. He could pass for white. His hair, although coarse-textured and glossy black, was almost straight. If he had it cut very short—like a Frenchman—and his beard trimmed close as well, he would look more Caucasian. His eyes were a light, gold-flecked hazel, his features straight and fine, and his skin, although tanned to a shade of creamy brown, was in truth no darker than the skin of many Frenchmen and Italians.

He smiled, showing even white teeth, but it was not an expression of either happiness or amusement. It was a grim commitment to deceit. The words from Ephesians came to his mind and he repeated them aloud, "Put on the whole armour of God, that ye may be able to stand against the wiles of the devil." Dear God, please forgive me, he prayed, for all I am about to do. I do it in Thy name. Make me Thy agent, Holy Father, as I act. I will never hurt the blameless or cause the innocent to suffer.

"I do it in Thy name," he added aloud, and then left the hotel, striding down Chartres Street with such remarkable physical grace and such aristocratic bearing that more than one woman watched him with interest. His destination was the jewelry shop on Lafayette Square, where he intended to sell his beloved wife's family diamonds for as much cash as he could get.

It was a cool, pleasant evening. The air was both fresh and spicy as it can be in New Orleans in autumn. The red sun hung low over the housetops, hesitating, a salty breeze blew over the city from the riverfront, and the smell of late-blooming roses perfumed the air. It was the hour of evensong and he heard nuns chanting behind a convent wall as he passed by. He walked more briskly, aware of the eyes on him from behind countless shutters, far from content but pleased to be en route to his future.

If he was successful in getting a good price for the jewels, he would dine at Antoine Alciatore's restaurant, an establishment he had heard about all his life.

And tomorrow he would begin immediately to investigate the possibilities of emigration to Brazil.

Although they had expected to see the green shores of Cuba on the horizon every day for the past two weeks, the passengers on the *Victoria* had seen neither land nor sail for twice that length of time. Misfortune seemed to have stowed away among the barrels of salt pork and meal, among the coils of rope and crates of hoes and plows, for not only were they unsure of their exact course, but the storms and squalls that had blown them across the Gulf of Mexico continued unabated when the waters changed from azure to deepest green.

Misfortune had been quick to find them in Galveston, and hold them there, for despite the hopes and best intentions of the Richlers and the other Brazil-bound colonists, their departure had been dogged by delays and misfortunes from the start. Their first setback was total and unexpected—the *Victoria* was not among the steamships and sailing vessels in Galveston harbor. In fact, as it took them a week's inquiries to learn, she had not yet left New Orleans, where there were many claims against her that all required time and money to settle.

The *Victoria* had been chartered by one of their number, the Reverend Willard Love from Macon, Georgia, who had visited Brazil the year before and secured a grant of land for a colony near the headwaters of the

Juquia River. In a visit to New Orleans, Reverend Love had hired the *Victoria* from her captain and owner, a lanky red-haired Yankee from Maine named Calvin Cash. Captain Cash had promised to meet the colonists in Galveston by the end of October, but when he failed to keep his word, they were without recourse, for they had all been obliged to pay their passage in advance. It did not help to know that Captain Cash had driven a very hard bargain for the terms of the voyage— they had paid $130 apiece—and that he was entirely without sympathy for the purpose of their emigration.

Weeks passed, and even the most optimistic became disgruntled. Some of the colonists were truly desperate, for they had sold their land and could see their money dwindling, but finally, at long last, the sails of the *Victoria* appeared in the harbor.

Only then did the Richlers move all of their possessions down to the waterfront. Elinor was privately dismayed by her first view of the cargo and the brig. There's more stuff here, she thought, than in Barnum's Museum, and a wilder variety.

The docks were crammed with baggage: mounds of farming equipment, grindstones, feather beds, crates of scrap iron, horseshoes, old chairs, stools, and mysterious crates, one of which, baying and bumping along the dock, turned out to contain a half dozen month-old hounds.

All of this they stowed in the hold, but after it was settled, leaving scarcely room to walk sideways in the long interior salon, the Yankee authorities arrived with another inspection warrant and it all had to be unpacked and redistributed.

Going below, Elinor was even more dismayed. The staterooms were no more than boxes fitted with shelves for human bundles, and ventilation was arranged by opening one of the two forward hatches. Poor Mama, she thought, however will she sleep on such a narrow hard bed? And none of us will have a moment's privacy.

"It is close," called out Darius Yates, who had followed Elinor into the hold. He could not stand near her, nor could she move easily to either side, for the passageway was several inches narrower than her hoops, which were nearly as wide as she was tall.

"Indeed it is, Mr. Yates." She smiled bravely in what he felt was an unsettling way. "Closer than Noah's Ark, I feel perfectly sure. I just hope we've packed as providentially as he did!"

"We shall all have to make certain sacrifices," Yates replied, and the ladies' hoopskirts were among the first. Even before sailing they all agreed to remove them, and stowed the mass of narrow iron rings in the main-mast cupboard behind the captain's cabin. On the third day out, it was discovered that they had miscalculated and had already run short of water. Everyone was put on short rations and washing was forbidden, but at the end of the first week, it began to rain, and the rain continued to fall.

"Do you realize that in forty days we have seen the sun only twice and the stars not at all?" Darius Yates asked Franklin Richler, when they were six weeks out.

"Without the rain, we'd have died of thirst."

"The scent of salt air doesn't make farmers into sailors," Yates said.

Nearly all the *Victoria*'s passengers were similarly rueful and resigned. They had never envisioned such a long, tedious voyage, never imagined feeling so lost and helpless on the high seas. Most of them suffered miserably from seasickness and some of them had lost considerable weight.

From day to day, the passengers' confidence in Captain Cash rose and fell. Cash was a habitual hard drinker, he had an explosive temper and a ribald sense of humor, he was a tyrant to his men, and was at odds with the bulk of the passengers on every conceivable subject.

"We are still afloat," Yates replied. "He lacks manners, of course. But then, he is a Yankee."

"I despise him," Zaidee snapped, bent over an embroidered collar. Zaidee was irritable this afternoon, and not just because any fool could see that the lavender silk was of hopelessly inferior quality and would never untangle, no matter what. "Drat!" she exclaimed, "I have stabbed my finger . . . again!"

"Oh, Zaidee! Take care not to spot the collar!" Elinor said anxiously. She was working on piecing a quilt from dress scraps, but she had lost the last half-hour in a daydream of green Brazil, in her mind a paradise of parrots and orchids. She sighed and touched a piece of flowered silk from a dress her mother had worn before the war.

"Double drat!" Zaidee swore. "I've broken the thread. Oh, I'd like to wrap it around Captain Cash's red neck!"

"An inadvisable notion," Yates drawled. "We are totally dependent upon him for our safety. He controls our lives, and I trust that all that is finest in his intellect and character will prevail."

"Do Yankees have any character?" Elinor asked. "If they had any, wouldn't they sell it?"

"Don't jest, Elinor. We may be overheard," Daphne

Richler said. Their mother had grown more silent than ever on the voyage. No one knew *what* she was thinking.

"Hell's skillet!" Zaidee exploded, hissing like a fuse as she threw down her work. "I give up! I can't bear to sit here another minute, not one! Oh, I'm sorry, Elinor, but I mean it. Mr. Yates, won't you walk with me on the deck? Thank you, sir. I don't care, Elinor, if it's raining above; it's always raining above, and I shall atrophy, I declare it, if I sit here another minute!"

"Go ahead, then," Elinor said with some relief. No one on earth was harder to manage than Zaidee in a bad mood. She did not envy Mr. Yates the task of calming her, nor could she guess at his own mood. He was always polite, but changeable: sometimes so easy and charming she forgot how old he was.

On the deck above, Zaidee and Darius Yates found themselves alone, save for the usual crew of sailors working the lines, and were immediately refreshed by the salt air. A fine rain was falling, and it was nearly sundown but—was it by a miracle?—the sky seemed to be clearing, and as they watched, it faded into nearly transparent pewter gray.

Zaidee's spirits rose. I suppose I was rude, she reflected. I saw Mrs. Love starin' at me, but I don't care! I am moody by nature, I have always been so and Elinor is not. She is *too* proper by half, but she can put up with me better than I with her, so that is the way it will be. Drawing her pale blue woolen shawl tightly around her shoulders she slid a few feet on the slick deck and laughed childishly when Yates stepped forward and caught her very firmly. How tall he is and how thin, she thought.

"Take care, Miss Zaidee."

Zaidee smiled flirtatiously. Jealousy of Elinor was

her purest and strongest emotion. She knew perfectly well Yates admired her sister, it was as plain as a pikestaff, and it followed directly that she wanted him to admire her more.

"Sir, I admit it," she said boldly in the sweetest of drawls, "I am tired to *death* of takin' care. I'm tired of everythin'! Aren't you, Mr. Yates?"

He laughed. "In a way I am, of course. We are all tired of sailin', Miss Zaidee." He narrowed his eyes, looking out across the utterly flat grayness of the sea.

What was she suggesting? She was as sexy as a whore. He could not help himself; his body was responding, his pulse racing. And yet, what did she mean? Something about her was false. He was acutely conscious of her even without meeting her eyes. The weeks of enforced proximity had given him ample opportunity for fantasies of every sort. He hesitated, confused and aroused, and his eyes caught a glimpse of something on the horizon. He turned, staring harder. "Look! Do I imagine it?"

"No, you do not!" For there far to the north, was a great whale in full view, spouting like a geyser and basking on the calm waters.

Silently, they stared, feeling the beauty of the moment and all that it promised. Tears filled Zaidee's eyes, and helplessly, for her emotions were swift if shallow, she whispered to Darius Yates, "Do you think it's an omen? I believe it is." She bent forward, so that he could smell her cologne, and whispered, "You may kiss me, sir."

Yates was frightened by Zaidee's capricious sexuality, and he backed away. "Oh, my dear, I could not."

Anger flooded her cheeks and snapped in her eyes,

as quickly aroused as affection and for reasons less mixed.

"I am sorry, Miss Zaidee," Yates said gently. He adored women, he revered them; nothing on earth could move him to mislead one. "I cannot love you," he went on clumsily and unnecessarily, "no, never, for I think I love your sister."

"You presume, sir," Zaidee said coldly. Her fury at his rejection was nothing compared with her jealousy of Elinor, Elinor who had done nothing to arouse this man's affections but be herself, whom everyone loved instinctively and faithfully and always had, unfair as it was. "Pray don't annoy her; she don't love you, Mr. Yates, and I know because she told me so. She dislikes you, sir, and is terribly bored with your company, so there."

And turning, she left him, her immense damp skirts clinging to her legs and nearly tripping her without the aid of hoops. Yates stood alone, rebuffed and bewildered, above all bewildered, as the sky darkened and the panoramic view of the great whale melted into the darkness.

And then even that, which had seemed a good omen, changed swiftly for the ill, and the winds that blew at the *Victoria* came from the north, came hard and cold, and struck the vessel just as night fell. Yates stared at the oncoming storm, black and glowering, his thoughts nearly as grim and cold, as long as he could, but the gale was freakish and carried hail and snow in icy gusts and he was driven below to see his fellow passengers kneeling in four inches of water, praying for deliverance.

"Dear Lord, we entrust our lives to Thy hand," Reverend Love intoned. "Save us, save us to do Thy will in the land we seek." Yates lowered his head in prayer.

"We are lost, we are gone up now!" someone moaned.

At one side of the main cabin Yates saw the Richler sisters with closed eyes and clasped hands, pretty as a chromograph of praying angels, but as he looked their way, Zaidee raised her head to glare at him.

# Chapter Five

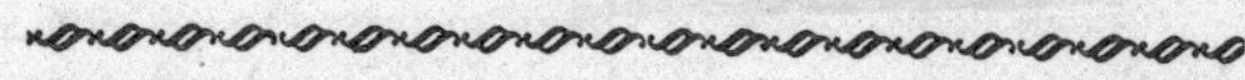

Tyler Ashby was certain of only one thing after a month in Brazil, a month after sailing into the spectacular harbor of Rio de Janeiro on a dazzling autumn morning. Brazil was not what he had expected. It was more beautiful, far stranger, more complicated, and more compelling.

Rio de Janeiro was a city unlike any he had ever seen. It was a city of sublime and spectacular scenery—the heights of the mountain called Corcovado towered above the semicircular Bay of Botafogo and were matched to the south by the far-famed mountain called the Sugar Loaf. Between the mountains stretched a wide beach with sands as white as the surf that pounded upon it.

Although it was a port, it was not at all like Mobile. Rio's beaches were scattered with palms and fishermen's small grass huts. The city's narrow, dark, mysterious streets were lined with huge granite and brick mansions in the Portuguese style. Most of these houses were of two or three stories but they spread out around courtyards, occupying acres even in the center of the city. The houses were flanked by gardens and orchards, banana and orange groves, and stone terraces and outbuildings, all set off by high stone walls and looking out at the street through tall, shuttered windows.

"We have arrived safely and been well received," Colonel Ashby wrote home. It was an understatement. Emperor Dom Pedro had met them as they stepped onto the beach, stumbling from small rowboats that had carried them in through the surf. The Emperor had waved all their baggage through customs and made a speech to welcome them to Brazil.

Dom Pedro, Tyler had been surprised to see, was a handsome young man, his shoulders squared with epaulets and his chest dignified with ribbons and medals, but with the look of a man who had never lived or worked in the real world. His pale face, framed in a dark beard, was soft and untried, and his body plump and awkward, reminding Tyler of the young Yankees from the Midwestern industrial cities, soldiers who had never marched or ridden or slept in the outdoors until the war forced them from their offices and factories.

"Welcome most cordially to Brazil," Dom Pedro had said, and called the *Talisman*'s passengers "the first wave of a welcome deluge of immigrants from the splendid Southern states." Then, with his retinue of white-bearded ministers, he had taken them to lodgings in a mansion called the Hotel por Immigrantes.

How luxurious that hotel had seemed to Tyler after weeks on shipboard. Its high-ceilinged bedrooms held soft wide beds puffed high with snowy linen; its sitting rooms were airy and cheerful with caged songbirds and massive, red-painted furniture, and its cuisine of sweet Brazilian fruits and spicy stews was delicious. And yet . . . how strange it was to be surrounded by curious, staring Brazilians and to have his ears filled with their unintelligible chatter in Portuguese, a language which he understood not at all, and privately doubted he would ever understand. It was a language so soft and melodious, spoken so rapidly, it sounded to him like birdsong. He could not tell when one word stopped and the next began, and he was always surprised when a speaker paused for his response.

"The Portuguese language is very difficult," Tyler wrote home. He did not add that most Brazilian attempts to pronounce English were equally inscrutable. And as for what seemed to be the prevailing Brazilian attitudes toward commerce, toward religion, toward women, and toward Negroes! He did not yet fully understand these attitudes, but already he understood enough to see that he had entered into a new world.

Again and again he reflected how everything in Brazil seemed to be both similar and different. It would take time to sort things out, to understand. He cautioned himself to reserve judgment and to learn all that he could.

To Tyler, Rio de Janeiro seemed to be a city of a thousand churches, and yet Sunday was a day of business like any other, even busier. Taverns and stores were all open on Sundays and theaters and opera houses attracted large audiences.

In passing through the city's business district on a Sunday, Tyler had seen Negro men wearing nothing more than scant loincloths over their bulging thighs and Negro women sitting on the sidewalks with only a thin chemise, all as unconscious of undue exposure as Eve in the Garden of Eden.

The city was full of half-naked women, many of them obviously prostitutes, some of them light-skinned and beautiful. Some walked or danced through the streets, but others rode in fine open carriages, displayed like jewels in their low-necked dresses.

Seeing them had stirred Tyler powerfully. At first he had stared so long that a carriage had creaked to a stop, with the woman inside smiling, laughing, beckoning to him, sending her footman rushing to him, bathing him in a torrent of unintelligible talk. He had stared quite stupidly, amazed at her elegant, bright dress and huge feathered hat. Then he had backed away, shaking his head in confusion.

Perhaps it is the tropical sun, he thought. Under the fierce Brazilian sun, everything was exaggerated. Everything seemed clearer, brighter, more forcefully itself. Not that things were less strange under the Brazilian moon.

He wondered what an American woman would make of these customs. Upper-class Brazilian women were nowhere to be seen. Women stay at home, their guide, Senhor Macedo explained; they go out only chaperoned and then usually to church. Neither Macedo's wife nor daughters had ever joined the men at the dinner table.

Senhor Macedo also explained the presence of so many light-skinned Negroes in Brazil. "It is the way here," Macedo said, his olive-skinned face gleaming with the considerable effort of speaking English. "In the first century, we were all bachelors. And now, we are all God's children, eh?" he said, winking and making a lewd gesture with his fingers.

From the Hotel por Immigrantes, the Ashbys had been moved to Senhor Macedo's own mansion, and they had passed two weeks there enjoying every possible comfort and luxury while Colonel Ashby was introduced to Dom Pedro's ministers and studied maps of the interior. In Tyler's case, the comforts of Macedo's hospitality had included the delivery of a very young mulatto girl to his bedroom on the first night of his stay.

It was an episode he had discussed with no one, but it had changed him, in a way, wakened him as a pitcher of cold water might wake a sleeper. He felt changed, felt more a man and less a gentleman, less a war-worn soldier whose army had been smashed into ignominious defeat. And, for a time, the girl's willingness and his intense reaction to her had put the face of the dark-haired Tennessee woman out of his mind. Some of the hopeful energy that he had known before the war came back into him and he looked at the world around him with new interest.

"Your father tells me you are a doctor," Senhor Macedo said to him.

"Not yet a doctor, but I have studied medicine."

"In Brazil, an American-trained doctor is a doctor," Macedo said. "You will need supplies."

I suppose I will, Tyler thought, and while his father was making arrangements for the next leg of their journey, he visited the pharmacies along the road to Petropolis. Many of the pharmacies were run by Frenchmen; they were as dark and dusty as alchemists' lairs.

Hesitant at first, Tyler found that the words "American doctor" won him not only cooperation but exaggerated respect. He bought ipecac, castor oil, and tincture of aconite for gastric disturbances and fevers of all sorts, as well as calomel, belladonna and quinine. At the advice of the pharmacists, he bought some powders derived from Indian remedies.

He packed the medicines and stowed them under his bunk in the *Vixen*'s small cabin; they were his ballast, they would steady him against the uncertainties of the future, as important to him as his father's five carpetbags full of gold.

After he had sold Marie-Anne's jewelry and paid his tailor's and hotel bills, Terrill Ruffin found himself in possession of a small amount of money. His next goal was to choose a way to get to Brazil, an easier matter than he had expected.

That spring all the lower South was burning with "Brazil fever." Daily, New Orleans newspapers carried accounts of Southerners setting off for Brazil, advertisements for books to advise would-be emigrants about where to go and what to take, whom to contact and what ships were taking on passengers to sail for Rio de Janeiro or the port of Belém in Pará, the Amazon region. The *New Orleans Picayune* published a series of letters from Brazil under the heading "All About Brazil," and it was estimated that upward of 50,000 Southerners were ready to turn their backs on Reconstruction and emigrate to Brazil. (Brazilian journals doubled the estimate and predicted 100,000 families of "provident, virtuous, and intelligent" people were on the verge of arriving from the states recently in rebellion.)

In the week that followed, Terrill Ruffin read some of the newspaper articles and letters from Southerners who had already reached Brazil. Not all of them were encouraging, but he was not primarily concerned with that. His first concern was any reference to Jesse Rall, but his name was not among the published lists of emigrants. He continued to search.

On November 15, Ruffin saw a notice in the newspaper that an official agent of the Brazilian Emperor Dom Pedro II would be receiving applicants and advising prospective immigrants in his suite on Royal Street. He called for an appointment and arrived there the next day.

Rafael Barroso, the Emperor's agent, was a wealthy, aristocratic young Brazilian who had accepted this important temporary post in a spirit of patriotism. He was the son of a large landowner. He spoke several languages and had traveled in Europe, an experience that gave him a perspective unusual for his age. Dressed like a European, he wore a tight-fitting frock coat, a flowing tie, and a full mustache over which his shining dark eyes regarded the world with curiosity. To date, he was half amused and half horrified by what he had observed of American customs and manners.

Barroso and Terrill Ruffin liked each other at once. Ruffin introduced himself politely and inquired if Barroso would prefer to speak in French or English. Barroso chose French, and he smiled as he told Ruffin he was the first cultivated American gentleman he had met, reaching for his hand and shaking it energetically.

Ruffin smiled back and explained that although he was American-born, he was thoroughly disenchanted with the state of his country since the war and desired above all else to emigrate to Brazil.

"Brazil is the land of opportunity," Barroso promised, passing his eyes boldly up and down Ruffin's supple, handsome body. "Monsieur Ruffin, you will do very well in Brazil, I can feel it."

Ruffin was surprised by the agent's frank appraisal

of him, but he was not displeased. His instinct was to trust Barroso. He seemed frank and completely at ease—his dark eyes gleamed with energy and his smile was open. Could it be that all Brazilians were like this? Perhaps he would find a more compassionate society there.

"I want to go at once," Ruffin said. Risking a confidence, he added, "There is nothing left for me here. All that I had is gone. I am alone. I hate it here—now. It's a chaos of mourning and mob rule."

"Monsieur," Barroso said, "I can see that you have suffered." He put his hand on Ruffin's arm. "Put the past behind you. Sir, it is in my power to provide you with passage to Brazil, and I'll do so gladly. As for now, I am tired of this office—it's such a beautiful day. Let's go together to the waterfront to see when the next ship sails."

"I'm in your debt," Ruffin said, responding to Barroso's show of feeling with more enthusiasm than he had felt in months. "Perhaps, later this evening, you'll allow me to entertain you. I have a certain knowledge of the city that might amuse you."

"Why not?" Barroso replied. "What a pleasure it is to have met you. I shall be sorry to see you go, my friend."

Ruffin smiled as they left the office. How unlike American white men this Brazilian was. Perhaps he would find a new race of men in Brazil. Perhaps even a new God and a new reason for living.

The freakish storm from the north tossed and battered the *Victoria* for five terribly days. On the sixth morning it ended as suddenly as it had begun, and both her crew and passengers were amazed to see that they had been blown into a sheltered cove. On three sides, land was in sight, presumably the mainland of Brazil, surely a mountainous landmass surrounded by broad sandy beaches.

"Praise the Lord, for He has delivered us," Reverend Love shouted, and in the first pink light of dawn the travelers joined arms and sang the doxology. Everyone's spirits were exalted and everyone talked at once.

"We have arrived at last!" Elinor Richler exclaimed. She stood with Zaidee at the ship's railing, delighted to breathe land-scented air and anticipate walking ashore after so many days of confinement. The breeze smelled sweet and grassy and the sunlight glinted off Zaidee's head like pure gold.

"Is that Sugar Loaf Mountain?" Elinor asked.

"It must be," Zaidee said. "Shall we sail in close to shore or go in longboats?"

"Why, I don't know," Elinor replied. "It's odd that I can't see the city. Can you?"

"Not yet," Zaidee admitted.

"It's said to be a large city," Elinor said.

"Where is the Captain, Papa?" Zaidee asked. "When can we go ashore?"

Captain Cash, as was immediately apparent, was still drunk from the night before, when he had shared his last three bottles of rum with his first mate. Both men had been convinced it was their last night on earth. They had never weathered a worse storm. Cash was roused, groaning and retching, and stumbled to his lookout position. Every trace was gone of the violent storm that had ruled the atmosphere with hail and hellish winds for five days; it was humid and hot, the sort of day when every movement leaves one exhausted.

Cash's head was splitting; he had never felt worse. He spit on the deck and scowled at the sight of the land.

"It ain't Rio," he said flatly. "I don't know why the hell it ain't, we kept our course steady as anyone ever did, but it ain't."

Franklin Richler stared at the captain with ill-concealed anger. He clenched his fists. In the army, we would have had him court-martialed a month ago for his blundering and unprofessional behavior, he thought despairingly.

Cash blinked at the sunlight and groaned, not yet glad he was still alive.

"If we are not arrived at Brazil, Captain Cash," Franklin Richler asked, shaking with anger, "why, then, where, in the hell as you say, are we, sir?"

Cash was roused to an equal anger. "I don't know, I tell you!" he snarled. "Can't you damn Rebs understand that? But I intend to find out!" Standing in the open door of his lookout, he winced at the sunlight glinting off the ship's brass fixtures and the glittering surface of the shallow blue sea.

"Papa, may we go ashore today?" Zaidee asked persistently. She and Elinor hung back just on the edge of earshot during their father's exchange with the captain.

"Of course we'll go ashore—all of us," Richler promised. Behind him, the other passengers were already making preparations to land. After so many weeks at sea, the nearness of land was irresistible. There were no cities in sight, but a flotilla of small open boats was approaching the ship from the land lying to the east.

"Papa, will you take down our hoops for us?" Zaidee asked. Wherever we are, she thought, we must show the natives that we are in step with fashion.

"Your hoops?" Richler had forgotten about the

women's decision to stow away their iron hoopskirt frames. "Where are your hoops?"

"We put them away there, in that cupboard." Zaidee showed him. "Please don't make us go ashore without our hoops. We must look civilized."

"In this cupboard?" Franklin Richler followed his daughter to the closet just behind the captain's lookout position and wrenched it open. A full score of iron dress hoops fell forward and bounced along the deck, clattering and ringing into the crowd of women and children, the crate of barking hounds, men who had already put on their Confederate dress uniforms, and the ship's crew hauling down the long boats.

Everyone turned to stare.

"How long have those damn hoops been there?" Captain Cash demanded from the door of his lookout. "Goddamn it! Who hid away those iron monsters?"

"They have been there ever since Galveston, sir," Elinor Richler said in a soft voice.

Drunk and weakened as he felt, Calvin Cash's vision was not so dimmed that he could not see clearly and at once what had happened. Understanding and outrage dawned swiftly. He stared, openmouthed, and then he swallowed, too astonished at first to let loose the stream of curses in which he intended to bathe the whole lot of ignorant landlubbers.

In the moment's pause, Franklin Richler began to comprehend. "The hoops?" he asked. "The hoops and the compasses?"

"Yes, the compasses, you goddamn Secessionist fools!" Captain Cash raved. "Your goddamn foolishness has sent us God knows where! Don't you mud-footed farmers know that iron will corrupt the finest compass in the world? We're off course and it's your fault, all your fault. Damn it to bloody hell!"

"Captain, there are ladies present!" Richler protested.

"No thanks to them, we're all still alive. . . ."

"Elinor, please take your sister and go below," Franklin Richler ordered. "I won't have you hearin' any more of this language."

"But where are we, sir?" Darius Yates asked. His voice was a wail of despair at the thought of going on with this terrible voyage.

"With that damn mine of iron aboard, we're lucky if we haven't sailed to goddamn Africa!" Captain Cash raved, and as it turned out, his guess was a good one, for when the open boats reached the *Victoria*, it was discovered that their dark-skinned occupants were residents of the islands surrounding them, not a mainland at all, but the Cape Verde Islands, just a hundred miles off the westernmost coast of the continent of Africa.

Looking at a map, when some of the furor had subsided, it was clear enough what had happened. Because of the iron hoopskirts, they had sailed straight east instead of east and then south. It was a reality at first hard to believe, and later hard to accept, but like all realities, it had its way, and a week later, the *Victoria* again ran up her sails and collected the trade winds, sailing southwest.

The week passed quickly. Minus hoops, which Captain Cash had ordered thrown into the sea, all the passengers had been ferried ashore in the *Victoria*'s open dinghies and had gorged themselves on oranges and sweet lemons, pineapples and fresh roasted meat. "It is no one's fault," Franklin Richler told his daughters, but it was obvious the Captain did not share that opinion.

"I believe he would just as soon dump all of us overboard," Zaidee speculated.

"God works in mysterious ways," Reverend Love declared. "Perhaps He wants to remind us of the vastness of the sea and the frailty of man."

# Chapter Six

Some weeks later, Tyler and Colonel Ashby stood together at the rail of a small coastal steamer engagingly named *Vixen*. The *Vixen* was carrying them slowly south from Rio to the port of Santos in the province of São Paulo. From there they would travel inland to search for property suitable for cotton planting.

As the *Vixen* churned through the choppy waters, the haunting, rhythmic chant of the Negro boatmen rose to the deck. Tyler looked up at the moon. Pale as a cloud, it hung overhead in a sky bright with stars. Thank God for the moon, he thought wryly. If the stars are all puzzlingly out of place, the moon is a constant.

"Do you hear that song?" his father asked.

Tyler nodded. The boatmen's chanting had grown louder and been supplemented by a drum beating monotonously.

"I have heard the same song in Georgia," Colonel Ashby said, and Tyler smiled, understanding that his father was also casting about for constants.

"Perhaps you have," he replied.

Santos, where the Ashbys arrived the next day, was a damp, dirty city built upon marshes that simmered in tropical heat and incubated yellow fever. After one night spent at a small hotel near the harbor decorated with the famous blue Portuguese tiles and smelling inescapably of coffee, they set out by railroad, climbing the coastal plain to São Paulo, the provincial capital, fifty miles inland. São Paulo, first settled by white men in the early sixteenth century, owed its prosperity to its fortunate location at the mouth of a natural gap in the mountains. All the riches of the interior passed through São Paulo on the way to the ocean and the city had already attained a population of 20,000.

After the heat and humidity of the sea-level cities, São Paulo's cool, brisk mountain atmosphere was invigorating, and the Ashbys lost no time in hiring a guide, two horses, and an oxcart to transport their baggage to the interior. They left the city at dawn on a day in late November.

"Next year, Senhores, we will have a railroad," the hotel keeper promised them, smiling toothlessly. "Or if not next year, surely the year after that."

But the Ashbys soon realized that not only was there no railroad but there was no road to the interior of the province. They made their way along the narrowest of ox-paths hacked through the underbrush, dusty in the dry seasons, and now, at the end of the rainy season, already worked into a mire by the passage of carts and feet.

At once, the cool of the mountains gave way to a suffocating heat in the flatlands of the inland plateau. There the wildness of the interior closed in around them. Mosquitoes, flying ants and beetles with jet-black pincers settled on their clothes and baggage, and the hushed silence was broken only by the sharp cries of brilliant parakeets and toucans, the doleful wailing of ibises, and the wild, fierce screams of jungle cats.

At the end of the second day they camped at the edge of a river, watching huge jabiru storks stalking eels and fish in the fading light. When they awoke, both the guide and the horses were gone. They continued on foot, never sure of the trail, crossing rivers and bending back the tangled vines that closed out the sunlight, their companions the black howler monkeys that swung through the treetops.

Ten days west of São Paulo, they attained a grassy plain. Here the land opened out into dreamlike vistas of greenwoods and glistening canefields in wide valleys between rolling hills. Slowly, they climbed one broad, sunbaked hill and looked out over a meandering blue creek. Tyler Ashby bent and took up a handful of earth. It was red and crumbled like gingerbread.

"Son," Colonel Ashby said, his voice rising with excitement, "it looks like cotton country to me."

"It looks like Alabama," Tyler agreed.

There was a settlement of railroad workers at the end of the valley. There they learned this was the Campinas region and that the nearest town was called Santa Barbara. When the railroad was finished, it would link Santa Barbara to São Paulo. First granted to Portuguese settlers by royal decree, this country had long been planted in sugarcane, and there were still large sugar plantations here, but in recent years it had been partially converted to coffee growing.

The more they saw, the more the Ashbys liked the land around Santa Barbara, and within a week they had made arrangements with a lawyer in Campinas to buy a plantation, or fazenda, as the Brazilians called it. It was a large fazenda, about five leagues square, and with it came a supply of Negro laborers. It had been previously planted in coffee and adjoined a large sugarcane plantation belonging to a Brazilian family named Barroso.

A two-story brick farmhouse in poor repair stood on the Ashbys' land. They settled into it, sent word to the family in Alabama, and began to make plans for the future.

The Amazon is more an elemental presence than a river. Nowhere in the wide world is there anything comparable to it. It is wider than any other river in the world, as wide as six Mississippis. Compared with it, the rivers of Europe are narrow trickles. It is four thousand miles long, dense and silty and fetid, muddy and green, swirling into the Atlantic to stain the sea for over one hundred miles. It is a river so vast no human eye can comprehend its dimensions—only the gods can know it is a river. It drains an area of almost three million square miles. It is so immense that an island the size of Belgium clots its estuary and is thought to be the whole world by some of its inhabitants.

The Amazon is more than a river, more than a congress of rivers. It is a tropical region bigger than any European country, a jungle that has never been fully penetrated or explored, home to some of the most primitive people in the world, home to Indians who have never heard of white men. Crossed by the Equator, the Amazon region is relentlessly humid, yet its temperature varies little. It is impenetrably swampy and thickly forested, a paradise for birds and animals escaping civilization, a vast, dark retreat for rare creatures of every species.

On Christmas morning, Jesse Rall woke by the

side of the Amazon River. Rall had been on the move for seven months; he had been in Brazil for nearly six of them. He had left Texas and crossed the sea without incident in a Mexican steamer bound for the port of Belém at the mouth of the Amazon. From there he had traveled upriver, following a rumor of an American colony, following his own lusts, indulging himself in dreams of vast wealth to be made in gold, in diamonds, in rubber, pushing onward into the interior past the reach of civilization or reason, moving onward nearly every day on a journey the nature of which he himself could not have clearly defined.

It was partly a journey into the unknown. Rall had a dark suspicion of the unknown, yet he craved it as a man craves a dangerous drug. In that respect the Amazon had stretched the limits of his craving—it was more in every way than anything he had seen in America: more vast, more untamed, more dangerous. Ostensibly, he sought the Americans who had gone upriver before him and established a colony, but in his heart he did not believe he would ever find them, or that they had ever or still existed.

In another way, the journey was simply a working out of his nature and a search for expiation of his sins. Rall knew he had sinned; he believed it as deeply as he believed he was damned, for he had been raised by his simple and pious mother, and although he had convinced himself that he was above the laws of ordinary men, he suffered remorse and remorse drove him to seek men more immoral than himself. Men of this stripe were easy to find in Brazil. He had seen them in Belém's saloons, slave markets, and whorehouses. He had drunk with them on the river steamer that bore him upriver, glorying in them and in beating them at their own games of cruelty and self-indulgence.

But the Amazon offered more, and he hungered for it. Traveling now with one other white man, a blackguard Georgian named John Satterlee, and six strapping black slaves he had bought in Belém, he moved on.

Rall controlled his slaves with a whip; they shared no other language, but he was used to controlling slaves. In Texas he had despised and feared the blacks under his supervision. It was a situation of extraordinary tension. All of them knew that the previous overseer had been murdered by one or more of the slaves, axed to death after punishing a man for some petty theft. Since the days at the Wilson plantation he had never gone unarmed and he had never slept sober, but as to his taste for drink, it was in his blood.

In the depths of the Amazon Rall's luck failed him and he fell ill with a fever. The rhythm of the boat's straining paddlewheel was a torture to him. His crowded cabin seemed an airless coffin. Begging Satterlee for help, he asked to be put ashore, and the steamer's captain gladly obliged, happy to rid his boat of the contagion of fever.

Rall and Satterlee were set ashore in a little village of leaf huts. It had been a thriving community once, in the time of the Jesuit occupation, but its residents had revolted against the priests, burned the houses, razed the church, and buried the church bells. The Americans did not know this: they knew only that one comes upon any settlement in the Amazon as a ship at sea comes upon an island. They saw cocoa-brown babies playing on a white beach, they saw tall palm trees and baskets of oranges. Rall sobbed and shook with the fever, and they went ashore.

"It's no more than a filthy Indian village," Satterlee said, "but it will have to do."

Rall drifted in and out of consciousness, and finally awoke unaware of how much time had passed. What did he remember? He had been very ill. He had hovered near death, but now he was better, and through the haze of fever and the hangover from drinking his last bottle of rum, he began to recall what had happened.

Satterlee was gone, that much was sure. Gone? Where had he gone? He sat bolt upright, and felt a wave of nausea as he began to remember. He had been delirious when they reached this wretched village, but he remembered that the Indians had been hospitable. Both he and Satterlee were given little huts. He had been too sick to protest when his slaves were taken away from him, but grateful to lie alone on a grass pallet with a roof to keep the sun and the mosquitoes away.

They had sent him a nurse. He had barely noticed her. She had been dark-skinned, of course, just an Indian woman with pendulous naked breasts and missing teeth, her belly hanging out of a fringe of grass and feathers. He had drifted in and out of delirium. When he woke she had fed him his rum and some unrecognizable vegetables. He had been constantly drenched with sweat and sometimes she had bathed him with cool water.

Later, when he woke, he could hear Satterlee's voice in a nearby hut, and understood by what he heard that Satterlee had been sent a woman, too, and was enjoying her. In his weakened state, Satterlee's lustful grunts and moans sounded obscene.

From time to time Satterlee had visited him. "We

are being held," the Georgian had insisted, "don't you understand? They are planning something for us, Rall. Can't you hear? They are watching us. When will you be well enough to go?"

But he had not been well enough even to listen. Sometimes he had not recognized Satterlee.

And then the men of the village had come to him, carrying a wreath of orchids. He had seen them but had been too weak to rise. Then he had heard them go to Satterlee. He had heard them lead him away. The woman who had been his nurse remained with him and with sign language she told him that there was a ceremony taking place, a feast. Then she left him. He had drifted off into sleep.

When he awoke, the nurse was sitting at his side. She drank something. She offered him a piece of meat on a manioc leaf. He remembered it—it had been gray-brown, hard like a lump of clay, rubbery. It revolted him for reasons he did not understand.

There was much he did not understand. Why was he being offered meat after days of vegetables and drink? Why were the nurse's dark breasts smeared with blood? Where was Satterlee?

Rall shook his heavy head. His eyes burned, the lower lips were swollen and reddened as if the fire of his soul sought egress. As his brain filled with poisonous memories of the night before, he struggled to hi feet. He was thin and weak. Rising made him dizzy. He staggered. He trembled with fear. He emerged from the hut where he had lain for so long, how long he did not know, to face a hideous and incomprehensible reality, even more terrible than his fears.

His nurse was gone; all of them were gone. It was a steamy and unnaturally quiet morning. The atmosphere was chokingly humid and the air smelled of death, a smell he knew well enough from the war at home, from the aftermath of Shiloh, where he had lain for two days on a wagon loaded with wounded men, stacked like bags of grain, men groaning and cursing and dying in their own excrement and putrefaction.

"No!" he shouted, wrung beyond reason by his detestable memories and the sight of the carnage that surrounded him now. The scattered bodies of his six slaves lay pierced with arrows; his nurse lay with an arrow through her throat. Why had his sick-hut been spared? Was anyone left alive? He did not know and would not stay to find out.

Screaming horribly, he ran toward the river, toward that immense milky presence beyond the fringe of jungle, still shrouded in the mist of humidity.

# Chapter Seven

Elinor Richler reclined languorously in a finely knotted string hammock, her fingers trailing to the floor. The fly that had roused her from her late-afternoon nap hovered over her bare knees and dropped to her raised toes. She yawned and swung herself slowly, drifting toward waking life, toward the reality of this large, whitewashed room with its high open windows framing squares of blue night sky, of heat—astonishing, down-pressing, breathtaking heat—heat that dictated afternoon naps and economy of effort, heat that smothered Rio, and of Carnival, the relentless festival that turned ordinary life inside out, the sounds of which rose to her window: drumming and singing, shouting and chanting.

The Richler family had been in Brazil only a week, and for nearly that length of time, the city had been celebrating its pre-Lenten Carnival. They had arrived on its eve, sailing, at last, past the rocky cliffs of Cabo Frio and into the deep blue harbor by the light of a full golden moon. The last leg of the voyage from the Cape Verde Islands had been mercifully smooth and uneventful.

At first the heat and the city had both seemed overwhelming. It was February, the hottest month of the Brazilian year. Rio baked in a heat wave, in a heat that dissolved will, muddled reason, incubated the growth of passion. The city seemed frantic, teeming, monstrous. To think that I considered Galveston quite a place, Elinor reflected. She smiled to herself, swinging her legs out of the hammock and dropping them to the floor. Zaidee still slept in another hammock, her mouth wide open in a childish pout, her red-gold hair streaming out behind her like an exotic fan.

Elinor stretched, reached for her petticoat and then thought better of it. It was really too hot. The singing and dancing, the steady, hypnotic beat of drums and the yearning, straining melodies of the brass and strings drew her to the window. It had not stopped all day, not while she slept and dreamed, not even in the hottest noon hours. How do they bear it? she wondered. Of course many of them are African, and they say black people do not mind the heat.

Leaning half out of the window, dressed in only the briefest cotton chemise and step-ins, she studied the scene below. It was twilight; to the west the sky was palest purple-blue streaked with orange and already the moon had risen over red roofs, green trees, and the palm-studded shimmering sands that fringed the great bay in the distance.

How beautiful it is, how beautiful, Elinor thought, her emotions stirring. She sighed and tightened her grip on the windowsill. It is so beautiful that I know I shall come to love it. All the confusion and misunderstandings of these first days will pass and come to seem only a tiny part of life in Brazil.

Of course, we shall not live in Rio, she thought, and it will not always be Carnival time, but whatever happens, I want to experience it . . . adventurously and in my own way. I want to understand Brazil, and its people and . . . all of life. Elinor's soul was thrilled by the idea. She knew herself to be extraordinary. Without being vain, she was very self-confident. Life had taught her to be so. She was accustomed to responsibilities, for her mother's illness was a lingering one, and while her father had been away at war, she had quietly taken charge of the family and the plantation.

I am restless, Elinor admitted, and dear Lord, I am so tired of Zaidee. Was there ever anyone more demanding and spoiled? Oh, she is clever, she can be charming when she will, but she is so willful she makes me seem foolishly proper by comparison, simply because I have better manners and try to practice restraint.

It was the night they had been waiting for all week. A special Carnival ball, the Ballo dos Americanos, was to be held in their honor. As soon as they arrived, the Richler sisters had heard about the ball and begged their father to be allowed to go. To their surprise, Franklin Richler had agreed, although no one had been properly introduced and it was even possible that liquor would be served. "The Emperor's invitation must of course be honored," Franklin Richler had said.

Tonight, she noticed happily, her father was again in good spirits. He had talked with American immigrants about several colonies already established and was interested in one said to be composed primarily of cotton planters from Alabama and Tennessee. This colony was in the province of São Paulo, inland from the sea and the mountain plateau, near a village called Santa Barbara. As soon as Carnival was ended, Richler told his family, they would sail to Santos and before the end of the summer they would likely be settled in a home of their own.

"I hope it is not a long sea voyage," Daphne said weakly. "I don't think I could bear another long voyage by sea, Mr. Richler."

"It is not a long way," he promised. "We will be through travelin' in only a few weeks." Daphne Richler had lost weight on the *Victoria* and had not recovered her strength. Even tonight, for the Carnival ball, she wore black and looked drawn and pale, but to her husband's eyes she was as handsome as ever.

"You look fine tonight, Mrs. Richler, and so do your daughters. I am honored to escort the three of you, I must say!"

"Thank you, Papa," Zaidee said pertly, but Elinor merely smiled. She was wearing her best dress, a ruffled and tucked pale-blue organdy with a deep blue sash; Zaidee was in watered green silk, and, at a shocking cost, they had managed to find hoopskirts to replace the ones Captain Cash had thrown overboard, but still, they looked like foreigners, and she felt out of place.

Nor did she feel less so when they arrived at Dom Pedro's huge and lavish seaside palace, as white and ornate as a wedding cake and glowing with yellow light at the end of a spit of land jutting out into Guanabara Bay.

A stream of carriages approached the Palace of São Cristovão along a white-shell driveway and paused at the front portico where a wide flight of stone stairs ran up to the ballroom and assembly rooms on the main floor and a crew of Negro footmen in livery waited to hold the horses' heads and help the guests out of their carriages. The ball had begun. Music floated down out of the second-floor ballroom, waltz music at first, as the Richlers' carriage approached, then changing to Brazilian music with a pulsing, insistent rhythm that Elinor recognized as the sort she had been hearing in the streets all week. Clinging together, the Richlers left their carriage and joined the crowd climbing the stairs into the palace.

"How wonderful," Zaidee said to Elinor, "it's like a romantic novel, isn't it?"

Elinor nodded vaguely but she did not agree. She tried to look everywhere at once, impressed by the size and grandeur of the palace—it was more elegant than anything she had ever seen before, but she was distracted by the crowd of Brazilians. Men and women in every manner of exotic dress were calling out greetings, falling into one anothers' arms, embracing, roaring with laughter. Many of them were in elaborate costumes and masks, some wore feather headdresses, and many wore garlands of orchids. A man in a black top hat carried a blue parrot on each shoulder, and some man—and why did everyone laugh?—was dressed as a woman, she could swear to it!

Oh dear! Where had the others gone? She had lingered, staring at the freakish man, and had lost her place in the slow procession moving up the stairs. The light was dim; it was cast by hundreds of candles flickering in sconces along the outside walls, the air smelled of flowers and smoke and liquor, and it was still dreadfully hot, so humid that everyone's face shone, so close that it was like breathing through a wet cloth.

The parrots screamed, and Elinor jumped. She could not help herself, her eyes filled with tears of fright. It was too much, too unfamiliar. Zaidee did not understand that this was not a romantic novel, this was their new reality, and that made all the difference. She shied away from the huge, black hand of a man dressed in bright yellow who reached for her at the top of the stairs. He smelled of rum, like a sailor. His eyes were too familiar, too probing, too frankly admiring. A sob caught in her throat, and she swayed unsteadily, her hoops quivering under her pale blue dress.

Inside the palace ballroom, Zaidee was swept away by the crowd and soon was lost. There were so many strangers, all chattering in Portuguese, many staring openly. Every way Zaidee turned she saw another amazing sight: a beautiful dark-eyed woman wearing a cat's mask and tail, preening and stroking her whiskers, a man dressed as a devil in a red satin suit and top hat, a coal-black woman in a fabulous cloth-of-gold dress over enormous hoops.

Perhaps the most astonishing thing was the number of Negroes in the crowd. She could not help but be shocked and battled with her lifetime's experiences to comprehend it. Evidently it was true that in Brazil black and white society intermixed. These must be free

Negroes, she speculated. Certainly they were not like American Negroes, who were all poor and uneducated and badly dressed and who, of course, as they said at home, "knew their place." Some of these people were very light-skinned. In fact, there were Negroes of every imaginable skin color: there were mulattoes, quadroons, octoroons, all the varieties she had been taught to recognize and not to mention. Of course, things were different here. These were Negroes—if they could be called so—who owned expensive clothes and knew how to dance, who felt more comfortable in the Emperor's palace than she did.

"You are American?"

It was a man, dark-skinned, very handsome, dressed as an elegant pirate in black silk trousers fitted tightly over his lean hips, an open-collared white silk shirt, and wide red sash. She stared, surprised to hear English spoken and then by the man himself. His eyes were bold and black, his face both aristocratic and frankly sensual, his mouth wide and full-lipped under a shining, jet-black mustache, curly and close-clipped. He smiled coolly and recklessly. Immediately she felt helplessly confused. She caught her breath.

"I have been watching for you . . . all evening." It seemed he could not stand still, he was all motion, he swayed and twisted in time to the music, he shifted his broad shoulders and shook his hips and his hands reached out for her. Still she could find no words. She felt the power of his sexuality like a hot wind. She had never laid eyes on a handsomer or more frightening man.

"Come and dance," he invited her. Her mind whirled with protests; it was impossible; she could not; he was too intimidating; he was too bold; she did not know him; they had not been introduced—and yet he was magnetic, he was irresistible. After a half-moment of hesitation she moved into his arms, thinking, I do not know this dance, and, How lovely it feels to give in to this music.

"I am a pirate." He laughed, showing straight white teeth. "I capture you, my lady." His English was clear but heavily accented; he was unmistakably Brazilian. I shall have to say something, Zaidee thought, or he will think I am a mute, but she smiled instead.

"You smile like an angel," he said, and Zaidee laughed, less frightened. It was a pleasure to move to the music; she loved dancing and the music of Carnival had had her tapping her feet all week. She allowed him to lead her; his hands were strong and possessive on her waist and he guided her firmly for a few steps until she caught the rhythm and began to move faster, her skirts whirling and fluttering, a rosy flush covering her neck and bosom, her eyes shining.

She was very conscious of her own body and of his. His thighs touched her in the sudden closeness of the dance, he bent her backward until she gasped, then scooped her up; she was as graceful as he; they were perfectly matched, and she forgot her fear and self-consciousness. Her pulse raced, she felt dizzy, felt a part of the swirling, frenzied crowd, felt as fluid and mysterious and intense as any Brazilian.

Perhaps more. Concentrating on the dance, on the wonderful unfamiliar sensation of spinning, of being in the arms of a man, she knew there had been nothing to compare with this heady ecstatic feeling in her life before.

She stumbled, but he caught her, holding her even tighter, so close to him that she could feel the muscular hardness of his body, feel it pulsing, so that she inhaled his smell of cologne and perspiration and tobacco. The music moved faster and sounded louder and she threw back her head for air. All of a sudden she was aware that they were no longer surrounded by the crowd, that a space had cleared for them and that hundreds of eyes were on her.

*"Brava! Brava bella Americana!"*

Zaidee froze, horrified. How conspicuous she was. It was terribly unladylike. Everyone was looking at her—everyone! She tried to break away, but he held her more tightly than ever. "Please!" she said, the one word wrung from her. She blushed deeper, but he spun her as the music reached a crescendo and stopped to a burst of applause from the other dancers and she was able to slip out of his arms, breathless, and run, she did not know where, just away. . . .

Before she had gone more than a few steps, Darius Yates caught her arm. "Miss Zaidee?"

"Oh! Oh, goodness! Thank heaven you are here!" she exclaimed. She clung to him, struggling for breath. Pray God he won't tell Papa what he's seen me do, she thought, but Yates's thoughts were far away.

Since the incident with Zaidee on the *Victoria* he had felt uncomfortable with all the Richlers. It had spoiled the spontaneity of his friendly feelings for them, and feeling more estranged than ever he had sunk into gloom.

The Richlers, like so many other Southerners, he had concluded, were pledged to preserving and even resurrecting the Dixie Kingdom, but he wanted none of it. He had to leave them or he would never escape the sadness and rage that accompanied all his memories of Georgia. I want no part of their colonies, Yates thought.

I will not live with a crowd of homesick misfits; I must go off alone. How can I be more lonely than I am tonight?

"Come along," he said to Zaidee in a stiff, uncomfortable voice, "we are all to be presented to the Emperor in the assembly room."

Zaidee followed him gladly and joined her family and the other Americans at the end of a long line filing past Dom Pedro on his throne. *"Os Americanos! Las Americanas!"* the crowd hissed as they passed through the room. The Emperor glittered with medals and wore white silk but no crown, to Zaidee's disappointment. His ministers were bearded older men in black who all looked alike to her as she moved down the line, bowing and curtsying with the others.

But at the end of the royal party was an unexpected sight that shocked Zaidee to the bottom of her heart, despite everything she had seen in the ballroom. Seated next to Dom Pedro on the royal dais was a coal-black Negro girl in a white gown covered with white feathers and seed pearls and wearing a diamond tiara. Zaidee's smile did not slip, but her lips went white.

"The Princess Luisa Maria," intoned the minister making introductions.

Zaidee trembled. How could this Negress be a Brazilian princess? Why, she was as dark as a monkey! Next to her, she saw Elinor's eyes fill with tears as she bowed, but Zaidee was less controlled. "This is just what we left the South to avoid seein'," she hissed, and turned on her heel rather than face the sight.

"Hold your tongue, Zaidee," Elinor whispered, but no one had noticed. All eyes were on the handsome Emperor, who rose to his feet, smiling, and led the

Princess Luisa Maria, his cousin, out onto the floor and into a waltz.

Some weeks after he and his father had settled into the big brick house on their land near the village of Santa Barbara, Tyler Ashby made up his mind to observe a Southern custom. He set out to call on his nearest neighbors.

Those neighbors, he had been told, were a family named Barroso whose ancestors had been granted land by a decree of the Portuguese crown some two or more centuries ago. Since then, the Barrosos had thrived and multiplied, planted sugarcane, bought slaves, and grown wealthy. Their land, which Tyler Ashby had been told amounted to several thousand acres, was adjacent to the plantation the Ashbys had bought, and bordered it along the lively blue creek.

It was a sunny afternoon in late February when Tyler rode along the creek road toward the Barrosos' main gate. He crossed a small wooden bridge and looked up at the small adobe-walled cemetery where white crosses and white marble mausoleums rose among willows and scraggly dwarf palms. A huge black iron filigree gate closed off the burying ground. A flock of crows spiraled, squawking, rising from the dusty road where they had settled on a smashed melon fallen from a passing wagon. A dog howled somewhere in the distance, breaking the quiet of the afternoon, undisturbed except for the buzzing of the usual flies and mosquitoes and a hot wind rustling the trees and sun-parched grasses along the edges of the creek.

It was a hot Sunday afternoon, one of a series of unrelentingly hot high-summer days. Tyler wore a straw hat and a dust-streaked scarf to protect his neck from the blazing rays of the sun, but his hands had burned a dark copper during these weeks of struggling to settle in, of buying horses and Negroes and supplies, of building an addition to the brick house, of planting fruit trees and directing the clearing of land. It had been hard work, all of it made more difficult by unfamiliarity with the Portuguese language, and of course it was only the beginning, but the land and the climate still reminded Tyler of Alabama, and he hoped the day would come when he would feel at home.

As soon as he crossed the little bridge, Tyler began to smell sugar. To the east he could see the fields of sugarcane, dense, tall green stands alive with spiders and toads, buzzing with wasps and bees and flies. The refinery, distillery, the mill with its big stone wheel, the cane-trash shed, boiling vat, and storage sheds stood just inside the plantation's main gate, all the refining machinery quiet now in the growing season. Tyler rode slowly past the whitewashed gatehouse. Inside, the guard was asleep.

Off to the west he could see a barnyard with stables and beyond it a long, low mud-brick house for quartering slaves, shaded by trees hung with hammocks and backed by the irrigation ditch that linked the cane fields with the creek.

How quiet it is, Tyler thought, surprised not to see more activity on such a big plantation. The slow clip-clop of his horse's hooves stirred the dust and echoed in the silence as he proceeded toward the red-roofed bulk of the big house at the end of the dusty drive.

But just as he came into full view of the house, the sleepy quiet was broken. A dozen leaping, howling, barking dogs roused themselves and charged for his horse's legs and a pack of naked pickaninnies rolled out of a few hammocks strung at the base of the immense white crucifix that stood in a little garden opposite the big house's front steps.

"Hello, hello!" Tyler shouted, struggling to keep his seat as the dogs snapped at his horse's legs and nipped at his own. "Easy, easy!"

And then a bell began to toll and from the open door of the chapel adjoining the house emerged the entire population of Barroso plantation, a full three hundred souls, black and white and of every imaginable shade in between, streaming out of Mass, sighing with relief to be free of the humid, close, incense-thick air inside, some chattering, some singing, the children running and leaping, men wiping their faces and necks with big handkerchiefs, old women bound in scarves and rosaries, young women stepping lightly in scanty red-striped gowns with huge golden hoops through their ears.

Astonished, Tyler searched the crowd for the master of the plantation. An ancient black man in blue trousers limped forward to catch his horse's head and another dozen black and brown-skinned children swarmed around him as he dismounted. The dogs had scattered, still barking, tails wagging, but the chattering had stopped as attention focused on the stranger.

"*Bom dia,*" he began, speaking awkwardly in Portuguese. Perhaps he had been wrong to come unannounced. He had hoped that so rich a man as Senhor Barroso would speak some English. But which was Senhor Barroso?

"Ah-ha! *Americanō!*" an immensely fat man exclaimed, the crowd parting around him as some of the women lifted shawls over their heads and scattered like hens. The fat man was Barroso, Tyler realized. He was dark-haired and middle-aged with a huge black handlebar mustache, wearing a rumpled white shirt and creased trousers, but his air of authority was unmistakable. "You visit, eh?" he said, smiling broadly to Tyler, extending a huge hand and laughing uproariously.

Tyler accepted the handshake. His own rather thin hand was lost in the big man's sweaty grasp, and his first instinct was to draw back, but he was helplessly swept into Barroso's embrace, a hot, sticky, engulfing embrace, like the hug of an immense bear, a bear smelling of bay rum and coffee and laundry starch.

"My son, Rafael! Alas, he is in Rio," Barroso shouted, and then frowned and gesticulated apologetically, why Tyler had no idea. Still laughing and apologizing, he marched Tyler across the dusty courtyard, one huge arm still draped wetly over Tyler's shoulder, turning back to call out, "*Padre, Padre,*" to the priest in his cassock with a silver cross a full foot in length hanging around his neck.

Passing under an orange tree fragrant with sweet-smelling white flowers, Tyler and his host reached the broad front veranda, strung with hammocks, and settled there, Senhor Barroso collapsing in a hammock with a grunt and a sigh, and Tyler accepting a chair next to the priest.

The priest, it appeared, was to be the interpreter, although Tyler was finally made to understand that if Barroso's son Rafael had been home, it would have been he, for his English was "as good as the Queen's," according to the priest. Barroso understood quite well, Tyler guessed, for he tossed question after question in his direction and listened to the answers closely. Barroso was as curious as a child. He wanted to know, in rapid succession, where Tyler had come from and how, how he had found the beautiful Santa Barbara valley, who else was in his family and where was each of them, how long he intended to stay, what exactly he intended to do, what he thought of Brazil, and how he liked Brazilian women.

Tyler answered politely and tried to follow some of the rapid exchanges between Barroso and the priest. He was offered cashew wine and drank the curious stuff gratefully, for he was terribly thirsty, and between Barroso's questions, he allowed his eyes to wander and tried to take stock of the situation.

Most of the slaves who had emerged from the chapel had disappeared, presumably into their own quarters, but they were still surrounded by some twenty or thirty, mostly women and children. All of them seemed to be on the most familiar terms possible with their master, who lay supine in his hammock, taking a brown-skinned baby onto his stomach, rubbing and kissing its naked body, touching and teasing the older children, twisting the curls of two or three sweet-faced little girls nearly light enough, to Tyler's eye, to pass for white.

The cashew wine was served by a mulatto girl with a shy smile and beautiful breasts. Her dark eyes fixed on Tyler coyly as she bent to refill his glass and offer him sweets from a tray. Another lissome dark-skinned girl hovered over Senhor Barroso, shooing flies, fanning him from time to time with a frond of palm, lighting his cigar and lifting it from puff to puff from his mouth, placing it meantime in her own in a manner that startled Tyler.

Dom Barroso's wife, a serene woman with a mountain of dark hair gleaming with coconut oil, who had been presented as Dona Aurora, sat at the edge of the veranda in another hammock, and although she smiled at Tyler, she did not utter a word. Her hands were busy tatting lace at the hem of a white baby's dress, and even had Tyler been familiar with such feminine pursuits, he would never have guessed that it was destined for the child expected by Dom Barroso's mistress, Dona Sophia, the woman who sat in an armchair at the other end of the veranda, her large belly draped with a floating garment of white muslin, her dark lashes resting on her cheeks as she napped.

Even so, even without fathoming this or any of the other moral irregularities that lay beneath the surface of the Barroso family life, Tyler Ashby received an impression of a family life very different from his own, or that of any other American slave-owning patriarch. He had never seen a master as much at ease with his slaves as Dom Barroso, swaying in his voluptuous couch with one brown baby after another tumbling in his lap.

"Dom Martim loves children," the priest said to Tyler, as if that explained it, but to Tyler, it did not. In America, these were not children, but nigger children, apart from the consideration that he had never seen any grown man so enjoy playing with babies. He saw no tension or formality between the master and slave, at least on this veranda; it seemed to be a tableau of easy integration of black and white, young and old, and master and slave. Tyler was amazed by this, and he was charmed. Was this, he dared to guess, a microcosm of a new world?

Tyler ate a pastry of coconut and sugar and drank more of the cashew wine. It served to purify the blood, the priest assured him. Perhaps this is what heaven is like, he thought, sentimentally, moved by the atmosphere of tranquillity and harmony. Here, they are all brothers and sisters of creation, just as Senhor Macedo told me. He accepted a cigar from Barroso and could not prevent his eyes from lingering on the young mulatto girl's half-bare breasts, as tan and gleaming as rich ecru satin as she lit his cigar with a bit of wood which she had run to ignite somewhere inside the house.

But Senhor Barroso had a surprise for Tyler, a surprise which did not banish his vision of paradise, but only served to remind him that Eden always has a serpent within. The subject turned to slavery and the terrible war just fought for its sake in the United States.

"Your war," Barroso exclaimed to Tyler, through the priest, "was a tragedy, a disaster in every way. Or so my son tells me."

Tyler nodded agreement.

"Here, we could not bear such a war," Barroso told him. "Nor could we exist without our slaves. Without very many slaves we could not produce sugar. We need them to plant the cane, to cut it, to carry it to the mills and to purify it. Our slaves are our hands and feet, and I would see all of their hands and feet cut off, yes, I swear it, even those of my babies here, before I would allow one of them to go free."

The image set Tyler's mind reeling. There was no doubt but that Barroso meant what he said. Was the man a saint or a savage? What, after all, was Brazil? It was certainly something quite new, of that he was sure, but he was no longer so sure it was poised securely on the side of the angels. Everyone said that abolition of slavery was inevitable, but apart from the legal status of integration, he saw it all around him already. He looked nervously at the priest, but the man smiled as if Barroso had said nothing unexpected.

A short while later, declining offers of dinner, Tyler rose and bid his host goodbye. His horse was brought to him and as he rode back down the dusty road, his mouth held a bitter taste and his mind was full of conflicting thoughts.

# Chapter Eight

Terrill Ruffin arrived in Rio de Janeiro on March 26, his late wife's birthday, after a smooth voyage broken only by a stop at St. Thomas. He had been lulled by the voyage itself, rocked into a sort of peaceful optimism, perhaps by the rhythm of the sea, for those long, rolling waves that swell inexorably like the inhalations and exhalations of a sleeping giant, breaking into snoring froth over their own weight, have been known to pacify the most disturbed men.

His companions on the voyage had been other Americans emigrating to Brazil, chiefly farmers from Mississippi, Alabama and Tennessee who had accepted him without second thought as a white man and respected him for his superior education, his increasing control of the Portuguese language, his gentle, Louisiana manners and his dignity.

The kindness of his fellow passengers touched and surprised Ruffin, although he did not show it. He was accustomed to keeping his own counsel, to waiting before he spoke, to listening to the speech of others carefully to determine their state of mind and mood. Try as he would he could discover no evil in these people. When he told a young farmer's wife that he had lost both wife and farm, tears of sympathy had come to her faded blue eyes. He was like the others; many of them had lost family and property; they were all ready to turn their backs on suffering and go on without asking questions, with hope for the future.

There had been many quiet empty days on the long voyage, and Ruffin filled them with reading, praying, and contemplation. As he read and studied, the ever-changing glitter of the deep sea—so constant in its change, ceaseless, eternal—played on his soul and dulled his anger and pain to a poignant awareness that he was still alive, still young, and charged with a mission of vengeance. Only time heals raw grief, but the voyage was long. Ruffin's moods changed, it seemed to him sometimes, by the minute, but he battled for peace and just as he believed he had achieved resignation, the little ship that had carried him from New Orleans drew into sight of Guanabara Bay. Ruffin stood on deck as the sails were lowered and looked out at his new world.

One of the Brazilian sailors approached him. "Brazilians say the Lord made the earth in six days and saved the seventh for making Rio," he said, and Ruffin smiled. It did not seem like sacrilege. It seemed to be the truth. The famous city lay ahead, hung between earth and heaven, resting on the blue waters of the bay. It was beautiful, but its bright beauty weighed heavily on his spirits. It was not his city. He was a foreigner here, a naïve immigrant. What place was there for him here?

Once ashore, he plunged into a bitter depression. He missed his shipmates' familiar accents. He had not felt so dislocated or so fearful since the terrible weeks after fleeing Texas with the image of his dying Marie-Anne searing his dreams. Why had he come here? What had he done? After all, he had run in terror from the hooded white demons, run in the fashion of all helpless black boys.

He sought revenge, but how could he find it in so strange and complicated a country? How could he ever find Rall? How could he find himself?

His confidence faltered. In pretending to be a white man, in dedicating himself to blood vengeance, had he defied the laws of God as he had been taught them? He shuddered with pain. Was this pain God's punishment?

How long would it be before he knew which path to take?

More than two months had passed since the Richler family had left the gay, busy streets of Rio de Janeiro and traveled south, first by steamer to Santos and then by mule train on a rough overland trail to the Campo region. Here, a small community of American immigrants was beginning to gather near the village of Santa Barbara. The village itself, to dignify with that name such a mean assemblage of dusty streets and alleyways, so few sun-faded and mud-brick structures and flyspecked places of business, was a disappointment to the Richlers, especially after what they had seen of Rio.

"When I think of what we left behind," Zaidee said, always the one to voice what everyone else was feeling, "when I think that we left everything and came all this way to live in a mud hut!"

"Hush, Zaidee, you know it's only the beginning. We'll have a fine house one day. Wait till we get started," Elinor said quickly, seeing her mother close her eyes and go pale, if it was possible for a woman already as white as a counterpane to lose color.

But the land was no disappointment. "I have almost forgiven our enemies all their wrongs," Franklin Richler said to his wife, "when I take account of the better place they have forced me to."

Daphne Richler nodded, hoping it was finally the end of their long journey. The land was only twenty-two cents an acre on four years' credit and as good or better than any she had seen either in Texas or Tennessee. She saw her husband set down his baggage in the doorway of the mud-and-straw hut and turn to the fields, turn to man's business with a feeling of thanksgiving.

She was left with the house and the girls. The house was worse than any she had ever lived in. The floor was mud, the windows had no glass, and the ticks and termites that nested in the thatched roof numbered in the millions. But what choice had they, now that they were here? They were forced to begin all over again, waging the slow struggle the younger generation had never experienced but that their parents knew well enough from the first days in Texas.

Some days Daphne could not work at all, but lay in the sunshine on a cot and coughed, leaving her young-lady daughters to work.

So they did, slowly and awkwardly at first, unused to physical effort, loosening the buttons on their high-necked cotton dresses, their bonnet ribbons drooping with heat and then sweat-stiffened as they dried, their small white hands turning red then brown. No use pretending they liked working outside. Bending to clear away vines and brush made their backs ache, and their arms and shoulders protested at lifting lumber out of the back of the wagon and breaking the hard red earth for a kitchen garden.

"It's nigger's work," Zaidee grumbled, and privately the others agreed.

Franklin Richler planted corn and cotton. He had managed to buy two Brazilian Negroes, a huge, barrel-chested man named Manuel, his coffee-brown arms rippling with muscles, and his wife, Joana, a statuesque black woman who wrapped her head in a white gauze turban and stalked across the barnyard with the air of a queen in a procession.

The worst of it, it seemed to Elinor, was the loneliness. Even the simplest transaction with Brazilians was made difficult by their ignorance of Portuguese and their American neighbors were few and far-flung. There was no American school or church as yet and so no natural meeting place, although anyone they met who spoke English was welcomed immediately to their home. Word spread quickly of Americans—two families who had been with them on the *Talisman* had settled ten miles away and they reported that there was a rich American family named Ashby living just past the Quilombo River, although the Ashbys had gone to Rio to meet others of their family.

It will be better soon, Elinor told herself. Things were different here and she longed to understand them. She endeavored to take pleasure in the smallest of the day's triumphs. They had plenty to eat, much of it novel—they had never imagined so many delicious tropical fruits.

Jesse Rall had lost track of time. He had forgotten to measure out the hours or count the sunrises and sunsets in order to count the weeks. He lost count of the weeks; they changed to months. The seasons were much the same: monotonously high humidity, high temperature, and high rainfall characterized the winter months, as well as the summer.

Every day, macaws and parrots flashed their gorgeous plumage at the rising sun and called out their existence in raucous voices; toucans cried at sundown, voicing a discordant plaint from tall vine-draped trees. Doves cooed dolorously through the hot afternoons, and at night the air vibrated with the *correos* of goatsuckers and whippoorwills.

Rall's struggle was to survive, to escape the undertow of his conscience, to exploit his natural energies and exercise his violent instincts for his own satisfaction and, whenever possible, his pleasure.

At the beginning, still racked with fever, he had been forced to linger near the dead village for some days, lying helplessly and listlessly in a hammock without food or water, through some negative will of mind trying not to remember or understand what had happened. He had watched the mist rise off the river, watched the huge black vultures, thick as flies, descend on the ruined village in the trees beyond. Bats by the million fanned the sky at night and he shuddered, knowing that some of them were bloodsucking vampires.

One night he awoke and saw a vampire bat fastened to his big toe. He shook it off, screaming so loudly that even the cicadas were hushed for a time. Also at night came the mosquitoes, relentless bloodsuckers, and the tiny black piume flies, the *jejenes*, which pricked his skin and swarmed on his uncovered flesh. Their bite made him itch and he scratched until his thin blood flowed and he thought he would bleed to death.

A few days later, with the devil's own luck, he

heard the splashing and hooting of a river steamer. No matter that it was a Bolivian rubber boat, headed downriver. Steamers were rare; they were inexorably slow and unreliable. No matter. He hailed the boat with his last strength and collapsed aboard, glad enough to see white men of any sort, relieved to be rescued from himself.

Almeirim was the steamer's next stop, a little town crouched on the Amazon's north bank at the point where the Rio Paru enters the main flow. In the town there was a mission clinic run by an order of Portuguese sisters who took Rall in.

For some weeks, weakened by fever and parasites, he lay among the white-shrouded nuns, their prayers humming over him like the droning of bees. He left the nuns in fair health and took a room in a run-down boardinghouse and bordello over a waterfront bar, an establishment known by the name of its owner, Loreto, and frequented by cockroaches the size of mice.

At first he was too weak and demoralized to consider moving. He could not think beyond his next slow slide into sleep. The difficulty of any journey provided reason enough to stay. Later, he was appalled by the town and used its one tavern and its few young whores vengefully, but it could not last. It was too poor a town; its few mud streets lacked men with anything to lose at poker, and it was overrun with Indians. He had come to hate and distrust Indians with the same venom he felt for blacks.

And so he had left Almeirim as abruptly as he had arrived and for the same reason—a steamer stopped there. This one was the *Monarch*, a regulation, government-run freighter with a two-hundred-ton capacity, making her monthly run from Belém to Manaus.

Among her passengers was a group of some seventy-five Southern emigrants, en route to a colony near the town of Santarém.

To Rall, the little group of emigrants was foreign. They seemed so pale and drab, so stolid, so determined and yet so innocently unaware of the dangers of this new land. He had little hope for their colony, if there ever would be a colony, but he was attracted to them as an illiterate to a bookshop, particularly the women among them, good women, all of them wives or maiden sisters. At first it was enough to hear their voices, soft and slow, drawling out the familiar rituals of Southern courtesy, inquiring politely for his health, and only later, with veiled curiosity, how on earth he had happened to join them so far upriver.

He could not relax in their company, but he enjoyed hearing them talk. They had left the ruins of the Confederacy later than he, and all their news was bad.

"Yes, I have come alone," he told his latest drinking companion, a former Lieutenant from Charleston, denying Satterlee without a second thought, refusing to consider what he could not bear to consider. But whiskey loosened memories, as well as tongues, and late that night he confessed to the man, "There was another man with me, another soldier, for a time . . . but he is dead."

The river was rising. Vast floating islands—*ilhas de caapim*—drifted by. These great grass islands swept downstream on the huge river's relentless push to the sea. The islands were as large and flat as pastures; they were made of water hyacinths, brittle grass and bastard cane. If a boat became entangled in one it might be totally engulfed and left to sink. The *Monarch* battled on and Rall drank with the Carolinian until the other man could drink no more, and then he drank alone, as he was meant to be.

"He is dead," he said aloud, thinking despite himself of Satterlee; men died quickly and easily in this region. Fevers dried them out, diseases swelled them until they burst, Indians shot them. There were many ways a man could die in the Amazon, none of them splendid, few honorable. How he hated the filthy, bug-ridden Indians who had killed Satterlee!

A group of drunken Indians appeared around the edge of the stern cabin, invading the deck where Rall had been alone. He stared at them with naked hatred. They laughed riotously, amusing themselves by throwing out scraps of garbage and watching, screaming with delight as the bloodthirsty fish that lived in the river's shallows, the piranhas, devoured them. "Damned filthy savages," he cursed, hurling his empty bottle out over the dark, misty river.

One Indian had a live cat by the tail and swung it out. The water flashed white, churned into a froth by the school of ferocious cannibal fish. The cat was gone with one helpless yowl. Rall watched the Indians with disgust. How ugly they were, how stupid. They played like children, jumped up and down like children feeding the dreadful fish as if it were a game.

Rall stood stiffly, watching, his eyes narrowed. All the Indians except one ran on along the deck. It was very late. No one else was in sight. He moved rapidly, smoothly, with deadly intent, shouldering the Indian boy roughly, using his height, tipping him over the railing with one push and watching with deep satisfaction as he fell into the midst of the school of fish.

It was over in less than a minute. The Indian's loincloth fell aside as he slid through the air. He hit the water headfirst and his screams were muffled as his dark skin paled and then reddened. In less than a minute the fish had stripped the body and the Indian's remains floated to the surface, a misstrung skeleton of snapped bones, white in the red-brown foam of blood and river water.

# Chapter Nine

Once the first settlers had paved the way, the region near Santa Barbara attracted more and more colonists from the American South, most of them farmers.

For many desperate Americans it promised to be a great adventure, a great exodus, one that so alarmed conservatives back home that they refused to print any news concerning the undertaking. "This is Brazil fever, it will sap our strength, and we must quell it," a Deep South editor wrote, but it was a movement spawned by despair and necessity and it could not so easily be quelled.

In the Campo region, their numbers increased daily, the Yanceys and Triggs and Smiths and Whitakers coming from Alabama, the Moncriefs and Budds from Louisiana, the Wards from Tennessee, the McFaddens and Meriwethers and Fergusons from South Carolina and the Quillens and McKnights and Waddells and many others from the state of Texas. They all came to begin life anew, and most of them were astounded by the primitive conditions they found.

The demands and privations of their new home took a toll on each member of the Richler family and pulled them apart. The friction between Elinor and Zaidee grew worse. Only a plea from their mother could stop their constant fretful quarreling.

Late one afternoon the sisters stood together over the outdoor laundry tubs. They had worked all morning and half the afternoon at the laundry, washing bedsheets which now hung over every bush and tree limb in the yard. They had carried water up from the creek, boiled it over fires of green wood, stirred the linens with saplings and wrung them out over the potato patch.

"Whatever are you smilin' at, Elinor?" Zaidee demanded. Her voice was sharp with annoyance and her face streamed with perspiration as she stood with her sleeves rolled up and her shirtwaist half unbuttoned.

"Just smilin'," Elinor replied, straightening her back and stretching her tired arms. "What a tirin' job laundry is. I never realized."

"It's all tirin'," Zaidee complained. "I hate it here. It's hot and wild and awful. Do you think Papa would agree to take us home?"

"No, honey," Elinor said, her eyes sympathetically taking in the fretful expression on Zaidee's face, seeing her mouth set in a stubborn line and her pretty blue eyes swimming with tears of frustration. "But don't worry, Zaidee, things'll be better soon. Come on, let's go down to the creek and bathe. Call out to Mama, will you?"

"Mama's napping, and I don't want to go. I hate the gnats in the open field, there may be snakes there, and the goiter is supposed to come from walking barefoot near the river. It's too hot, anyway."

"Too hot for bathing?" Elinor asked, but she didn't care. It was a relief to escape from Zaidee in a bad mood and outdoors was her only possible escape.

"And it may rain," Zaidee called out after Elinor.

Elinor was content to go alone, humming a song as she made her slow way across the fields. Along the edge of the twelve acres planted in cotton already, cotton crossed with rows of corn in the American style, marveling at the free soaring flight of a red-winged bird, ignoring the hum and whir of a million insects.

The riverbank was shaded and delightfully cool. She left behind the shallow ford where she had hauled out water for the washing and picked her way upstream, lifting branches and ducking under vines that crossed the narrow path, admiring a cluster of fragrant, grape-purple orchids drooping luxuriantly, and then gasping in delight as she surprised a small deer drinking from a secluded pool at the base of a silvery waterfall.

At Elinor's gasp the deer disappeared, leaping crazily into the tangled underbrush, a flash of fragile brown legs, startled soft eyes, melting into the green and brown of the forest so smoothly that it was gone at once, although she obeyed an irresistible desire to follow it and clambered up some mossy rocks, her boots slipping, falling to her knees. It was gone, completely gone, but it led her on, into the forest, deeper than she had been before.

She climbed more rocks. At the top of the waterfall there was another reach of mossy stones, another cataract glinting green and silver, another reed- and grass-fringed pool, and to this one she succumbed, sitting on a rock that caught the sun and still lent an easy view of the falling water, succumbed to the green watery beauty all around her and the lulling, hypnotic sound of falling water.

Time passed and Elinor forgot it. She pulled off her boots, tossed them aside, and removed her long pale-pink silk stockings. The sun was delightful; its power flowed into her and persuaded her to pull off her shirtwaist and petticoats. How she loved the caress of the late-afternoon sun, no longer strong enough to scald, invading without being beckoned, knowing her flesh, brightening it, calling it to life.

She played in the pool, then, purely naked and completely without self-consciousness. Here I am completely myself, she thought, looking down at her own sleek, wet breasts, their roundness familiar yet unfamiliar, rarely glimpsed in sunlight. She touched them, tentatively, and then let her hands slide further down to her cool wet hips and legs, satiny to her own touch, flaring out, palest pink and smooth. The sound of the water pounded in her head, deafening her to any other sound, persuading her absolutely of her privacy.

I am content to be myself... Elinor thought, but I do not want to be alone. She thought often of the excitement of dancing at the Emperor's ball. Remembering it always stirred strong feelings that were slow to subside. Sometimes she even remembered the young soldier in Texas, but it was not he whom she wanted, it was someone, but someone she did not know... someone new.

Alone, Terrill Ruffin took on Rio. He walked for miles in the summer heat. Battling fear and self-doubt, he forced himself to explore the city.

Rio connived to seduce him. Even before he had found his land legs he had rubbed shoulders with well-dressed businessmen, half-naked fruit vendors, sailors from every corner of the world, beautiful dark-eyed women and fat priests. He stared, he struggled to understand signs and street talk, he gulped down new sights, he swallowed fear, he walked on.

All the streets were crowded and crazy with color. The gutters ran with urine and stank with refuse. The air smelled of coffee and flowers and ripe fruits and a distinctive pungent odor that drifted down from the green hillsides, the strong odor of growth and decay that is the essence of the jungle. He saw fine stone houses and huts worse than any slave's cabin back home. He followed wide, tree-lined boulevards that led into wretched muddy alleys where pigs and children fought for crusts of bread.

Days passed and he felt more at home. He saw men of every possible complexion and physique. He saw couples of every age and class walking arm in arm—mixed couples of every type: black, brown, yellow, white and every combination of these, smiling and courteous. He looked at them, his curiosity barely veiled. And what did they think of him? Two shabby youngsters selling cut flowers addressed him as *doutor*. He laughed.

*Doutor!* To them he was a doctor, a man to be respected. To them he was an educated man, by his face and bearing, and likely an American by his clothes. So he appeared to the people in these streets, so, in fact he was. Everything he had seen argued that this was a city and a country where he could be whatever he wanted to be. This was a place where he could live any way he wanted to live.

One day just after sunset he was tired; he had walked for hours and before going on, he needed to stop and rest. Across the avenue was a huge church in the baroque style. He had seen many churches during his walks—Rio seemed to be a city of churches—but the dull, steady tolling of the vesper bell drew him toward this one. He entered it through a side door, at once feeling at ease in the familiar dimness. He was used to churches like this one; he made the sign of the cross as he felt the coolness of the cavernous interior, vast and ribbed like the hull of a ship turned upside down.

This was the church, the Roman church, the one true church that had given him so much—he had been raised and taught by the Jesuits, he had been given faith and the gift of acceptance, that gift which had made it possible for him to live in the world. But hadn't it failed? He had not been able to live honestly and peaceably in the world, after all. Everything he had lived by had turned out to be false. The white man's blind prejudice and hate had struck him down, killed Marie-Anne, wounded him deeply and marked him with a desire for revenge, an unholy desire blended of hate and despair. He still reeled from it; it had brought him here. It was unslaked and robbed him of peace.

He stood abruptly. He did not feel right in this church. Then he saw an unusual man kneeling in prayer—a tall, sandy-haired man dressed like himself. He paused as the man rose and sat back so that he needed to climb around him to reach the aisle. The man clasped his hands. His light blue eyes were open but his lips trembled in audible prayer, and to Ruffin's amazement, it was in English.

"My God, how can I go on? Must I go on? My

God, my God..." he murmured as Ruffin stared, his embarrassment at eavesdropping lagging behind his astonishment at hearing English spoken. He forgot what he had been thinking, what he had been doing, as the tall man turned to face him, feeling all his anonymity dropping away, feeling again a black boy facing a powerful-looking white man.

"Who are you?" the tall man demanded.

Ruffin had a terrifying if irrational sensation that the white man could see right through him, through his fancy New Orleans clothes and his light skin into his black heart. He battled with conflicting emotions: relief, fear and hate. It was wonderful to be seen, really seen, really looked at as this man was looking at him. It was terrible to be judged. It was exciting to feel the hate in his heart find a target; it stirred his spirit to be challenged by this man.

"I am an American," he said, finally, battling for control. He owed no other explanation.

"Oh, are you? An American? You put me in mind... for a moment there... of a young Brazilian I knew. Well, no matter. So you speak English, eh?" The tall man held Ruffin's eyes with cool assurance. His voice was clear and deliberate but accented with a slight Scottish burr.

"Yes, sir, I do. I have just arrived in Brazil." Ruffin fought for calm. He was a white man; to this man's eyes he was white. He was American. He was anything he wanted to be. "My name is Terrill Ruffin."

"Ruffin? My God, it's a Scots name!"

The tall man laughed. Ruffin's legs felt like water, but he forced himself to smile. He stood with the tall man in the gloom. The nave was beginning to fill with people and he was aware that they were causing a disturbance. He stepped backward. The other man followed him.

"Ah, Ruffin, I'm in a black mood, damn it. I have reason to be, I promise you. Let's get out of here, Ruffin. Come and walk with me. Do me good to speak the Queen's own tongue."

"Yes, sir," Ruffin said and led the Scotsman out of the church.

"Let's have a drink, Ruffin," the man said, as soon as they were standing on the wide, scallop-shaped marble staircase. "I'm James Barnes. Eh? Shall we?"

Feeling as she did, that it was a day when something important must happen, Elinor Richler was not really surprised to see that her father had guests when she returned home from bathing at the waterfall.

"My daughter, Elinor," Franklin Richler said, as she approached the shaded veranda where he was sitting with two young men.

Elinor could tell from the tone of her father's voice that he was pleased and excited by the men's visit. She listened carefully to their names. One was Dr. Tyler Ashby, the eldest son of the family living just past the Quilombo River, and the other was a younger man, an American recently arrived from Rosedale, Mississippi, who lived with his father on a farm right near the town. Ernest Gregg was always smiling. Ashby, on the other hand, looked severe, even forbidding, and scarcely met her glance.

How proud and conceited he looks, Elinor thought. She had rarely taken such an instant dislike to anyone, and it was unfortunate, really, as there were so few Americans living nearby.

She studied him. His face was handsome, in an

intelligent way, but completely spoiled by the arrogance of his expression and the careless way a lock of his light hair crossed his brow. Tyler, aware that he was being studied, grew tense, and a flush of embarrassment rose above his collar. When he stood up, as much to escape Elinor's scrutiny as to examine the fields of cotton Franklin Richler pointed out in the distance, his posture and movement were awkward and constrained. When he reclaimed his seat, his foot shifted nervously, and his smile was tight.

Elinor lingered on the veranda, standing alone, leaning against one of the pillars watching the men, with the last glow of her secret hedonistic plunge into the waterfall coloring her complexion. She did not understand why, but although she had decided she did not like Tyler Ashby, her eyes lingered on him.

"There is no perfect climate," Franklin Richler was saying evenly. "Unless we get some rain, the cotton will not take its full height. Have you had red ants in your fields?"

"The red ants are troublesome," Tyler Ashby said. He leaned forward to stroke Ernest Gregg's hound, a yellow puppy that wriggled and licked at his hand. "I am not the farmer my father is, or my brothers, either, but they believe it possible to destroy the ant colonies with hoes."

"They are optimistic," Franklin Richler said. "And what of the gnats?"

"The Brazilians have shown us how to twist cotton strings, pin them to our hats, and set them afire."

"Yes, I have seen that," Richler said. "There is so much to learn that is new."

Smiling, Tyler Ashby said little, patting the puppy when the dog climbed into his lap. But even his smile irked Elinor. Why is he laughing at Father? she wondered. How provincial and poverty-stricken we no doubt look to him—such a rich gentleman doctor from Alabama. Angrily, she left the porch and went into the kitchen to help her mother with the dinner.

How stiff he is, and stubborn, she thought at the dinner table. How proud and rigid. Yet, despite her disavowal of him, he commanded her attention, and she had no appetite; indeed, there seemed to be no room in her for food, so complete were her lungs full of caught-up breath, so tight her throat and so unsettled her stomach that she could not swallow a bite. His presence made her uneasy; it pulled at her in a thousand powerful ways, as potently as the moon pulls at the tides and as inevitably, for whenever she lifted her eyes through modestly lowered lashes her glance caught his.

Tyler Ashby, for his part, was intoxicated with Elinor and engulfed with giddy, optimistic feelings he had not thought he was capable of having. Elinor was, he thought, quite the prettiest girl he had seen in years, but beyond that, he sensed, romantically, something special about her beauty, a quality of intelligence, of sympathy, of fineness and depth, of hidden mysteries. Her shyness, obvious to him, arrested his attention and convinced him of her fineness. Perhaps she was high-strung and delicate by nature. It was not unbecoming in a lady. It never occurred to him that he himself was a factor in the equation.

Neither Tyler nor Elinor was to remember much about that dinner, or the hour of conversation that followed; whatever was talked about jumbled in their memories, all of it far less clear than the unspoken emotional signals that passed between them, signals of inquiry, awkwardly restrained and parried and then, just as irresistibly returned. For Elinor, the hour was endless and miserable. Wherever she looked, her eyes inevitably returned to his face and always found him looking her way. At the end of the time, she felt exhausted.

Thank goodness he is going, she thought when both men rose and thanked her mother and father for their hospitality. Thank goodness this is over . . . and yet, her eyelashes were wet when she rose to say goodbye and she followed Ashby a few steps from the edge of the veranda, helplessly, as if she were being pulled along by a strong cord.

He turned. Seizing the moment, he spoke, and his voice was gruff and choked. "Miss Elinor . . ."

She stopped short and swayed on her toes. How tall he was, she thought, and, trembling with emotion and anxiety and a sort of fear, she turned her face away.

His voice was low. "I am happy to have met you. May I see you again? May I call on you?"

A tide of relief washed over Elinor, an emotion that surprised her nearly as much as the dislike she had felt toward Ashby all evening. She despised him, she was sure of that, but at any rate she should see him again and this strange awareness between them would work itself out, be exorcised by time and familiarity. She did not like him; she could not bear his presence; she was delighted to see him leaving; still . . .

"Soon," she whispered. "Yes, Mr. Ashby."

# Chapter Ten

"I like Americans," James Barnes said to Terrill Ruffin after the men had drunk whiskey until the sky was black and the streets near the cathedral were yellow with torchlights.

Ruffin smiled self-consciously and nodded. The two men were riding in Barnes's carriage, a spanking-new two-wheeled cabriolet swiftly drawn by two sleek black horses. Barnes was carrying him home to dine and meet friends. Ruffin had the sensation of swimming in deep water, yet of swimming powerfully and of having conquered the dangers.

"Americans are energetic, innovative, ambitious," Barnes went on. "At least the ones I have met. Like yourself, they do not look back."

If so I seem, so I will be, Ruffin thought. He was certain that Barnes liked him. Their meeting had been sheer coincidence and their first conversation unusually confidential. Barnes, like himself, was a recent widower and still suffered painful grief for the loss of his wife. Like himself, Barnes was widely read and knew the classical philosophers. Ruffin had enjoyed their conversation, found that he could understand and amuse the Scotsman, and if no one could keep up with the pace at which Barnes drank whiskey, perhaps it was the whiskey that had made him feel so at ease.

As their carriage stopped in front of the Villa Barnes, two others drew to a halt almost simultaneously, and Barnes called out greetings to two men dressed in dark suits like European businessmen. Together they entered the big front door which was opened by a dark-skinned manservant.

Inside the front room, a square chamber with ten-foot ceilings and shuttered windows, Barnes introduced Ruffin as "my friend, the American." The other two men were Jorge Machado, a young man who was dark-eyed and smiling, and Juracy de Almeida, an older, heavy-set man inclined to corpulence whose shirt-front was already dark with perspiration, and whose hand was clammy when Ruffin shook it.

Chatting of matters Ruffin knew nothing about, half in Portuguese and half in English, James Barnes led his guests through the darkened entrance hall and a fragrant central courtyard where a fountain played and birds in wicker cages whistled and sang. Beyond the courtyard was a dining room built with huge windows like the front ones, but these stood open to a glittering view of the city and beachfront below.

"Ah," Jorge Machado said mournfully. "How is it that a foreigner has the best view in Rio?"

"I think I have paid for it." Barnes laughed and the others joined him.

"Champagne, my friends? Or cognac? Scotch whiskey?"

Ruffin accepted whiskey, intending to sip it. He was not used to strong liquor and he had already drunk more than ever before in his life.

"They ask, my friends, what you Americans have heard of the war in Paraguay?"

"Very little, nothing much at all," Ruffin answered.

"You see?" de Almeida shouted, jumping to his feet, obviously much disturbed. "We fight in vain. No one cares or heeds us."

"We have been at war with Paraguay for two years," Barnes explained. "A disastrous waste. Everyone hopes it will be over soon."

"In a war, everyone loses," Ruffin said.

"You are wise," de Almeida said. "For a young man, you are very wise. And in this war, an epidemic of fever has carried off more Brazilians than the enemies' bullets."

"It is disastrous to trade," Machado said mournfully.

Trade, Ruffin soon understood, was the main bond between the three men. Barnes had told him that his business was investing in and outfitting expeditions into the province of Minas Gerais, that province of Brazil famous for its mineral wealth, especially for gold and diamonds. At the start of the evening Ruffin had no sense of the size or importance of this business, but as time passed and he listened to what the others said, he began to understand that Barnes must be very successful and very rich.

Barnes's partner, he was told, was a Brazilian named Armando da Silva. Da Silva had been expected for dinner, but had instead sent a note, delivered to Barnes by a servant.

"Where is Armando?" de Almeida demanded, at one point.

"Ah, he was called away," Barnes said with a wink. "An errand of charity, I presume."

The other men laughed and Barnes leaned over to Ruffin. "A charity of the heart," he said.

"Were it not for Armando's saints and his mistresses,"

Machado said, "the firm of Barnes and da Silva would be very rich indeed!"

"It's true," Barnes said, "but we do well enough." He clapped his hands and dinner was served to them by two mulatto women dressed in white. The food was delicious, but as he ate roasted squab and well-spiced mouthfuls of rice and vegetables, Ruffin began to feel very drunk. He smiled and nodded and laughed, enough intoxicated so that he believed he understood more Portuguese than he actually did, enough so that he did not refuse the cognac Barnes served after dinner.

When Machado turned to Ruffin and asked, "And you, American, what is your business here in Rio?" Ruffin was startled and for a moment, he could not reply.

But Barnes spoke for him. "Mr. Ruffin is newly arrived, but if I am fortunate, I will persuade him to enter my firm."

Hiding his surprise, Ruffin nodded and when he did speak, his voice was strong and clear. "Mr. Barnes has much to teach and I am eager to learn," he said.

"Be sure he does not become the pupil of da Silva!" Machado said, and then the two Brazilians laughed as if it was a great joke.

Ruffin had no idea why it was so funny, but he knew that he would find out.

A week passed before Elinor Richler and Tyler Ashby were to meet again, and although neither of them had been able to think of much else but the remarkable and confusing impact of their first meeting, their second meeting was by coincidence.

It was the edge of the rainy season and for five days the skies had darkened with clouds and cracked with thunder. It rained relentlessly and Elinor had been forced to spend every day inside. Sewing, cooking, occupied with endless minor domestic duties and the major one of bearing with Zaidee, the five days had seemed an eternity, and her own state of mind was no less troubled than the weather.

I do not like that man, she thought at first, as if thinking it could make it so. Never had she been so stirred and scared by any man. Never had she felt so devastated.

It did not help that her mother and sister made the visit of the two men a prime topic of conversation during their long hours of confinement in the small stuffy house.

"He seems the finest sort of Southern gentleman," Daphne Richler said.

"Who?" Elinor asked dreamily. Certainly not Ernest Gregg, although Gregg had been declared "polite enough" in a previous dissection of the visit.

"Dr. Ashby, I expect," Zaidee said. "I thought him stuffy and proud. He is too old; I believe he's nearly thirty. Anyway, I have heard that he is engaged to be married." In truth, Zaidee had thought Ashby wonderfully handsome, but she had seen clearly that he was falling in love with Elinor.

"Oh, really? Engaged? To whom?" her mother asked.

Zaidee felt two pairs of eyes on her. "To some rich girl, I believe," she said airily, casting a sly glance at Elinor to see if she looked disappointed, but Elinor did not; she had fixed her gaze as if repairing her father's everyday overalls were the most fascinating task in the world.

"It's a shame there are so few nice young men

nearby," Daphne Richler said, "but no doubt there will be more coming in as the community grows. I'm sure you both will have opportunities. Did you like Mr. Gregg, Elinor?"

"I hardly noticed him," Elinor said, biting her lip.

"There was nothin' to notice," Zaidee said. "He scarcely spoke. He was as charmin' as a corpse. And he smiled like a Chessie cat. I wonder if he's simple."

If he is engaged, why did he ask to call on me, Elinor wondered.

Two days later, Elinor felt as if the wide swings of emotions had finally cleared her mind and that she had regained her equilibrium. Her first sight of Tyler Ashby proved that this was not so.

Elinor had ridden into the station at Santa Barbara to collect the family's mail. When she emerged from the station house she confronted Tyler Ashby standing by a two-horse carriage outside. The shock of beholding him so unexpectedly disarmed her and she lost her hard-gained composure to a fresh tide of muddled feelings. Her first instinct was to hide, but it was too late; he had seen her.

"Miss Elinor!" he said. "I am surprised to see you here."

She stared. How confident and elegant he seemed; how tall and lean and neatly dressed. Oh, why must he be so handsome?—everything she had ever imagined in a lover.

He smiled, then removed his hat and bowed. She inclined her head as slightly as possible. "Hello, Dr. Ashby. Why are you surprised?"

"Because I had planned to drive out to your home this afternoon, after putting my sister Amelia on the train for Rio."

"Oh." Elinor stopped, far more shaken by his presence than she wanted to reveal. She twisted the strings of her satchel in her gloved hands. "The train is not here yet," she said and then blushed. Of course he knew that. Meeting his eyes was even more upsetting than before; it caused her heart to pound and spread confusion like fever through her body, and her head was so full of questions she could not ask that she could think of nothing ordinary to say.

And then the train and Amelia Ashby Scott arrived at once, the train whistling and belching black smoke, and Amelia, dressed as smartly as a Paris model, looking out of place on the dusty station platform.

"How do you do?" Elinor managed to say, as Tyler Ashby introduced them, and then stared at Amelia under the cover of the train's arrival. She was nearly as tall as her brother and wore her shiny, chestnut-brown hair extravagantly piled up and looped around the pale green straw of her tiny bonnet, a wonderful shade that exactly matched the green watered silk of her dress and her green eyes shining with curiosity and confidence.

As the train rattled to a stop, all three of them spoke at once.

"My sister is an artist and is going to Rio to paint and study," Tyler said.

"I am very glad to meet you. Why, you are just as pretty as Tyler told me," Amelia said in the friendliest of voices. "He described you very well." A girl of about six clung to her hand, a pretty child, very like her mother. "This is my daughter, Susan Jane."

"Will you be travelin' all that way alone?" Elinor asked, and then blushed again. Of course it was none of her business.

And then the noise subsided and all three of them

laughed, for their remarks had come so fast on top of each other that no one was quite sure what had been said or heard. Elinor felt relieved and more comfortable. If any woman looked capable of traveling alone it was Amelia, she decided.

"Come, let's walk out to the train together," Tyler suggested. He led the way, carrying two suitcases and followed by a servant carrying a trunk.

"You are from Texas?" Amelia asked, and Elinor nodded, swept along by the Ashbys and their mood of excitement.

The train, it turned out, would pause only briefly in the station as it was already far behind schedule. Neatly, Tyler settled his sister and niece in their carriage and returned to the platform to stand next to Elinor as they waved goodbye.

And then, in the settling cinders and the last roaring and rattling of the departing train, they were left standing alone. Elinor waited without speaking. She had no idea of what to say as the silence grew and felt increasingly ill at ease. Oh, why had it been so comfortable with Amelia present and why was it now so different?

At last, Tyler took her arm and turned her gently to face him. "I have thought about you a great deal since we met," he said simply. "I wanted, very much, to see you again. Please do not think me forward, Miss Elinor, but I am very impressed with you."

Elinor gulped and swallowed. She could not lift her eyes. Feelings of excitement and confusion engulfed her. But what about his engagement? Was he teasing her or lying to her? She looked up through her long lashes at his face and could not believe that he was—he looked so serious and intense. More than anything she longed to make him happy, to see his seriousness dissolve into a smile and to hear him laugh as easily as he had at his sister's conversation. And yet, she could not. She was frozen with the importance of what he was about to say to her.

"Circumstances have brought us together," Tyler said, "far from our native land. We do not know each other yet, but in such a small community, it is likely that we will. Miss Elinor, I want to be completely honest with you. I want to speak frankly, to tell you the truth . . ."

Elinor was overwhelmed with dread. So it was true. He must be on the verge of telling her he was engaged to another woman. Obviously, he was apologizing for something and what else could it be? She could bear no more. She twisted away from him and began to run away.

"Stop!" he cried out. "What's wrong?"

"Leave me alone!" Elinor called back, embarrassed at the strangled tone of her voice, nearly drowned in tears. "I don't want to hear your excuses, sir! Don't call on me! Leave me alone!"

All the Brazilians on the station platform were staring at them. Tyler began to run after her, but she had a twenty-foot lead and burst through the open-sided station house. In the street, she untied her horse and jumped astride, all thought of the mail and her other errands forgotten.

"Miss Elinor!" he shouted as she turned the horse's head away.

"Leave me alone!"

"I trusted you, Ruffin, from the moment I met you. I am never wrong about these things, never,"

James Barnes declared. He and Ruffin were alone in his office on the second floor of a warehouse overlooking the docks of Rio. It was the end of the second month Ruffin had spent in Barnes's employ. "They say the Scots have second sight," he added.

"I want to deserve your trust, Mr. Barnes," Ruffin said. In the past months he had learned many things, among them how fortunate he was to have found a patron like James Barnes.

"You work hard," Barnes said. "You know what I need. Let me put it bluntly. I need a junior partner, an honest man with a sharp eye and a strong pair of legs."

"Yes, sir."

"I am still, thank God, a strong man, but I am not a young one, and my partner . . . well, do you know what is wrong with da Silva?"

"He is going blind, sir." Ruffin liked Armando da Silva; there was much that was likable about the good-tempered, enormously fat Brazilian who had accepted him as willingly as had Barnes, who had invited Ruffin to dine at his house, had taken him to cockfights and horse races in the country, who had shown him night-clubs where exotic women danced dressed only in feathers.

"Yes, he is dying. Of the domestic disease, a scourge that is so prevalent here that they pass it around like measles, but it is deadly, deadly. You take my meaning, Ruffin?"

"I believe I do, sir." Ruffin knew how common syphilis was among the Brazilians of all classes. The newspapers were full of advertisements for remedies, of elixirs and nostrums proposing fantastic cures. The walls of the churchyards were plastered with religious prints, showing the infant Jesus surrounded by little angels, for babies born syphilitic died at once.

"Of course you do, *you* are not blind." Barnes looked out of his window toward the sunset. "They call it the Gallic disease, but it could be called the Brazilian one. Da Silva is dying; he has six sons; they are infected also; he has dozens of useless relatives who would kill to pick up his interest in this business. I will not leave Armando while he is still alive, but when he dies, I will need you. We will sell out my interest and begin again."

Barnes's voice had grown excited as he speculated. "Does it interest you, Ruffin? Eh? Why would it not?"

"It does, very much. . . ." Shall I thank him, Ruffin wondered. He felt much more emotional than he revealed. Shall I tell him that meeting him has given me a chance at a new life, that I have begun to hope as I never hoped before? He hesitated. "Thank you . . ." he stammered, at last.

"Don't thank me, for Christ's sake," Barnes said simultaneously. "I shall work you like a nigger. It could be someone else, Ruffin, but it is you because I trust you."

"Yes, sir," Ruffin said, struggling to control the relief and happiness in his voice.

"It is a business arrangement, no more," Barnes said. "Now what did you come here for?"

"Two things," Ruffin said, straightening his shoulders. "First, I have a small amount of money that I brought with me from America. I'd like to put it into the next expedition to the mines at Sabará. And, secondly, sir, I have uncovered a reprehensible case of stealing and sabotage in the warehouse, and I believe I know which men are responsible."

"Excellent!" Barnes exclaimed. "You justify my judgment. Of course I like that!" He laughed. "We shall show these lazy Don Juans what sort of businessmen the Anglo-Saxons make, shall we not?"

# Chapter Eleven

When she rode away from the station at Santa Barbara, Elinor Richler had no idea where she was going. She wanted only to escape from the sight of Tyler Ashby and then to be alone to recover her composure.

Blinded by tears of humiliation, her breath strained, and racked by confused emotions, Elinor was not equipped to manage a successful escape. When she should have ridden east, toward home, she headed west, toward the unbroken forests, along the roughest of roads, ordinarily rutted and now worked almost into uselessness by the five days of rain.

Duke, the sturdy but stiff-legged gelding her father kept for both riding and hauling, reacted to her panic and began to saw at the bit. Whinnying, he balked. He splashed through a huge puddle, drenching Elinor's skirt with mud; he skidded sideways, he feigned lameness when Elinor tried to force him into a canter.

"Come on! Duke, giddy-ap!" she shouted. Of all the times to be stuck with such a miserable piece of horseflesh, as broad and stubborn as a cow. Duke stumbled, tossing her forward to his neck where she clung, feeling if possible more foolish and out of control than before. "Oh, Duke!" she cried. "You wretched beast, oh, please!"

Taking advantage of her desperation, Duke got his head and ran wildly, crossing the road, jumping puddles and nearly throwing Elinor off his back. Her helplessness made her cry harder, but she was too shaken up to think, and when she heard the sound of horses and a buggy behind her, she was glad to be rescued by anyone, even Tyler Ashby.

"Whoa, whoa there," Tyler shouted at Duke, seizing the gelding's bridle and pulling his head in close to the carriage. Duke obeyed, abruptly, and with a shriek, Elinor slid off his other side, landing breathless and on her backside in the muddy road.

"Are you hurt? Are you all right?"

"I am well, but . . . furious!" Elinor admitted, and then took Tyler's hand. She laughed. She looked down at herself: her dress was dripping wet and caked with mud, as were her boots, and when she raised a hand to straighten her bonnet, she felt her wind-blown hair escape its pins and cascade over her shoulders.

"How wonderful to see you smile," Tyler said. "I thought I should never again have that privilege. Miss Elinor, we must talk. Please grant me that favor. Grant me a hearing, as I have saved you, as well as your sight and soul."

At least he has a sense of humor, Elinor thought, while Tyler was thinking the same thing. He is not stiff, not at all. "I . . . have no choice . . ." she gasped. She laughed again.

"None at all."

"Well, then . . ."

Tyler took a deep breath. This was his chance. He must speak seriously; he must persuade this elusive and beautiful creature to look kindly on his suit.

"I am an honest man, Elinor, and a doctor. I believe that all suffering is evil and that love is always good. Do you believe that also?"

"Yes." She had stopped laughing and the look that she gave him was wild, yet cold. Her eyes glittered with emotion and she had not yet caught her breath.

"I think I love you, Elinor. No, I know that I do."

"Have you any right, sir?"

"Every right!"

"Oh!" She turned away. Her heart was beating terribly; she felt it in her throat; it would choke her, but she must speak. "Is it not true that you are engaged to another woman?"

He caught her hands. "Not true. Not true at all! Whatever makes you ask it?"

Elinor paused. What was important was that she believed him—believed him free, honest, and sincere and that she felt the current passing between their connected hands.

"My dear Elinor," he said without embarrassment, "I love you and no other."

"Can you feel it?" she asked, meaning the wonderful current.

"I have been feeling it ever since I met you."

She nodded.

Their eyes met, his blazing, hers wide open with surprised delight and she stepped forward into his embrace.

"My darling, my darling," Tyler whispered. Her acquiescence had flooded him with a sense of relief and hope more potent than morphine. The sensation of her small body against his delighted him. "I will never hurt you," he promised. "I want only to make you happy and live with you all of our lives."

Darius Yates had left Rio the morning after the Ballo dos Americanos. He left without a farewell to any of his fellow Americans, seeking adventure as well as an independent new life, seeking escape from the feelings of lethargy and despondency that had dogged him since the war and had not been exorcised by the long and misdirected voyage to Brazil.

Applying himself assiduously to the study of Portuguese, he soon mastered the rudiments of the language and set out to explore the backlands, following whatever road or rumor led him from one city to the next. He traveled through the curious baroque cities of Minas Gerais, north to the splendid port of Salvador, west to Sergipe, moving rapidly and at will, rarely stopping for more than a few days in any town.

Yates was diverted by what he saw, although it would not be accurate to say he understood it all. He was not an ordinary traveler, even for the most eccentric epoch of the nineteenth century, nor was he an ideal one. His vision was too often clouded by introspection and melancholy, and his curiosity blunted by horrors already seen. He thought often, surely too often, of his late wife. Sometimes he mulled over his pleasure in the company of Elinor Richler. Had it been innocent or had he imposed his presence on a girl scarcely out of childhood? It had been innocent. He had meant her no harm. And her sister? She had confused him. However would the two sisters adapt to Brazil?

No doubt Yates presented a curious figure—this

aristocratic-looking, soft-spoken man, the last of a refined, privileged family, traveling around provincial Brazil dressed in an increasingly rusty black suit with the white shirt and sapphire cravat pin he always wore. He traveled alone, for the most part, occasionally finding companions for a few days or weeks, but always glad to leave them when their routes or interests diverged. From fellow travelers he learned of various American colonies, but he chose to avoid them.

As the months passed, he grew somewhat weary of travel and ceased to marvel at even the most verdant of valleys or precipitous of waterfalls. He was alone in the most remote part of the province of Sergipe, that part of Brazil natives call the Sertão, not far from the watershed of the wild and irregular São Francisco River. On a ramshackle riverboat, he met a bronzed German planter, his white beard stained with tobacco. The German told him about a river valley, some hundred miles west, which was eminently suitable for the cultivation of cotton.

"From what I have heard," the German said. "But 'tis you Americans who are the world's best cotton planters. At least the more old-fashioned among you. Tell me, sir, were you involved in that American civil conflict of late? You were? Ah, do you count yourself among the winners or losers?"

"The losers, Herr Schmidt, the losers," Yates said bitterly, but with wry amusement. As soon as he could he excused himself and retired for the night, but the next day he left the riverboat, hired four mules, and set out to look for the land.

He traveled west along a tributary of the São Francisco, following a narrow trail. The stream looked shallow and sluggish but had a silent, strong current.

He fished. He enjoyed the isolation of the wilderness. By night he camped in a clearing and slept under a mosquito net in a string hammock, laughing at how well he had adopted Brazilian customs.

At dawn on the sixth day of his solitary journey, a flock of noisy parrots flew over in pairs and a bottle-green toucan hovered over his cookfire with fearless curiosity. It had rained at night and the air was cool. He picked up his shotgun with the notion of shooting a partridge for breakfast, but as soon as he stepped out of his camp, he had the unmistakable feeling that he was being watched. He stared into the green density of the underbrush and the immense moss-hung trees. He saw nothing. He jumped nervously at the sound of a tree frog, heard the mules eating and stamping their feet. The muscles of his shoulders tensed and the hairs on his neck bristled. He could see no one but he knew he was no longer alone.

Carrying his gun, he carried water to the mules and brewed coffee. He ate, feeling himself watched. The green jungle was oddly silent. Uneasily, he banked the fire to put it out, but as he straightened his back he heard a slight rustling.

He turned. More than fifty naked Indians surrounded his camp. They were small in stature but painted with black-and-white geometric designs over every inch of their brown bodies, and wore long feathered pendants in their ears. Each held either a lance or a bow and arrow, and all of them were aimed at him.

# Chapter Twelve

Elinor Marietta Richler and Tyler Lamar Ashby were married, in the sight of God and their families, fifteen days after they had met. Both families were delighted with the match. Colonel Ashby and his wife, who had arrived in the Campo region with the rest of the Ashby clan shortly after the Richlers, thought Elinor just perfect, a truly lovely little Southern lady; Franklin Richler pronounced Tyler a Southern gentleman of the finest sort. Everyone could see that the young people were outrageously in love. They had scarcely left each other's sight for fifteen days. Under the circumstances it seemed best that the marriage ceremony take place at once, and Elinor and Tyler agreed, wreathed in happiness and glowing with self-satisfied sexual delight.

The Reverend Pritchett Henry, newly arrived from Fayette County, Georgia, was invited to perform the traditional rite on the front veranda of the Ashbys' modest brick house, since it was much the largest space available. Zaidee Richler stood up with Elinor, barely controlling her jealous resentment by recalling that Tyler Ashby was positively the last young man Elinor would entrance. From now on, Elinor would be a matron—off limits to romance. It was a gratifying thought.

Daphne Richler had surprised them all by producing her mother's wedding dress, an eighteenth-century confection of old silk, French lace and fragile ribbons. "I was married without it," she told Elinor with a wan smile that lighted the delicate skin of her pale face, "but I always hoped and prayed, dear Elinor, that one of my daughters would wear it—for all the Pecks and Kimballs in Tennessee, for their remembrance." Elinor agreed readily. She smiled when she shook out the yellowed silk gown in a narrow-skirted Empire style. Not only was it lovely, but she would be comfortably free of hoopskirts on her wedding day.

The day of the wedding dawned cool and cloudy but, by noon, the sky had cleared to a magnificent blue. All the family members—all the Ashbys and Richlers—declared it a beautiful day for a wedding and an authentic old-fashioned Southern one, and it was true that all the traditional words were spoken—both during the ceremony and among the guests—and that most of the men wore their Confederate uniforms, but it was not a typical Southern affair. It could not be.

No Southern bride ever held a bouquet of huge purple and pink orchids, stood under a trellis where wild green parrots shrieked and quarreled, or ate wedding cake concocted of manioc flour. Probably, it never hailed on the morning of a June wedding in Georgia, as it did for Elinor and Tyler, while the hissing of flying ants and the far-off howl of a hunting jaguar filled the silences in the minister's prayers. It is true that back home the "people" of a plantation often assembled for their masters' weddings, but here black and brown men and women had come unbidden from miles around, camped in the Ashbys' fields and stared openly at the ceremony and the guests, particularly at the pink-and-white beauty of the bride.

"Sometimes I feel just like I'm in Africa," Zaidee

whispered to her mother, who shuddered and said, "Hush, dear, that's foolishness," although she knew perfectly well what Zaidee meant. The blacks were different here, and there were too many of them. It was hard to say how it was different from being at home, but it was, as different as hell and heaven. She didn't feel comfortable here and didn't know if she ever would, but it was an immense comfort to see Elinor marrying so well; it was just exactly what she wanted to see. Her bridegroom was so handsome, both tall and blond and a natural-born gentleman as anyone could see, and from the very richest of the emigrant families. If any union was designed to preserve the highest values of the old Southern civilization, this was it.

But Elinor and Tyler wanted something else, and they, too, were satisfied that they had found it.

"In the flesh and spirit, we are already married," Tyler said to Elinor, speaking in the bold and poetic manner they now cultivated between them. They stood together, hands clasped, a bit apart from the others on the low, wide veranda awaiting the minister's arrival.

"We were never strangers," Elinor said softly, her eyes flashing through her veil. "You had no need to court me, nor I to flirt with you. I do not fear you or worship you, I only love you."

With a rush of emotion, Tyler lifted Elinor into his arms and held her close against his chest. His feeling for her closed out the rest of the world. Someone among the crowd of blacks squatting beyond the veranda laughed, but he did not hear, nor did she. She was completely lost in the sensation of her blood beating in time with his, suffused with the pleasure of loving so freely, of being exempted, she hoped forever, from playing any role.

"I adore you," he said in a low voice. "At last my inner and outward desires are completely in accord."

"Together we will flourish, living in a new world, nothing like the old one," Elinor murmured. "I promise you that."

"Don't promise me anything," Tyler said. "You—you are everything. You are enough." He wished with all his heart that this social occasion were already over. To be in her presence was to be overwhelmed with desire; his body ached to be alone with her. When he touched her like this he could barely preserve control and celebrated the feeling. How good, how natural it was to feel so. How much, how *much* there was to look forward to!

Colonel Ashby stood erect at the center of the veranda as the wedding guests filed past. White-haired, proud, the Colonel smiled with the same easy hospitality he had liked to extend to his guests back home at Spring Bank plantation. He was well pleased with everything—with the day, which the sun had warmed from a frosty dawn to a pleasant springlike afternoon; with Tyler's promising marriage; with the crowd of wedding guests.

It was odd. Except for his own family and one or two other families from Dallas County, Alabama, he had known his guests for less than six months, and yet they had so much in common that he felt as if he had known them all his life. He liked them—most of them—as much as he had liked his neighbors back home. Oh, perhaps Kinch McCall was a bit of a rowdy; he who had announced his intention of setting up a liquor distillery like the one he had run in Tennessee. Perhaps some of the settlers were not quite as refined or well educated as his own family, but they were all good folk, good honest Southerners with attitudes and accents he could understand.

And the land was wonderful. He was well pleased with the progress already made. He had preserved the existing coffee and canefields, planted cotton and corn, set out an orchard of peach trees and a stand of bamboo. This winter he would clear the acres of tangled growth along the Quilombo River. Before his family had arrived, he and Tyler had supervised the addition of a fireplace, a dining room, an American-style pantry—the sight of it had brought tears of relief to his wife's eyes, for he had modeled it exactly after the one she had left behind—and enough bedrooms for all the children. Now the house was a fine-looking one—red brick with shutters and some colored window glass imported from England. It was quite the finest one in the community, he thought.

Colonel Ashby turned to watch his son with his bride. She was a beauty, a shining-eyed beauty among beauties . . . both Richler girls were pretty as princesses, but he guessed Tyler had married the prettier one. What a relief it was to see Tyler so in love and married, just like that, in the traditional way. Tyler had worried him, he didn't mind admitting that now. His mother had been worried, too. Back in Alabama it had seemed he was frightened by the sight of a pretty girl. He had suffered terrible sleeplessness and had seemed moody all the time.

"Well now," the Colonel said to his wife, "so the dancin' is beginnin'." He looked out over the crowd. The musicians, six of them already and more coming forth from the crowd, were busily tuning up and already Tyler and Elinor had begun to dance, turning around and around in each other's arms as if they heard the music of a New Orleans hotel orchestra.

Franklin Richler, moved to a point of almost unbearable emotion at the sight of his elder daughter dancing in the arms of the man who was now her husband, turned away from the sound of the scraping fiddles and walked toward the barbecue. Richler cut a fine figure, dressed in his gray trousers and tunic. He had hesitated before packing his army uniform, but he was glad now that he had. Tyler Ashby was wearing his dress uniform too, and looked equally fine.

How lovely Elinor looks today, he thought. He could see her perfectly, even as he stood alone and let his eyes follow the line of bamboo trees out to the edge of the fields planted in cotton and corn. She is like an angel in that old white gown, so lissome and graceful, so rosy and bright-eyed.

"Luck to the bride and groom!" Yancey Ashby shouted, offering the flask to Franklin Richler.

How splendid this day is, he thought, inhaling the tantalizing smell of broiling meat, seeing the sun glint off the silver brandy flask, hearing the lilt of the fiddles playing for the dancing and the pounding of dancing feet. He admired the fresh physical strength and beauty of the young men clustered around him. How much better it was for them to be here than mixed up in a vengeful violence as his own dear son, Laray Holt, had been.

Laray Holt! His head began to swim with grief, as sharp and specific as an arrow to the heart. He would *not*, he would not spoil Elinor's wedding day with grieving. He had determined not to brood over his lost son, and he would *not*. With a manful effort, he cleared his throat and spoke to the young men.

"Don't you all be missin' the dancin'. Hearts will be breakin' if you all stay out here and let those pretty girls languish."

"You're right, sir," Yancey Ashby said, smiling. "Hey, boys!"

And Franklin Richler trailed the pack of them back to the party. There were more than a dozen couples dancing now, and in the midst of them Elinor and Tyler, radiant and wordless, entirely wrapped in each other's gaze. Franklin Richler paused at the edge of the crowd, next to his wife, and admired them with the rest.

Darius Yates had been captured so quickly and smoothly that he had neither cried out nor struggled. A struggle would have been purposeless; he was alone and the Indians were many. One seized his rifle and hunting knife and three others quickly tied his hands behind his back. His chief emotion was not fear but astonishment, for his capture had been so unexpected and his captors were so curious—it was like being transported into an adventure novel or a long-gone age.

To his eyes, the Indians were primitive and inscrutable savages. He could share neither language, motive, nor understanding with any of them. How odd I must look, how very odd, he thought, seeing himself as a tall, pale man, overdressed in his sweat-soaked black suit, stumbling behind the small brown men in penis strings and body paint, part of a single file heading deeper into the green thickets.

Very soon, astonishment was succeeded by suffering. Vines and thorns caught at him and his boots split. He kicked them off, and then his jacket. He stumbled, his hands bound, struggling to keep pace, every inch of exposed skin penetrated by insects, drenched in a constant running sweat.

After two days and two nights of continuous forced marching he was finally given food and water and allowed to sleep under a shelter of palm leaves tied onto a frame of fallen branches. The night was cold and every muscle in his body ached from the strain of walking but nothing pained him as much as the uncertainty of the future. Was all this a prelude to a violent death?

After the two days of marching, the Indians settled into a slower pace and stopped every night to make camp and sleep, traveling only from dawn to dusk. Yates tried to keep track of the days. By his count he had been captive for ten days when the pace picked up. From the rhythm of their speech, he could tell the Indians were excited.

At sunset on the eleventh day they entered a village at the side of a river. Yates felt himself the center of attention for several hundred curious, naked Indians. Men, women and children crowded around him, staring and jostling each other for a better view. In the background were dozens of small, palm-thatched huts. Dogs barked and macaws shrieked from the branches of trees.

Yates struggled to remain calm. Had he come so far, survived the years of war and the terrible shock of having his life destroyed, just to die here, in a lost Indian village? If God so willed it, he had. He steeled himself to reveal none of his fear and confusion, determined to retain his dignity to the end.

A white-haired man stepped out of the crowd and beckoned him aside. Following his orders, a very old woman stripped off the rest of his tattered clothes and he heard a wave of laughter at the whiteness of his skin. He stood quietly, waiting, and then the chief led him into one of the huts.

There was a fire inside and the air was both dank and smoky. Motioning Yates into one of the hammocks that hung along the side, the white-haired chief sat down in another and began to talk in a rapid singsong.

Yates understood not a word.

# Chapter Thirteen

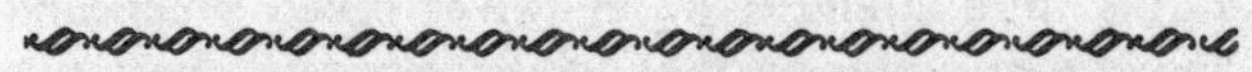

Before the memory of the marriage of Elinor and Tyler Ashby had faded, the American settlers had another occasion to pause and rejoice.

That same month Tyler Ashby's sister-in-law, Lucinda Rose, the willowy, brown-haired Alabama girl married to his brother John Bradlaw, gave birth to a healthy baby boy, the first American child born to the community. John Bradlaw and Lucinda named the child Clifford, after the Colonel. He was the Ashbys' first grandson.

Tyler, who was beginning to be known as Dr. Ashby, attended Lucinda Rose at her confinement, riding to his brother's house in the darkest hour of the frosty June night under a sky flashing with stars. Every woman has her baby at night, and everyone dies at night, he thought as he crossed the rounded hills that bordered the river. So his first teacher, the Ashbys' family doctor in Mount Pleasant, had told him. He felt a surge of confidence recalling Dr. Windham.

Windham, who had seemed ancient even when Tyler was a boy, who had been white-haired and slightly stooped even then, had died during the war, working in a soldiers' hospital in Mobile. When Tyler was twelve and first declared his ambition to be a doctor, Luther Windham had encouraged him, taught him, and taken him along to visit the sick, and that experience stood Tyler in good stead now, for his medical education had barely touched on mundane and practical matters such as childbirth, and now it seemed those were, after all, the most important.

Tyler had learned that it was not the Brazilian custom to have a doctor present at a normal birth. Births were attended by midwives called *practicars*, and of course, hundreds of babies were safely born this way. He acknowledged it. An experienced midwife was all most women needed, Brazilian or American, in his opinion, but there were other Brazilian customs that seemed both strange and dangerous. After a birth, it was the custom for a Brazilian mother to be kept in bed for forty days, fed nothing but broth. Brazilians believed if she got up or ate solid food it would kill her.

"Why, a new mother needs more food than she has ever in her life!" Tyler had exclaimed to Elinor. Elinor was almost sure she had felt life quickening inside her own body, although she had not yet told him so. She did not want to tell him yet. As happy as she would be to have a baby, she did not want this time to end, this golden time of mutual exploration, of discovery and celebration of their astonishing love and inimitable good fortune.

They had moved a few miles away from their

families, after the wedding, and until they could afford a big house of their own they lived in a simple, two-room house, a house built of mud and sticks plastered over with whitewashed adobe inside and out. It was a laughably poor house, little better than the houses the slaves had occupied on the Ashbys' plantation back home.

Tyler would never have thought that he would take his bride to such a house, but none of it was as he would have thought. He would never have expected that the size of the house to be so irrelevant to them, that their love would change it to the finest of castles-in-the-sky. He thought of Elinor as he had left her, smiling drowsily in their bed amidst a drift of hand-stitched white sheets and the blue-and-white double-ring patchwork quilt her grandmother in Tennessee had made. Uncovered, her slim, firm thighs had been creamy in the pale morning light.

They had passed the evening and half the night in lovemaking, falling into an exhausted sleep only minutes before John Bradlaw had pounded on the door. How he loved her body—the luxurious pearl-white silk of her skin, the cool and warm texture of it, the surprising and maddening musky smell she exuded when she was excited. How he delighted in her kisses, passionate openings-up of her most powerful self that stirred in him a desperate explosion of feeling, as if a volcano were bursting in his brain, its lava spreading from his heart to his loins.

She was so small and light in his arms, and yet so surprisingly passionate, so powerful as she clung to him, devouring him with her own desire, breathing with his own breathing, baring herself and daring him, with her so-saintly blue eyes to bare himself before her as he had not ever before another human being.

Elinor! He called to her in his thoughts. There is not a moment that I do not think of you with love. And your love gives me strength.

When he entered his father's house, his mere presence seemed to give Lucinda Rose the courage and comfort she needed to deliver her child. The baby was born in minutes; his squalls rang out into the brightening moment of dawn; his clear skin was as pink as the sky, and his mother slept sweetly and soundly, dreaming of her son's future.

Tyler left his family within the hour, stopping only to drink some of the powerful Brazilian coffee they had brewed from the beans raised in the valley. This thick black brew never failed to elevate his mood and give him a surge of energy. His parents were well. Charley Owen was away on a hunting expedition in the hills, and his sisters were excited beyond giddiness by the arrival of the new baby.

Tyler had no premonition of trouble as he rode away from his father's house. It was a clear, cool morning. A crescent moon clung to the last of the night. The rising sun had painted the pink sky with a streak of pure saffron over low clouds hunched like a range of rounded hills. As he rode along the creek, it seemed every bird in existence had awakened to sing its morning song from the solid green wall of trees and bushes that crowded together, gasping for light and air, along the bank.

On an impulse, he turned into the mud road that led to the Richlers' farm. He would stop for a visit with Elinor's family. Perhaps he would take her sister home with him for a brief stay; at any rate he would give

Elinor's family the news that they were well and that Lucinda Rose's baby had been safely born.

A dead armadillo, or *tatu*, as the Brazilians called them, in the front yard of the Richlers' house was his first intimation of neglect. It meant nothing; the little creature, crushed by a wagon wheel or horse's hoof, splayed in the dust like a bloodied crab, was nothing to mourn, and the ants were making short work of the *tatu's* remaining flesh, but Tyler shuddered unaccountably at the stench that rose from the dust.

Why had no one removed the dead creature? Had no one passed this way?

It was strangely silent, even for early morning. Tyler slowed his horse and dismounted, looking for signs of a fire, expecting the smell of coffee and the appearance of one of the family or some servant. Probably his father-in-law had gone out to the fields, but he expected the women to be at home.

"Miss Zaidee? Miss Daphne?" he called. "Hello! Who's home?"

He entered the low doorway into the house. Nothing seemed amiss. A clock was ticking on the mantelpiece and the round table in the center of the room was still covered with a cloth and a few plates from last night's supper. Beyond a curtain was a small bedroom with a big spool bed. Perhaps someone was ill and still abed.

Tyler stood silently for a minute before he called again.

"Hello! Good mornin'!" He felt awkward going into the bedroom unless invited.

"I'm here," Zaidee said in a flat voice from the doorway of the bedroom.

Tyler was embarrassed. Zaidee had been asleep

and appeared in a long, high-necked white linen nightdress. Her red-gold hair was tousled and tangled, and the collar of the nightdress fell aside to reveal a strip of very pale, gold-freckled skin. Her expression alarmed him—she looked dazed, almost drugged.

"I was asleep," Zaidee said unnecessarily. "I knew someone would come eventually."

"What's wrong?"

"It's Mama. She's been very ill. Papa is with her now, but he won't let me see her."

"Where are the servants?"

"Papa sent them away."

"And where is he?"

"Both of them stay in the house back there—the little house." Zaidee's voice broke. "He won't come out, Tyler!"

"Dear Lord!" Tyler sprinted across the barnyard, scattering a flock of hens. He ran past the kitchen garden, past the grape arbors and the terrace Franklin Richler had built for his wife.

The door of the little back house was closed. He knocked politely at first, and then pounded with all his strength.

"Mr. Richler! Are you there? Open up, sir!"

The silence was frightening. He could not wait another minute. His imagination ran wild. All the tension of approaching a locked house while foraging for supplies during the last year of the war was reborn in his mind. He expected screams, half-heard shots and the explosion of cannon. He was horribly frightened and felt weak, as if his body had been drained of all its blood.

He pounded on the door with his fists.

"Open up!" he screamed. Zaidee, still in her white

nightdress, had followed him out from the main house and stood behind him at some distance watching.

And then, very slowly, the door of the little house swung open, outward, and Franklin Richler stood in the doorway. He was fully dressed in a high-collared white tucked shirt and his best black cord suit, and wore over it his Confederate Army sash, all badly creased and rumpled. His hair, gone completely white in the past few months, was mussed and stood up stiffly around his bare head like an eagle's ruff. His face was ghostly pale and out of it stared his watery blue eyes, glassy with tears.

"She's gone," he said. "She's passed on. At the end she asked to go home and I promised I'd oblige, but she was too sick to travel anymore, don't you see? Now she's gone to heaven, although I believe she would have rather gone to Tennessee."

Ashby felt a rush of terrible sympathy for his father-in-law and then the feeling mixed with horror. A sickening smell of putrefication came from inside the darkened house. "Good Christ!" Tyler exclaimed.

He peered into the dimness and saw Daphne Richler laid out on a white patchwork counterpane, her pale face oddly yellowed, set and stiff, her dark hair dusted with silver and spread out on the lace pillowcase that had been part of her trousseau. How long had she been dead? He gagged at the smell.

"Jesus Christ!" he said again.

Franklin Richler lurched forward and broke into sobs.

"She's gone! Your mother's gone!" he moaned, trembling with grief. Zaidee led him away, back to the main house and Tyler shut the door again before he followed. First, he would give Franklin Richler a sedative and see that Zaidee was strong enough to care for him. Then he would see about making arrangements to deal with the dead.

# Chapter Fourteen

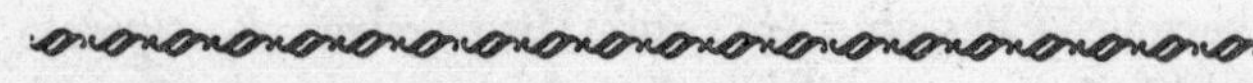

The river city of Santarém is 475 miles upstream from the mouth of the Amazon. The steamer *Monarch*, carrying 109 American colonists and Jesse Rall approached that city at dawn. Rall stood at the rail of the *Monarch* as the first strip of white beach came into view. He had been awakened from a tortured, dream-troubled sleep by the noisome squawking of parrots and the ceaseless hammering of cicadas, a pulsing sound that matched the aching of his head.

The *Monarch* drew near a shoreline marked by a row of low houses. In the distance was a range of rounded hills filigreed with feathery black palms. An alligator floated by. Rall saw it and laughed his bloodthirsty laugh. It was a country full of predators, a land of killers. All right. He was ready for them. He was a man who had killed and killed again, a killer among killers. All right. He breathed deeply of the cool, humid early morning air, slapped at the relentless mosquitoes, and saw an arrow arc out from a lower deck. An Indian had taken a shot into a flock of giant jabiru storks. The arrow found its mark and one of the long-legged birds dropped heavily onto the deck.

The river was a full thirty miles wide at this point. Here the Rio Tapajoz, enormous and black, enters the Amazon from the south and here its inky waters stripe the yellowish main stream. This effect can best be appreciated from a cloud, or the back of a bird; Rall did not appreciate it. From the water's level, the Amazon is a flat sea of streaked silver-gray. It is this aspect of the river that the Indians call the "ocean-river," and in fact it is now generally supposed that the Amazon, at a time too distant for comprehension, was a shallow sea separating the Andes, the highlands of central Brazil, and the mountains of Guiana. If this were so, then it was the rain and rivers from these highlands filling up the vast shallow sea with rich silt that created the world's largest jungle.

Rall was on the edge of it again, on the rim of the jungle, and as he sensed its power, a wave of fear rocked his body. Even from the protective vantage of the boat, the jungle threatened to reach out and engulf everything. Above the town, the vast greenness was black in its impenetrable density. He could smell it all around him—the rich odor of moisture and mold, of millions of plants and animals living and dying, crammed together in a vast soulless world where man was an invader. Already, in his heart, he had learned to hate the jungle and to believe that it was unconquerable.

But this time he was not alone. He would travel with the Americans aboard the *Monarch* to the land selected for the colony about fifteen miles from the town on the right bank of the Rio Tapajoz. The land had been purchased a year earlier by the colony's leader, Ransom Bailey, one of the great promoters of emigration to Brazil, author of an *Immigrant's Guide* which had inspired many to set sail. Unfortunately, Bailey, who had returned to America, had died on the voyage, but the land he had contracted for still awaited them, and the Brazilian government had agreed to build the colonists temporary shelters, finance the needy for three years and exempt their goods from all import duties.

Rall had heard all this from the other Americans and he had agreed to go with them to the site, although he did not share their spirit of hope and enthusiasm. He had already seen too much of Brazil and the Amazon to anticipate an easy time, and now, as the town of Santarém came into closer view, he uncorked his pocket flask and took a drink of rum to bolster his courage.

"So this is Santarém."

Rall looked down. Under his elbow was a small woman in a shiny black dress many sizes too large for her. It was Bailey's widow, the Alabama girl who had become his bride just before sailing and who had pinned herself into borrowed mourning two weeks out from St. Thomas. Rall regarded her mistrustfully. He had not spoken with Mrs. Bailey before; until today she had not left her cabin. He was tongue-tied at the sight of her—so tiny, so prim and pale, her smooth, shiny red-brown hair piled high off her neck, her eyelashes fluttering over clear hazel eyes at the sight of the wide river and the landing ahead.

He cleared his throat and wished he could take another drink. It had been so long since he had seen a white woman like this, a Southern lady, and all his responses to her were conditioned by a lifetime of conventional social intercourse.

"The Amazon is no place for ladies, ma'am," he said gruffly.

"Indeed it is," Eva Bailey replied quickly, "or my husband would not have brought us here." Her voice was soft and slow but utterly confident and Rall felt at once the amazing power of women.

And yet this woman was so frail. She could not weigh one hundred pounds, her wrists and hands were tiny, and she was so pale as to be wraithlike. He felt a rush of protectiveness, such as that he had once felt for his own sisters. Mrs. Bailey had no idea what sort of a country she was facing.

"The Indians bear watching," he said to her. "They're not good people, you know. They're worse'n niggers. They're bloody savages, those Indians."

"We shall save them," Eva Bailey said. "We shall teach them through our example of the good Christian life. We shall lift them from the dark hell of heathen beliefs into the light of Christ."

The *Monarch* touched the first of a chain of rafts tied together with thick vines, and a pack of naked Indian children, their brown bodies glistening, swarmed onto the decks of the steamer. Ashore a line of Indian women stared out at them, also naked except for necklaces strung of seed pods and bright-colored beads. Rall was embarrassed—not for himself but for Mrs. Bailey and the other American women. The Indian women were hideous, to his eye. Their pendulous brown breasts and foolish smiles insulted the modesty of all women, but Eva Bailey looked past them and marched directly ashore, stepping neatly over the swaying rafts, and stood under an immense silk-cotton tree on the riverbank.

There she unfurled her parasol, a yellow-and-white ruffled silk—obviously a relic from happier days. From a distance, it looked as if a bright butterfly had settled onto her shoulders. After stopping to drink again from his flask of rum, Rall followed her ashore, a desultory hunter keeping his prey in sight.

* * *

Most of the responsibility for arranging Daphne Richler's burial had fallen onto Tyler Ashby's shoulders. Franklin Richler was too shocked to do more than sit in a chair on the veranda, slumped among pillows, his frame shaking with silent sobs, and the rituals of death called out to be observed.

It's not fair, Zaidee thought, none of it's fair. None of it has to do with me. The war didn't—it was Papa's and General Lee's war. Coming to Brazil—that was for Laray Holt's sake, as much as anything else. And now I am left here, in this terrible place with Mama gone. She could not bear to think of her parents lying together in that little house, in this awful heat. She could not bear to think of it, but images of it crept into her thoughts and flashed around the edges of her mind.

By the morning of the second day, all the arrangements had been made and the funeral service took place in the front yard of the Richlers' house. Nearly fifty members of the American community stood in dignified silence around the family and the coffin and the sun beat down on their bent heads as Reverend Henry pronounced the familiar words of the Methodist funeral service.

We should have an American church, Elinor thought. In my mother's name I shall start a subscription campaign for one. It is only right that we should have our own church.

There should be a hearse, Tyler Ashby thought, riding behind the coffin. We make a ragtag procession. Well, we can't help it. So it is. We are not yet used to death here. We did not expect it so soon.

Even at a distance of twenty feet Tyler could smell the odor that all of them were pretending did not exist, although most of the ladies held white handkerchiefs over their faces. Daphne Richler had lain unburied too long.

The procession moved slowly. Tyler looked up at the sky and saw, to his horror, that their procession was being followed by huge buzzards, circling high in the dull sky, a sky that mirrored the mourning below, overcast with gauzy gray clouds that held down the heat of the earth and the moisture of the river like the lid on a kettle. It was an intensely humid morning. The hooves of the horses and the wheels of the wagons raised a red dust that clung to everyone's skin and clothes; it was a fine dust mixed of clay and sand but held moisture so that it caked like mud.

The cemetery gate stood open, and as the American cortege approached, another funeral procession moved toward the gate from the rear of the cemetery. Tyler looked out over the crowd. There were a lot of mourners—a hundred at least, many of them dark-skinned and dressed like laborers. At the head of the crowd were two priests in long robes and another, all in black, with a crooked gold-tipped staff and conical headdress.

And then, as the Americans stared, the priests turned to each other, appeared to confer, and then called out to some of the men behind them. A dozen men filed out of the cemetery and surrounded the Americans, blocking their entry.

"What is it? What do they want?" Franklin Richler demanded, suspicious and annoyed. Some of the women began to cry. Tyler dismounted and walked toward the big, open gate. At the gate, the buzzards flapped over his head, cawing, and settled in the top branches of the trees.

Kinch McCall had come along behind Tyler Ashby, and so had Charley Owen. "They don't want us in there," Charley Owen said to Tyler in a low voice.

Kinch McCall spit into the dust. Tyler wished he hadn't. It didn't look gentlemanly, or respectful. "It don't take second sight to see trouble," Kinch said.

"No, it don't," Charley Owen said. Tyler did not speak. He set his jaw and felt the sweat streaming off his neck. His collar felt tight. It was hotter than it had been in weeks, blistering hot.

"Does anyone here speak English?" Tyler asked. "*Fala inglês?*"

One of the priests stepped forward, his huge silver cross swinging in the folds of his dark robe. He bowed slightly, lowering his head in acknowledgment of the Americans.

Tyler Ashby bowed in return. "We have come to bury Mrs. Richler," he said slowly. "Senhora Richler."

"There is a problem," the priest said. "We cannot allow interment of heathens in the holy ground of this cemetery, dedicated to São Joao de Reis two hundred years ago."

Tyler stared at the priest. He was a bald-headed, round-faced little man. Tyler felt he had seen him somewhere before. He looked at the head priest. He was glowering, his eyes narrowed, a remote expression of cold outrage on his face. The interpreter spoke to him briefly, and the head priest answered at length in rapid Portuguese, but Kinch McCall spoke even as he was speaking.

"Heathens? Who is he callin' heathens?"

"We are all God-fearing Christians here," Charley Owen said in a loud ringing voice that all the Americans could hear.

"We are Christians," Tyler Ashby said simply. The head priest was a fearsome figure, thoroughly intimidating in his foreignness and his pompous, unworldly headdress. Tyler thought of the old Creek chieftains he had seen in the northern part of Alabama when he was a child; they had been copper-colored and inscrutably angry with all white men, just like this priest. Just like this priest, they had worn ridiculous headdresses.

"The Monsignore is distressed at your arrogance," the first priest translated. "We cannot permit you to enter or violate our sacred funeral grounds."

"We must leave at once," Tyler Ashby said to his brother and Kinch McCall. It was unthinkable that they would be turned away from the cemetery, but it was even more unthinkable to stand here and argue, to suffer any further humiliation. Daphne Richler could be buried on his father's land; there was plenty of it. It was best to go at once. He fought anger, thinking, I shall never understand these Brazilians, I shall never forget this awful moment.

The next moment was too late.

"Your customs are not our customs," the priest raved. "You are heathens. The unbaptized cannot be buried in holy ground."

"Who's unbaptized?" Kinch McCall shouted, his voice raw with rage. Behind him, near the coffin, a fight erupted. A young dark-skinned Brazilian and Ernest Gregg fell on each other. The sound of blows set off a woman's screams. Reverend Henry jumped off the wagon and was immediately knocked flat.

Tyler Ashby saw the flash of a knife blade, heard a bone crack.

"Watch out!" Zaidee Richler shrieked. "Mr. Gregg! Look out!"

"Dirty nigger!"

"He's killin' me!"

And behind him, more of the Brazilians burst out of the cemetery and encircled the Americans like a small army. Panic rose in Tyler's throat like a clot of blood. Years fell away and for a moment he was at Antietam again, seeing his men surrounded by a battalion of Yankees during that ghastly afternoon on South Mountain. But then he had been armed, he had been ready to kill every damn Yankee in sight to save himself and his men, and he had done so, to the absolute limit of his strength. . . .

"Stop!" he yelled. He dove forward to restrain Ernest Gregg, and saw Kinch McCall baring his teeth as he jumped another Brazilian. Reverend Henry struggled to his feet, gasping, and moaned, "This is a travesty! It's a sacrilegious abomination! Desist, in God's name!"

"Stop, please stop!" Tyler Ashby begged. He held back Ernest Gregg and backed him away from the crowd. It had all happened so fast that most of the mourners still stood in a flock.

"Stop!" Tyler shouted. "There's no good in fightin'!"

"You are right. This is mistake, misunderstanding," the interpreter priest said at Tyler's elbow. Behind him now stood Senhor Barroso, whom Tyler Ashby recognized at once and whose presence made him recall that he had seen the bald priest at Barroso's plantation and realized that all these ruffians were Barroso's men.

"Most unfortunate," Barroso said solemnly. He put out his hand. Tyler hesitated before he took it.

"We are sorry," the priest went on. "Senhor Barroso

regrets this misunderstanding, but we must bow to the edict of our prelate, who is come here from Campinas for this ceremony. Senhor Barroso's cousin is dead. But it is altogether impossible to bury an American here in our holy ground."

Tyler Ashby stared at Senhor Barroso and saw Barroso shrug and wink. "Very sorry," he said.

Battling rage and humiliation, Tyler turned away from the two unctuous men.

"Turn the wagons around," he yelled. "At once! We must go." And slowly, the crowd of Brazilians parting, the mourners moved on, wagons creaking, horses shying nervously. No one spoke and there was no more fighting. A sad, strained silence prevailed as the horses and wagons and mules and mourners retraced their steps and then took the road to Colonel Ashby's farm, where they were able to finish what they had set out to do and lay Daphne Richler to rest in the earth.

Tears came easily, then, to all the men and women standing around the grave, for they had more to mourn than a single death. It was not the time for resolves or resentment; such feelings dishonored the dead, but all of them knew it was a turning point. They could not blend into this community; they must create a community of their own.

Santarém was just as Rall expected: dismal and forlorn. It was a last-ditch trading post inhabited by a few Americans and Europeans involved in trading rubber, gold dust and tonga beans and hordes of half-drunk, half-corrupted natives and *mamelucos*. Santarém was the second largest trading center in the Amazon, after Pará, but jaguars prowled its streets on dark nights, and as the Americans soon learned, the road they had been promised had not yet been cut through the jungle.

Nor were any of the promised shelters yet constructed. After a brief stay in Santarém's disreputable boardinghouses, the Americans set out on their own, carrying their provisions on their backs, forced to walk the fifteen miles to the land they had contracted to settle. The land was fertile, that much was true, and they set to work at once, digging wells, choosing the sites for their farms and clearing the land. There was lumber in abundance. Felling a single immense evergreen oak yielded enough wood to build three of the open-sided huts that were sufficient shelter for this season of the year, but it was brutally hard labor, all of it, and discontent and disillusionment grew up among the colonists as rapidly as the greedy vegetation of the surrounding jungle.

Rall watched the discontent grow with a measure of detachment. He was not surprised, nor was he exempt. Like most of the others, he had never been a laborer. There were too many gentlemen in this colony, and not enough practical men; not enough wheelwrights or farmers, blacksmiths or carpenters or farm mechanics; and there were no Negroes at all in this region. At first, the colonists tried to hire Indians to help them, but the Indians did not prove to be good workers and most of them ran away, some of them carrying important farm implements with them—for what reason, Rall did not know, perhaps for curiosities or to kindle cookfires.

As the weeks passsed and became months, Rall became convinced that the colony would not last much longer, but he had his own reason for remaining as long as he could. That reason was his desire for Eva Bailey, a lust that had begun with amazement at the fierce ruthlessness of her idealism, and had been corrupted by their continued physical proximity to a deluded need. Her purity and primness tormented him; he longed to destroy them and to see her waver and fall; he ached to despoil her, but was arrested by her innocence and her seeming disregard for him as a full-blooded man.

He had never known a Southern lady more completely confident of the tradition. Brazil had made no impact on her, and could not. Wherever she goes, she will be in Alabama, Rall realized. She sees only what fits into the old, ruined framework of customs and conventions that have no place in this green wilderness. Her blind confidence fascinated him. She was simply not equipped to see life except as it had been before the war, even if it assaulted her, like the Amazon's heat and humidity.

He wondered what her body would be like without clothes, what she would be like in bed. He thought about it, imagined what it would be like to peel the dress and petticoats off her tiny, childlike body, for her to respect him as a man. Perhaps at the bottom of his desire for her was desire for his mother, for she had originally reminded him of his mother, but her own personality had soon driven that similarity out of his mind.

Eva Bailey was her own person. She was twenty-eight, and until she had met Ransom Bailey, had expected to pass her life as a spinster. She had expected the half-life of a maiden aunt, turning a polite ear to other women's coy complaints about husbands, baking cookies for other women's children.

The truth was clear: there were so few men left in the South. So Eva Collins, a woman who had seen her world shaken up like a bottle of salts until it bubbled fearsomely and erupted, changed in character and became uncontrolled, had thanked God when she first met Ransom Bailey, a leader of men, a man who had already been to Brazil and explored it and declared it was ideal for Southern colonization. Bailey had traveled 19,000 miles the year before he arrived in Jasper, 10,000 on his Amazon inspection trip. Then he had returned to Alabama to recruit emigrants and had met and married Eva Collins in the space of two weeks.

The two weeks, ending with the wedding and a flurry of farewell parties and packing trunks with all the best that was left from her own and her mother's trousseau, had been the happiest in Eva's life. Ever since then, she had been caught in a downward spiral of shattered illusions and disarray; the physical side of marriage to Mr. Bailey had been surprising and disconcerting; the long sea voyage uncomfortable and his sudden desertion by death monstrously shocking and nightmarish.

Rall misjudged her when he saw her as calm and capable, unruffled by the fearful absurdities of the Amazon. In fact, it was largely his presence that made her seem so; she had cast her net for him the first time she saw him. She needed him desperately. She did not reveal it, but she was frightened into blankness by the jungle, the Indians, the isolation of the land Bailey had selected for his colony, and the prospects of pioneering life.

Eva Bailey had an intense need to attract, enthrall and control a man. It was the essence of her training as a Southern belle. She had wanted and needed a husband until she almost gave up hope, and then she had found one. Having lost him, she knew with clear poignancy how much she needed another, all the more in this horribly strange setting.

Although she was frightened, she was resourceful, and the recent reverses of her life had lent her a pragmatic outlook. She was in need and Jesse Rall was available, so to him—although in the world she had grown up in, in those easy, careless days, she might have scorned his bad grammar and looked down on his status as an overseer—she was conciliatory and charming, she was pliable and admiring, she was shy and yet confident that he could provide all she needed, all she asked.

And so Rall was drawn to her. He needed a woman and this one seemed pretty and pure and serene and polite, a perfect lady. He wanted her, and he wanted to destroy her. His hatred and fear of women was checked by a deep-held desire to please and love them, and in the balance, he pressed his courtship, in his own way.

# Chapter Fifteen

"Now, 'course, the seasons are reversed," Franklin Richler said to Zaidee. They sat together on the narrow veranda in front of their mud-brick house. Zaidee had planted morning glory vines at the bases of the unpeeled pillars that supported the veranda's thatched roof. The vines had climbed the poles in a month, growing so rapidly it was almost possible to measure the days by it, and bloomed now, both morning and evening, hanging heavy with large, bright purple blossoms that gave off a musky-sweet scent in the humid air.

"The seasons are reversed," Richler repeated with an air of saying something marvelous. "Back home, it'd be winter now, Zaidee, think of that."

"I don't care to think of it," Zaidee said softly. As long as she spoke softly, her father never heeded her words. She had endured his observations about the seasons a hundred times, anyway, and had already thought on the reversal far more than she cared to do. The worst aspect of her father's absentminded ramblings, if there was a worst, if the content of them was not in itself the worst, was knowing that he had said just exactly the same things in just exactly the same tone of voice to her mother, when the three of them had sat here on evenings just exactly like this one.

Now that Daphne Richler was dead, Zaidee had the awful feeling that she was being slipped into her mother's life, cast in her role as mistress of the household. It was a role she had no desire or inclination to play. None at all. I was never raised to be a dairy-maid, she thought. I work harder than a nigger back home. . . .

"Well, I wonder how Cousin Bert's doin' this winter," her father said, his level, dull-dreaming voice undercutting the raw, rushed feeling of panic that engulfed Zaidee. This was no place for her; she would rot here; she had to do something; she had to escape. Sometimes she felt like jumping up and just walking away, walking down the road to town and from there to the next town that would put her farther from this and nearer to home.

But of course she could not. "I expect Cousin Bert's well," she said in a choked voice, knowing her father would not notice. She looked down at her hands. They were rough and red from laundry and butter-making. There were ugly spots of buttermilk on her black silk mourning dress.

The woman servant Joana should have taken care of the butter, but she didn't know how, or pretended she didn't—it amounted to the same thing. Zaidee heard Joana's voice, deep and rich, singing as she carried water from the well to her own house. Joana was difficult to manage, and because she could speak only a few words of English, no company at all. Zaidee's method of managing her was to repeat her orders, loudly and clearly, several times, always with increasing bad temper, and then, as a last resort, to use sign language, although she believed that Joana understood when she wanted to.

Papa did better in communicating with the field hands, although it was also a constant struggle. Ever since Mama had gone he had been drifting away. The light in his blue eyes seemed dimmed; he repeated himself and forgot mealtimes and wandered away alone for hours at a time.

"Company's comin'," Franklin Richler said, lifting his head and brightening at the sound of a horse approaching on the road from town. "Now who can it be at this hour, Zaidee? Who can it be?"

No one at all, Zaidee thought peevishly. No one of any interest.

"Why, it's Ernest Gregg," her father announced a few minutes later. "I expect he's comin' to call on you, Zaidee. He wouldn't be callin' on me."

"Just as I thought, no one at all," Zaidee murmured. Ernest Gregg had come courting, if you could call it that, several times since the first time he had come with Tyler Ashby. At first he hadn't the sense or wit to say what he was about, but lately it had become obvious, and even the sight of him curdled Zaidee's temper. Ernest Gregg was not at all her idea of a beau—the only man who could interest her would be a gentleman, rich and handsome and courtly. When she married, it would be to a man with style and manners, not a rough farmer. Perhaps a knight, or even a prince. She was sure she hadn't met him yet, although she sometimes remembered the man dressed up as a pirate she had danced with in Rio. He might have been a prince in disguise.

"I'll get some lemonade," she said, and pulled off her faded percale sunbonnet. No need to look like white trash even if she did work like a hand. When she returned to the veranda, her father was talking about the corn crop and Ernest Gregg was seated on the top step, turning his hat by the brim. Zaidee looked at him with loathing and handed around the lemonade. How crude he was. His face was as coarse and brutish as a mule's and the dark hairs that curled out from his cuffs revolted her.

As the night birds began to call and broad-winged swallows circled in the darkening sky, Franklin Richler's voice dimmed and slurred. Finally Ernest Gregg rose and stood, again turning his straw hat by the brim.

Perhaps he has forgotten this isn't his home, Zaidee thought, but when he did say goodnight she found herself being drawn into step with him as they walked by lantern light to the rail where he had hitched his horse.

"I sure have enjoyed this evenin', Miss Zaidee," he said.

"Pleasant," Zaidee said flatly.

"Yes, ma'am. Well . . ."

"Well, goodnight."

"Yes. I jest wanted to say, well . . . I've not got much, yet, Miss Zaidee, but I've got prospects."

Prospects? Did he call a chance at his father's farm, a farm just as much in the first stages of settlement as her own father's, did he call that prospects? What a boor he was! His presumption was sickening. The anger she felt at her whole life welled up in her and she laughed.

"Prospects, Mr. Gregg? Why don't you wait till you've struck gold, prospector, before you come botherin' me anymore!"

And then she laughed again, uncontrollably, and swung back into the darkness with the lantern, leaving Gregg to find his seat alone, but it was Zaidee who felt most alone. Alone, she crept into the darkened house and cried herself to sleep.

Jesse Rall built Mrs. Bailey a simple house on her land. He dug her a well and cleared trees for a small kitchen garden, setting out in the rich well-drained soil some of the seeds and tubers that she had carried from Alabama. He drew her water, cut her firewood and he built her fires. For a time things went no further. It was the setting-up time, the time of an unspoken struggle for power between two determined personalities.

At the end of the second month, the rainy season began—not gradually with a slow loosening up of the glowering heat, but explosively, with a sullen threatening sunset sky. Rall and Eva Bailey ate their simple evening meal together, as was their custom. As usual, conversation between them was slow and strained. Eva Bailey was tense, white-lipped and silent, her anxious face barely concealing despair. Rall spoke hesitantly of crops and the weather.

After the meal, Rall prepared to leave for his own house. Eva Bailey lit a candle and set it down. A snake dropped off the roofpole and coiled itself into a hissing pyramid on the table.

She screamed.

Rall pulled out his small pistol and blasted the snake's head off with an eruption of blood.

"I can't bear it," Eva Bailey sobbed. "Not another minute of it!"

Her sobs fell into the heavy, hushed silence that precedes a devastating change in the weather. They both felt it, although they did not recognize it—even the birds were hushed, only the incessant cicadas whistled and pulsed.

"Don't cry," Rall said in a choked voice, "I hate to hear a woman cry."

"It's a monstrous country," she moaned. I wish I had never come, she thought, but it was a thought too regrettable to voice. She buried her face in her hands, and above them, high above at first, above the tall trees that closed out the sky and stars even on the clearest nights, the rain began to fall, crashing through the leaves, splashing up from the black earth, falling in silvery sheets, closing out the rest of the world as if a curtain had been dropped around them.

"I s'pose it is," Rall said.

He picked up the length of the snake with the butt of his pistol and tossed it out the open door. A stream of water was already running into the hut and the heaviness of the rain-soaked air made breathing palpable. The crash of thunder was the only sound loud enough to be heard over the sound of the rain, and the occasional flash of lightning was like a flash of sun. He replaced the pistol in its leather holster and moved across the room, straight to her.

But to her surprise, when he took her in his arms, she shuddered with violent distaste. He was not what she wanted. She wanted not comfort, but salvation. He was too big and raw for her; he was too like Brazil, too forceful and predatory. She was oppressed by all of it and craved something small and familiar and manageable. She did not want a lover but a servant, a man who would do her bidding and then go, a man who would smile and bow like old Uncle Henry, the driver her father had kept before the war, when men, like reality, knew their place and kept to it, observing conventions. All those conventions had protected women but none of them could protect her now.

She struggled in his arms, twisting and writhing helplessly, fighting him for more than he was, fighting all of it, the absurd loneliness of this doomed and isolated colony, the jungle, the night and the terrible storm.

"Let me go. You may not touch me," she ordered, her voice fretful and imperious.

He moved closer to rage. How dare she address him so? He had done everything for her; he had given her everything he had and she had accepted it. He had worked for her like a dirty slave, he had dug and built, bent and carried, and until now asked nothing in return. He had planted for her, he had fished for her, he had even cleaned her little house after he had built it, feeling far from generous in these gifts of labor, but aware that there was no other way, for she was a lady in mourning and in need. Her need was so immense it was obvious.

"Eva."

She broke away from him and faced him with eyes blank as buttons, narrowed like a cat's. Her color had risen, she was breathing with effort. Her borrowed black crepe mourning veil was limp with moisture and had collected mosquitoes in its foolish trailing length. Rall reached for the veil and jerked it off.

"What are you doin'?"

"Give up mournin' him. It's time to forget him."

"I'll never forget him!" She snatched at the veil, but he dropped it into the water running in the open door and stepped on it.

"Stop!" She leapt at him, clawing at his throat and neck.

Her temper set off his. If she was no lady, then he need use no restraint. Rall was never far from the limits of his own self-control, easily lured over the brink into the chaos of rage and will that was always there inside him, just under his skin, just behind his red-rimmed eyes. The minute she started for him, he knew how it would end. He knew he would have her now; she was all his; she had ended her mourning and her marriage in that moment. Now he would have her his way, any way he liked; now he was her master.

He smiled as they fought. Her efforts to scratch him glanced off his tough skin like an insect's bite. He caught one arm and held it; it was thin and as brittle as the stalk of a fern, but he did not snap it, he merely bent it around her back so that her body was forced up against his, and with his other hand he pulled off her dress.

Her underwear was white and she was even smaller than he had imagined. He had thought about her body so often that it had few surprises, or else he saw only what he expected. Her breasts, when he had stripped away the fragile white camisole, were tiny, delicate white waterlilies with dark-pink centers, nipples that stood out boldly, fully mature, beautiful and provocative.

Afterward, when she tried to remember, their tussle seemed like a dance routine. She had seen a Russian ballet once, on a visit to Natchez, had seen the dancers turn delicately toward each other and then twist away, but this was no dance. Rall held her, lifted her, set her down, then picked her up again. For all her twisting and flailing, she was completely helpless and she knew it, as surely as a child knows it is an inconsequential creature in its father's grasp. She gave up the physical fight, but her eyes blazed at him.

He had hurt her; her bones ached and his rough fingers had reddened her thin, pale arms.

She could still hurt him, too, and she wanted to.

"You are too common to touch me," she hissed. "I hate your dirty hands and your ugly, common face."

He flushed dark-red, panting, then buried his face in her flesh, scratching her with his dark beard. He unpinned her long, soft, reddish-brown hair and combed it roughly with his fingers, bringing tears to her eyes, but she did not cry out. No one could have heard her, anyway; no one would save her; there was nowhere she could run. Somehow, God had sentenced her to this and she believed, unthinkingly, that she deserved it, for she did not question fate; that was blasphemy.

She could not stop him, after that, and it was even more than she had feared. It had never been like this with her husband; he had been a tentative bridegroom and Rall was not, but her cry aroused him further and he drove himself at her again and again, holding her thin body against the table's edge with her arms bent back and her mane of hair sticking to both of their sweat-slick bodies.

She had never known passion or even imagined it, never suspected its strong ties between men and women she knew, and, in the end, it was his passion that awakened her. His passion, not her own. His was sufficient.

"Oh, yes! Eva! Oh!" he cried, and her eyes opened wide with pain and astonishment and she was lost in the feeling even as she feared it, and clung to him.

And after the rainy season had begun, it rained incessantly.

# Chapter Sixteen

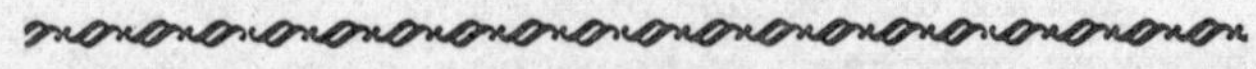

Some months later, Terrill Ruffin found himself in the most unlikely and impossible situation his mind could conceive. James Barnes called him into his office, early one morning, a day Ruffin had expected to devote to examining the accounts of an expedition to the highly successful gold mine Barnes owned in Minas Gerais.

"Da Silva is worse today," Barnes said. A frown settled onto his broad forehead as it always did when he thought of his partner's illness. Barnes rose to his full height. At six feet four inches, he towered over Ruffin and Ruffin felt, not for the first time, like the Scotsman's surrogate son.

"I am sorry to hear that."

"He is so ill, in fact, that all of his sons are at home with him. Perhaps this is the beginning of the end.

Consequently, I must ask you to take care of a certain business that I generally leave in da Silva's hands."

"Yes, of course."

Barnes frowned. "I despise this business, understand that. Perhaps it's hypocritical of me to send da Silva or his sons out to do it each time. It is a necessary business, but I believe it an immoral one. As an educated Christian, you doubtless think so, too."

Ruffin waited without speaking. He was beginning to understand and hoped his anxiety did not show.

"Nonetheless, our society demands it. Brazil is not a modern nation. Of course you are aware of that. To you she must seem a very backward nation in many ways . . ."

Barnes began to pace the floor.

"What is it, sir?" Ruffin asked.

"I refer of course to slavery. We have spoken of this before, Ruffin. Brazil's wealth is founded on two rocks: her natural resources and the slaves who toil to extract them. But slavery is a false foundation. A rotten one. Poisonous to all involved. It's hard to say who suffers more—master or slave."

Ruffin thought he knew, but he remained silent, listening to Barnes, hearing him out.

"You have seen it in your own country, no doubt. Oh, the most wretched Negroes carried across the sea have improved their lives. And many have become Christians. But to the higher race which has imported him, the Negro has done great damage—incalculable injury, moral as well as physical."

"Yes."

"The truth is that where slaves labor, all labor becomes servile. Whites prejudiced against labor, and especially against the most important form of labor for a young country—agriculture—impair their own future. Good Christ! Slavery is doomed, we all know that. Dom Pedro is a moralist and the greatest abolitionist in the government and he will have his way—already no slaves can be imported, but until the last day possible . . . white men will exploit dark ones for profit! You know it is so!"

"What is it you want me to do?"

"Oh! Forgive me. I rave on. It is a simple matter. I want you to go to the slave market and buy, let us see . . ." Barnes studied a sheaf of papers before him on his desk. "Buy ten or twelve healthy men to send along to the mines with Perrera's expedition next week. Yes, just ten or twelve."

Ruffin had broken into a cold sweat as Barnes talked. Blessed Christ, Barnes had no idea how such cold-blooded discussions affected him. Alone in his employer's elegant two-wheeled carriage he mopped his face again and again. Leaning over the side of the carriage he emptied his stomach, then sat back to feel it tighten in pain.

Feeling dazed, Ruffin stumbled through the great, arched doorways past a long, low table and a roped-off area containing antique and secondhand furniture, old pictures, Dutch cheese, Yankee clocks, kitchen utensils and crockery, old books in crates, shoes, jars of pickles . . . but these would be sold on another day. These were the daily goods of sale. Today, on this one day each week, the merchandise was human beings.

The slaves for sale were ranged on benches behind a railing and the low pulpit of the auctioneer set up before them so that the buyers could face both. Ruffin took a seat and looked at the auctioneer. He could not yet bring himself to look at the Negroes up for sale.

The auctioneer was a tall, black-whiskered man of

about thirty-five, a master of his profession if Ruffin could judge from the fluency of his patter and the occasional ripples of laughter that swept through the crowd. His speech was so rapid that Ruffin could not follow all of it, but with the aid of the auction bill and the numbers hung on placards around the necks of the men and women for sale, it was not difficult to understand the procedure.

For a few minutes Ruffin just stared, forgetting that he was there to buy ten healthy men. Because of his sheltered life in the monastery, he had never seen a slave auction in New Orleans. Of course he had known they existed, but it was impossible to generalize about the sight before him.

He sat very still, his eyes meeting those of the slave being sold, holding them, searching them for hints of the poor creature's character. A man of about his own age stood up for sale. The auctioneer released a flood of words. A bidder stepped up to examine the man, baring his legs and fingering their muscles appraisingly, testing his grip, then smiling.

Ruffin looked down at his printed bill. If this man was number 29, then he was "Perez, Romeiro," a barber-surgeon, also a "*bom sangrador e musico,*" a singer and musician. The man went for eight hundred milreis.

According to the bill, all the men would be sold first. Most of them were between eighteen and thirty years old, and most of them were trained to be carpenters, masons, field hands, coffee carriers, and coachmen.

Of the females to be sold, the oldest was twenty-six and the youngest between six and eight. They were advertised as being "*muito prendada*"—very accomplished. Two of them were dressmakers, others were washerwomen, sewers, cooks, some made shirts, others were accomplished at dressing ladies' hair. A couple were wet nurses, *"con muito bom leite, com cria."* Ruffin realized with a shock that *cria,* the word for colts, was also used for the offspring of Negroes.

The minutes passed, as lives were disposed of and the auctioneer's voice rose and fell. Ruffin stared, feeling by turns obviously black and then invisible, staring at the slaves seated on the benches, devouring their fear and imagining their feelings.

He could not help himself from staring at the women coming up for sale. They were of every skin color from jet to nearly white. One young woman standing with hunched shoulders was as white as himself. As white as himself!

He nearly choked. How could he sit here and be part of the audience of bidders? What strange joke was God playing with him or to him? Struggling for composure, he felt ill again. At any moment, he expected to be exposed as a fraud, jerked out of his seat and hung with a placard, examined by bidders like a carriage horse . . .

"Number 89," the auctioneer called out and Ruffin saw that if he was to buy, he must do it soon. How could he return to Barnes and say he had made no purchases? Almost blindly, he bid on the next dozen men brought up, won ten of them, and stood up to pay and go.

"Barnes and da Silva," he told the cashier. It would go on the company account. For all he knew he had bought men who were diseased or surly; he did not know; he wanted only to escape from this unholy place.

But as he arranged for the delivery of the men and signed the promissory note, the auction of men ended and that of the women began. He could not resist looking back to see what would happen to the young woman whose skin was the same shade as his own.

She was number 5. He waited, heart pounding.

And then the clerk went behind the rails and dragged her forward. How thin she was! Her legs were sticks, her shoulder blades stood out like wings, and her pale bare arms were no thicker than her wrists. She stumbled, still hunched, still looking down, but she was not alone. A girl child clung to her hand, weeping, obviously dreading to be torn away from her mother, and the look on her face was more than Ruffin could bear.

The child did not cry out, but tears chased each other down her face and her narrow chest heaved violently. The auctioneer exchanged fervent words with a prospective bidder, then waved his hand to include both of them. The bidding began and Ruffin was astonished to hear his own voice lift the price.

He was even more surprised a half hour later when he found himself helping the woman and her child into Barnes's trim carriage. Why on earth had he bought the female slave? And what was he going to do with her?

"How I hate everything," Zaidee murmured. She stood alone in the barnyard that stretched from the kitchen door to the little garden behind. It was a sunny morning, as quiet and full of domestic details as every other sunny morning: Franklin Richler had gone out to the fields, Joana was at work in the garden, and the hens basked in the dust as the turkeys scattered, rustling black-tipped red feathers as they trotted to roost on a broken-down fence pole.

I cannot bear it here, she thought, stamping her

feet in the red dust. Her boredom and loneliness were crippling, but she was lent some share of energy by the spirit of the day, for it was Elinor's birthday, and she and Tyler were expected for a visit. If only for a time, I must get away, she decided, and walked purposefully toward the stable, now that she had a plan. She would take Duke out for a ride, no matter if she was not at home when Elinor arrived.

Elinor could wait.

Zaidee loved riding. As a child, she and Laray Holt had kept twin ponies and had ridden out together on countless sunny afternoons, disappearing into the grassy meadows along the river, beating down the buffalo grass into secret paths, pretending to chase coyotes, free as the hawks that circled over their heads. She thought of Laray Holt with a twinge of sadness; they had been close in age and close friends. She missed him, and perhaps if he had not been killed, they would never have come to Brazil. Now she wrestled with Duke, forcing him to trot along the dusty road next to the cotton fields until she reached the main road that ran from her father's land into the town along the rim of the foothills.

It was here that the bed for the railroad was being dug and the tracks laid. The new railroad would be a tremendous advantage for the town—everyone said so. It would open them up to trade and enable the cotton growers to reach their markets. It would connect them with Campinas and beyond to São Paulo, but to Zaidee it would be a personal lifeline. No one had understood her interest in the building of the railroad, but in her own unfocused dreams she could see herself, clothed in some wonderfully stylish traveling dress, satchel in hand, boarding the train for a long journey.

I believe I'll ride over and see how the tracks are coming, she thought. Won't be long now till they're done, everyone says.

On the main road, Duke found a more secure footing and settled into a smooth canter. Zaidee leaned forward, enjoying the familiar feeling of a powerful horse under her, her black skirts and wisps of red-gold hair flying, her knees pressed tight to Duke's flanks as the forest on either side of the road flickered past. She was exhilarated, and the speed of the ride cleared her head of the dull malaise that possessed her. She coaxed Duke to a greater speed with a good snap of her riding crop.

Like a colt, he raced along the road, then climbed the narrower trail that led to the railroad embankment. Zaidee sawed on the bit to slow him, but he found new strength, and she laughed, thrilled by the element of danger, and clung to his back as leaves and branches scratched her hands and bare arms like hooks and claws.

Perhaps I shall ride clear out of the country, she thought wildly. I should never miss home, if I did, and when I was rich and married to a fine gentleman, I should come back on the train. She laughed, and the gelding crashed on through the underbrush, the sound of his hoofs silenced by the soft green moss and drift of dead leaves underneath.

There ain't a man in the whole region who's my type, she thought. They're all oafs, wors'n Mexicans. The only man in Brazil who had stirred her imagination was the pirate at the ball in Rio, and she thought of him again now, the rhythm of the ride calling him to mind, for it was not his dark-skinned courtliness that she remembered most powerfully, it was the ecstatic feeling of being swept into the dance.

"Come on, Duke," she yelled, forcing him onward toward higher ground. Duke's eyes rolled and he glistened with sweat, but the top of the rise was the site of the railroad bed. The gelding danced into a sun-bright clearing. There were the tracks already laid, stretching out to the east, hard iron ribbons set in red earth; to the west only a tunnel cut through the dense forest.

And in the center of the clearing, clear as noon, there was a sight Zaidee had not expected: a gang of half-naked men wielding picks and shovels. She came up short and so did the men, all turning toward her, six or seven men made of muscle, their bare brown backs and corded shoulders sweat-shiny above brief tattered trousers.

How ugly they are, she thought, a pack of dark, dirty animals. She shuddered, and then jerked on Duke's bit, driving it into his jaw. The horse ducked his head, then bucked suddenly; Zaidee lost her seat and flew off, her skirts flipping upside down to show short white lace pantalets as she landed in the dust with a force that left her breathless.

It was all dark. She could not see, nor hear, nor move, and then she gasped and opened her eyes to shattering brightness. The sun was directly overhead, no higher than the treetops and burning, blazing down on her, searing her like fire. No, the fire had settled into her ankle! It shot through with white-hot pain when she tried to move. She fought for breath and then looked up.

They were all over her, all around her, and worse than the pain was the sure, instinctive fear that they could do anything to her. Even the sight and smell of them sickened her. "No!" she shrieked. "Duke! Oh, help!"

The silence that settled in after her cry was stunning. She struggled against her own weakness and winced in pain. The men shuffled around her, barefoot on huge flat feet. Their calves were massive knots of muscle, their dark faces outlined against the light were square and intent.

"No," she screamed again. She could smell them—they reeked of sweat and rank masculinity and the worst of them, a hulking man with hair to his shoulders, leaned down over her.

"Don't," she gasped, thrashing, hot with fear and outrage, pinned to the earth by the pain in her ankle. All the terrible stories of violence and violation that she had ever heard rushed into her mind, all jumbled and pierced with pain.

"No . . ." she wailed, miserably sure she was on the edge of death, and then, still heavy on her back, she sensed the men melting out of the shimmering circle of light and heard the sound of a horse's hooves.

It was a mirage of rescue. Was she dead and dreaming? It was a well-dressed white man sliding out of a silver-trimmed saddle, off a sleek black horse, holding Duke by the reins and bending over her. It was a man she vaguely recognized. She blinked, wide-mouthed, and then slid into a dead faint.

"Can it be you?" she asked, a few minutes later.

He held a flask of liquor to her lips. She gulped, then shivered at the strength of it. Her head throbbed and the shimmering lights at the edges of her vision flashed still, but his arm was under her shoulders and the ugly men had retreated.

"I might ask, is it you," he said. "I might ask what an American angel is doing here?"

Zaidee sighed with a feeling of deliverance. Of course it was meant to be. He had saved her again—the elegant pirate. His eyes were still as bold and black, his smile as reckless and irresistible. Just as before she was helplessly confused and could not think of a word to say.

"Are you living nearby?" he asked, making sense of it. "Are you one of the Americans farming here?"

"Yes," Zaidee managed. Now here was no struggling dirt farmer; he was a nobleman at least. Perhaps he was a prince. She stared at him, too astonished and fascinated to speak. His suit was cream-colored, soft-looking linen tailored in a fashionable style. His riding boots were rich, dark leather and gleamed like the silver trappings on his saddle and his riding crop, and . . . she lifted her wide-eyed stare, the light in his laughing brown eyes.

"I am Miss Sarah . . . well, Miss Zaidee Richler," she said at last, more conscious of the drabness of her rumpled, dusty, ill-fitting gown than of the coincidence of their meeting. After all, Brazil was a small country, not like the vast one she had left behind. Pray God he did not notice the spots on her skirt.

Of course he did not notice. He was amused, and surprised, and quite satisfied to admire her red-gold hair and her pretty face, across which a variety of expressions quickly passed. There was no doubt but that she was the American woman he had danced with at the Emperor's ball. How curious that she should be living here, in his town. Perhaps it would not be so dull at home, after all. Perhaps his self-imposed exile here would prove to be a lively diversion.

He laughed. He had always thought life amazing. There was no end to its surprises. Zaidee winced at his laugh and blushed.

How pretty she is, he thought, and how charmingly confused. They say these American women are very independent and straitlaced, but this one does not appear to be straitlaced. He looked at her bare arms with surprised admiration. Perhaps she is running away from something. No Brazilian lady would ever ride out alone. Of course, no Brazilian lady of her age would be unmarried, either. Brazilian women married at twelve, thirteen, or fourteen years of age. A family with an unmarried fifteen-year-old daughter made desperate promises to St. Anthony and St. John. They said that a girl would spoil from overripeness if she were not plucked in time. Why should the Americans be different, he wondered. He smiled, thinking that he would like to find out.

Gently, he lifted Zaidee to her feet. She stepped cautiously on her twisted ankle. It hurt, but after all, it was not broken. She clung to his arm.

"Excuse me. I must introduce myself, Miss Richler. I am Rafael Marcio Cristobal Barroso, senhorita, at your service."

"Oh," Zaidee said. "Yes . . ."

Barroso! Her mind raced. Oh dear, he must be one of the family whose land adjoined the Ashbys'. Why, he must be one of that dreadful family who had humiliated all of them at the graveyard, who had refused to let her poor mother be buried in peace. Not this one, but perhaps . . . she thought quickly, probably his father. Her father hated all those Barrosos, or said he did; of course he had never met them . . . but still, he would not like her to talk to this one.

"I shouldn't be here . . ." she murmured distractedly.

"Certainly not," Rafael Barroso agreed. "I must take you home."

"Oh, no!" He must not take her home. Not yet. Her father would not approve, and he would be disgusted at the smallness of her home. There was no doubt but that they must meet again, but it must be secretly. She was sure he was all she desired in a beau—he was handsome and aristocratic and surely as rich as sin, but there was no place for him in her ordinary life. He would be the instrument for her escape; he would save her once again.

"I am better already," she said in a strained voice. "If you could just help me mount?"

"Yes, of course." Very carefully, Barroso lifted her onto Duke, and if his arms held her a bit longer than was necessary, and both of them knew it, it was a sensation that only promised more.

I cannot let her disappear again, Rafael Barroso thought. He smiled. "Miss Richler, in this country a gentleman may sometimes call on a lady, if she likes."

"Oh," Zaidee said softly, weak with relief that he had spoken out. Papa would not permit it, but perhaps...

"May I call on you?"

Whatever Papa thinks, I must see him again, Zaidee decided. I must. "Perhaps we could meet again, out riding," she suggested.

"Yes? But where and when?" Rafael smiled. So he was right. She was not a lady; she wanted a private assignation with him. Like all the others, she could not resist him. He was immediately excited at the thought. "When shall we meet? Tomorrow?"

"No," Zaidee said decisively. "In a week's time. At the base of this little trail, just where it departs from the main road. At midafternoon."

"Oh, I will be there," Barroso promised. "Now take care, pretty lady, Miss Zaidee. Do not fall off your horse again!"

Zaidee frowned. Fall off, indeed. In the distance, the gang of workmen was still bent over their shovels in the bed but now they looked menial, not menacing. This is certainly the most interesting thing that has happened to me in Brazil, she thought.

There was nothing under the Brazilian sun more unlikely or intolerable than that Terrill Ruffin should become a slaveholder, and yet that was the result of his impetuous bidding at the auction on Santos Street.

Had it not been so terribly sad and serious for all concerned, the situation might have been funny, or so Ruffin thought as he drove away from the dreadful warehouses and auction hall. Beside him in Barnes's elegant carriage were two human beings; an emaciated, light-skinned young woman and her small daughter, whose eyes, as bright and round as copper coins, were fixed unswervingly on her new owner, asking what would happen next.

What indeed? Possibilities and solutions raced through Ruffin's mind. The immediate needs of the woman and her child were shelter, food, rest, kind care, privacy . . . all the ordinary needs of human beings. But Ruffin was living in a hotel; he had rented rooms from Ralph Carson in Carson's English Hotel on the Rua Catete, rooms sufficient for a bachelor but in no way spacious enough for two. . . . He hesitated, trying to define his relationship to the woman and her child. Certainly they were not to be his slaves.

Their freedom was a need as pressing as food and shelter. They must be freed, at once. Whatever the mechanics of manumission might be, he would set them in motion before the sun set that day.

"You shall be freed," he announced, forgetting for the moment that the woman could not be expected to understand English. "You shall be freed," he repeated in careful Portuguese.

The woman looked at him timidly, her terror and anxiety clearly written on her thin, pale-tan face.

"Don't you understand?" he asked. "You and your child shall be free."

"Yes, master," she said softly.

Ruffin could see that she did not yet understand, and that freedom would not end his responsibility to her. Freed, where would she go? What would she do?

"Can you cook?" he asked. "Can you keep house?"

"Yes, master."

"Very well, then," he said. He drove the carriage along a narrow street within sight of the harbor and was forced to stop for the passage of a gang of coffee carriers, a file of slaves trotting with bent backs in close formation, each with a full two-hundred-pound sack of coffee beans balanced on his head. The gang's leader set the pace with a rattle, as desperate and ominous as a snake.

Ruffin winced. There were over a million slaves in Brazil; he could not set them all free, and although it was probably true that the Emperor favored emancipation, it was unlikely that he should see it in his lifetime. Nonetheless, he would do what he could, whatever he could.

I shall have to rent a house, he thought, and nearly laughed at the pattern of his decision making. He had hired a servant (hired, for by nightfall the woman would not be his slave) so now he must hire a house to put her in. So be it.

"What is your name?" he asked the woman.

"Estrella," she answered.

"And the child?"

"Marianna."

Marianna. Had God sent him another Marie-Anne? He searched the child's plain, frightened face. The two of them, the woman called Star and her child, had been placed in his care, two beings more helpless and unfortunate than himself. Before God, he would do his best to give them a happy and comfortable life. He turned into the Rua Catete. He would leave them in his rooms for the balance of the day, asking his landlady to feed them and bring them water for bathing.

Meanwhile, he would report to Barnes and arrange to rent a house and find the papers that would set them free.

Ruffin's hands were shaking when he arrived at the offices of Barnes and da Silva, but he felt more purposeful than he had felt in months.

# Chapter Seventeen

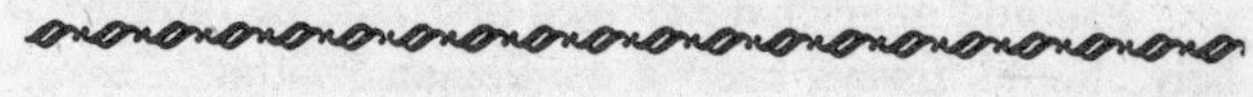

Rafael Barroso was late. Perhaps he is not coming, Zaidee thought. She waited at the agreed-upon spot, the clearing at the base of the wooded trail, and as she waited, her mood changed and her confidence began to wilt in the midafternoon heat.

Why had she come? "I have come because I want

to," she said aloud. Duke danced on the narrow trail and she sighed. Lifting her pretty straw hat, she smoothed an escaping strand of hair into the knot she had arranged before her mother's mirror. With her hair in place, she had invaded her mother's jewel box for the seed pearl earbobs that made her look, she hoped, both rich and sophisticated.

A good part of the excitement of meeting the Brazilian was the secrecy of it. She had told no one, but the prospect had enlivened her thoughts for the past week.

But where was he? It was rude for a gentleman to be late to meet a lady. Perhaps he had come and gone. I will wait only a few minutes more, she decided. I will count to fifty and then go. She began counting, but before she had passed ten, she heard a rider coming up the trail.

"Whoa, Duke, whoa!" Duke fidgeted, stiff-legged, excited by the tension in Zaidee's hands and the approach of the other horse.

When he came into view she was surprised at his size and the whiteness of his suit, gleaming like parchment against the wall of green leaves. Rafael smiled. "So you are waiting for me, my pretty lady, Miss Zai-dee!"

I should never have arrived first, Zaidee thought; a lady should always keep a gentleman waiting. "Yes, I am," she said, feeling at a disadvantage.

"But why do you frown? You are looking very pretty and I am delighted to see you," Barroso said, his voice as smooth and rich as a preacher's. He slid off his horse and seized Duke's bridle. "Come, dismount. Walk with me in the shade. It is too hot to ride, isn't it?"

Zaidee obeyed, although when she slid out of the saddle and his hands closed on her waist, she felt embarrassed. Should she permit him to touch her so? Was he mocking her? She studied his face and his eyes. They were unfathomably brown and crinkled in mirth.

"Why are you laughing?" she asked crossly.

"Only in happiness to see you! You have fixed your hair differently. It is very charming."

Zaidee blushed. She was pleased by his compliments, but felt vaguely uncomfortable. His eyes seemed to examine her.

On the other hand, she thought, perhaps he was justly appreciative. She was looking her prettiest. The earbobs made her feel elegant and she had unpacked her flowered green silk with three tiers of ruffles—her very favorite gown. If she had precious few occasions to wear it he needn't know that. He would see that she was a lady.

He was even more handsome than she remembered. He removed his straw hat and offered Zaidee his arm.

"And how have you passed this long week, Miss Zaidee?"

Dismayed, Zaidee thought of it—boring days of household chores, struggles to accomplish the cooking and gardening, and laundry and dairy work, the sad silences that filled their quiet evenings now that both Elinor and Mother were gone.

"At home," she said finally. "With my family. Quietly. Oh, reading . . . a little music. And you, sir?"

He laughed. "Not so quietly. We are a very big household." Dramatically, he waved his arm to include the universe. "And I am busy, with my father, directing the sugar milling. Now it is a busy time for us."

The way he pronounced busy, so slowly and importantly, built the image of a hive of bees in Zaidee's mind. She smiled, at the same time amused by his accent and fascinated by his physical confidence and aristocratic air.

Rafael walked swiftly, gracefully and surely, as he did everything, swinging along the narrow trail away from the point where he had tied the two horses. Zaidee struggled to keep up with him and answer his questions. The trail was rough and more than once she caught a toe under a stone or root. Soon she was breathless.

"So? Do you like Brazil? Do you find it very different from your homeland?"

"Oh, yes, different in every way . . ." Thinking that she hated everything about Brazil, Zaidee ducked under a thick green vine and looked straight into the eyes of an immense green tree frog. "Oh, dear Lord," she gasped and staggered so that she nearly fell.

Rafael caught her easily and, of course, laughed. "The *hilideo* is quite harmless, Miss Zaidee, unless you are a mosquito!"

"Oh, but I hate it!" Zaidee fumed. "I hate such things!" Where was he leading her? She had never gone so far into the forest. It was foreign and threatening—strange birds and insects pulsed and chirped, faint green light filtered through the overlapping leaves. Was that a long green vine—or a snake? It moved. It was a snake. She screamed.

"What is wrong?"

"It's a snake!"

"Most are harmless, dear lady."

Zaidee's eyes filled with tears. She turned her head so that he would not see. Why was he dragging her out here? She could not understand it. It was not chivalrous of him to endanger her. Should she be insulted? Oh, why did his presence confuse her so?

"Only rest a moment." Taking her hand, he pulled her down to a mossy log and sat at her feet, as much at ease in his white linen suit as if he sat in a drawing room. "I find it beautiful. A green heaven. See? We are at peace with God in the jungle. Do you say jungle?"

Zaidee nodded. Jungle. One might say jungle. She started as she felt his hand settle on her knee. She could not look down at him, but stared at her knee, covered by layers of green silk. Without speaking he stroked it gently, easily, as if he had every right to do so, as if it were a gesture of long habit, as if she would not mind.

She trembled. Surely he would stop. She was too embarrassed to speak.

"How beautiful you are," he said.

"Oh!" She was both surprised and gratified. Beautiful? His touch was friendly and at the same time exciting. When she put out a hand to stop his, he took it in a firm grasp and stroked her other leg with his free hand.

His touch sent chills of fear and dread along her spine. What did he mean? What did he intend? Did he love her? Surely he knew she was a lady. As she hesitated, his hand slid down to her ankle and then up along the inside of her silk-stockinged leg. She pulled away.

"No. Please! You mustn't!"

"Why? When you are so beautiful to see and to touch . . ."

"No!" Confused, Zaidee jumped to her feet. "I must go!"

Rafael shrugged. So be it. She was not ready, yet, but he felt confident that she soon would be. He had never seen a woman dress more seductively. This dress bared her shoulders and bosom and it was still afternoon. And she had come to meet him in secret, he was sure of that. He wanted to make love to her, wanted it powerfully, but he could wait until she was ready.

"Of course," he said. "Let us go back to the horses. Here, take my arm, Miss Zaidee. But we will meet again? Next week? Next week I will show you a hidden spring where the water is delicious to drink."

"I don't know," Zaidee said, but she did know. She knew that she could not resist meeting Rafael again and that she would come, as he asked her, in a week's time. I shall do as I wish, she thought petulantly, with a sort of half-understanding of what it was she did wish.

Often, in the past few months, Eva Bailey had thought that she must be mad, must have gone mad. What she was doing was wrong and more than wrong and she was not the sort of woman who did wrong repeatedly so if she did it, she must be mad.

On the afternoon she woke in bed next to Jesse Rall in the shabby waterfront hotel in Belem, she thought it at once. Am I here, is this me? I am not myself. She lay half dressed on the edge of the bed. It was not a large bed and Rall was spread out across it, his trousers crumpled on the tile floor, his sweat-soiled shirt open and unbuttoned. He was sleeping deeply and snoring in a manner that she had gotten used to hearing.

Several months had passed since the first night of rainy season when Jesse Rall had first made love to her. Since that night he had been with her constantly and her world had been turned upside down. After a while, she had been forced to tell the other members of the colony that they were planning to be married, although he never said anything about marriage. No one had asked her, but she felt obliged to give some explanation: everyone could see the way he treated her. He treated her as if she were already his wife.

A sob caught in Eva's throat. Her head was hot and ached when she tried to lift it. They had arrived in Belem this morning, coming down the river in a steamer, and they had eaten lunch in a noisy crowded café he remembered from his stay here before.

The lunch had been simple enough, the usual Brazilian fare of fish and farinha, but he had drunk more than she had ever seen him drink and she had drunk more than she had ever before. The drink was a fruity punch of *cachaça* and *caju* juice, strong and sweet and delicious and for a time she had been happy. But she was not happy now, she was sick, and she could remember everything too clearly.

Belem was a big city compared to anything she had seen in Brazil before, although it was not a nice city, in her opinion. It was dirty and crowded and hectic, and of course it was terribly hot.

She felt a little stunned—by the heat, the drink, the feeling of helplessness she had never become used to, and yet when she looked down at her hands, she shivered. He could do anything he wanted to her. Her small, pretty white hands were reddened and bruised. They ached as much as her head and she clasped them softly, cradling one in the other, remembering how he had bitten them.

He had led her back here, to this hotel, wherever it was, after eating and drinking, and then he had taken her to bed, right in the daylight, right in front of that open window with only the thinnest gauze curtain over part of it. Blinking, she looked up at the window now and saw by the color of the sky that it was late afternoon, almost evening. He would wake soon. And what would happen then? She trembled, imagining, and then closed her eyes and forced herself to lie still, remembering what had passed.

Less than two months after the night of the rainy season and their affair started, the general exodus from the American colony at Santarém had begun. Only a fraction of the original colonists now remained there; the bulk of them had left. They had sent a plea for help to the American Consul in Pará. Their venture was a failure, they acknowledged. The land was badly chosen; it was isolated and insect-ridden. The Brazilian government still had not made good on its promise to build a road to Santarém and a monopoly on the sale of provisions made them too expensive for the colonists' limited funds.

Amid the general complaints and recriminations, there were good reasons for the colony's troubles. Some of the settlers were disinclined to physical labor; few of them were experienced farmers; there were no Negroes to do the heavy work; they could never learn the difficult Brazilian language; and the Amazonian insects and reptiles were more ingenious than any of them.

Eva shuddered, remembering the snakes and insects that had overrun her house. She could never set down her feet without crunching on cockroaches. She could not have lived there alone; no woman could have. The whole colony had been overrun with biting red ants. There had been ferocious fish and fever-bearing monkeys. There had been hideous crocodiles—the natives called them *jacaré*—that lived in the stream where they bathed in the dry season. The *jacaré* were fierce carnivores, and one American boy, Philip Davis, had been lost to them. Two other children had died of the bite of a diseased monkey they kept as a pet.

The Amazon is far too hostile for white people, Eva thought. My husband was hasty in choosing it. She blushed as she realized she was criticizing her husband. In the months since his death she had canonized him, in her mind. He had become a saint, although sometimes when she dreamed of him she felt angry as well as guilty, for it was he who had brought her to this ghastly, godforsaken place. It was he who had exposed her to such dangers and put her in the position where she was forced to take protection from such a man as Jesse Rall.

Finally, when it had seemed certain to many of the Santarém colonists that they would never get out of the jungle, word had come from the Consul in Pará that he would provide passage to Belem for any who wanted it. From Pará they would be transported to American colonies in other parts of Brazil or could book passage back to the United States. Some American vessels already in Brazilian waters offered to receive emigrants who wished to return, as much as there was space for them.

And that was what Eva Bailey planned to do. As soon as possible she would go home. The intention gave her courage, but she had another fear. What if she could not escape from Jesse Rall? What if he would not let her go?

For something very unexpected had happened between them, something Eva had never imagined and had no way to deal with. She had become dominated by

Rall in every possible way. Giving in to him at all had led to total capitulation, but most difficult to believe, and impossible to understand, was that she had come to tolerate it, to expect it, even to enjoy it.

How could she enjoy it? She did not know why, although she had asked herself often enough. Only that she did, not purely and not indefinitely; she had every intention of leaving him as soon as possible, unless he promised to change, that is; but in the months she had just passed in Brazil, their congress (for even she could not term it love) had been the sole source of excitement and surprise in her life and it had often been . . . again she struggled to admit it . . . fulfilling in an unbelievable way, a purely physical way, but a real way, a way that had provided for her—for both of them—temporary escape from the boredom and misery of life in Santarém.

Rall gave a moan and a sigh and she looked at him cautiously. He was wearing a white cotton shirt that had been her husband's. There had seemed no good reason not to give him her late husband's clothes; she had taken charge of his trunk and Rall was in need of clothes. The two men were nearly the same size. Her late husband had been thin as a result of travel and asceticism. Rall was thin from fever and lack of food, his dark hair was as long and wild as an Indian's, and his naturally florid face was burned brick red from the Amazon sun. He was not handsome, but his brutish self-possession and confidence made him attractive.

Looking at him, Eva began to tremble. The trembling started in her vitals and she began to breathe deeply, deliberately, in an effort to still it. Below the window, she heard two men begin to quarrel. She could not understand their words, but the anger in their voices was unmistakable. Oh, be quiet, she begged under her breath, be quiet, or he will wake.

Rall did not wake, but still half asleep, his eyes still shut, he rolled toward Eva and seized her.

"Jesse? Are you awake?"

"Uh."

"No, Jesse. Please. No!"

He did not seem to hear, but ran his rough hands over her breasts and stomach as if evaluating a strange object in the dark. She wore only a thin batiste underslip; it was too hot to wear more; it was as humid as it was hot and everything adhered to everything else—her skin to the rough bed linens, her gown to her legs as if plastered there. She wriggled and was immediately bathed in perspiration. Oh dear, she thought, how I wish I could take a bath, and that he might, too. She wrinkled up her nose at the strong odors of sweat and drink and spicy foods that clung to him, hoping that she did not smell so herself.

And yet, what if she did? She would be gone soon. She lay still, but he did not. His strong fingers caught and rubbed and twisted, they invaded; he pulled her onto him and she felt her skin flush, felt her heart beat faster, felt her lips part and fasten themselves onto his shoulder as he lifted her like a rubber doll.

"Oh, Jesse," she sighed.

"Uhh . . ."

He is like an animal, she thought. Why doesn't he speak to me, sweet-mouth me?

He opened his eyes to see hers narrow with resentment and it pleased him. She's like a little cat, he thought, secretive and spite-eyed, staring at me. The idea delighted him. Sex was a source of great pleasure, and an easy source. Some of the other things he liked:

good horses and the fellowship of like-minded men, the mastery of weaker creatures, winning at cards, and of course whiskey, were harder to come by.

But women, women were everywhere. This one, a little spitfire, it had turned out, despite her prim and prudish pose, had just fallen into his life. Who would expect to meet a high-toned white woman on an Amazon steamer? He was a fortunate man. He laughed. He had sure made her forget her husband. He had sure taught her to want it, and to beg for it.

"Don't. Don't hurt, you dirty man," she whispered.

He took it as an invitation. She'll not soon forget me, he thought before he forgot thinking, and little does she guess I'll be gone tomorrow.

Eva did not guess it; there was no way she could. Her body accepted his and her mind went dark. His heart was like a beating drum and his weight as immense and intolerably wonderful as the depths of the sea. She felt the trembling engulf her, and she stretched out to him her tiny hands, pale as starfish. When he began to bite them her eyes lighted up and she began to moan with pained pleasure.

Some time later, Zaidee was walking along a dusty, tree-shaded road that bordered the farthest of her father's fields when a man on horseback caught up with her. It was early afternoon and the sun was hot; a flock of parrots set up a ruckus from the topmost branches of a cinnamon tree.

Zaidee turned around curiously, and then blushed with confused embarrassment. It was Rafael Barroso, the man in her thoughts, her increasingly muddled thoughts. She had not seen him in more than a week and hated to be caught wearing her faded pink percale with her hair drooping, carrying home the empty dinner pail like a servant.

"Drat!" she whispered, wishing she could run. Her romance with Barroso was not going well at all, if you could call it a romance. She was more confused than ever. Her elegant gentleman, who had at first seemed to offer the possibility of true love and honorable escape, had disappointed her. He was not what he had seemed to be. Every time she had met him, his sexual demands increased, and she could not meet them, could not and would not. She had decided not to meet him today and had not gone to their appointed rendezvous.

He does not understand me at all, she thought, accurately. Tears glinted in her blue eyes as she turned to face him.

"What are you doing here?" she asked petulantly.

"Good day, Miss Zaidee! How charming you look!" Rafael sang out, gay and flirtatious as ever, handsome as ever, seeming more in control of the situation than Zaidee could bear.

She turned her back and walked stiffly on, faster than before.

Rafael jumped off his horse and caught up with her.

"Are you angry, dear lady?" he asked. "Have you tired of me?"

If he laughs, I shall lose my temper, Zaidee thought. She walked on without answering.

Barroso laughed. "Have you missed me so?"

Zaidee turned on her heel and slammed the pail into his stomach. He knocked it aside easily and caught both her arms, pulling her into an embrace, amused as he would be at a capricious child.

"You must care for me," he said, "or why are you so naughty?"

"I do not! I am not!"

"Little spitfire," Rafael said, holding her in his strong brown hands and feeling her struggle. It was a delightful sensation. Zaidee intrigued him, and he knew that he did not understand her. At first she had seemed so seductive, so flirtatious. Her dress, her demeanor, her body itself suggested that she was a woman of rare sensuality and passion. But she did not respond. She was hot, then cold. She invited, she suggested, and then she pulled away, seemingly unaroused by his touch. She was so unlike a Brazilian woman. Perhaps all American women were so. He would always regret that he had not met any in New Orleans.

"I was coming to call on you," Rafael said, still holding Zaidee's arms in a grip that she could not shake off or twist free from.

"No! Don't ever come to my house!"

"You are ashamed to receive me?"

"Don't be foolish! My father would not approve."

"But you approve?" Her efforts to break out of his grip had ended, but he felt the strength and tension in her arms. It aroused him, as much as her lovely red-gold hair, as much as the pulse beating under the paper-white skin of her throat.

"No!" A shiver, partly temper, partly fear, rippled down Zaidee's spine. "Don't harm me!"

"Harm you? Not at all, pretty lady!" Rafael was truly confused. The mystery of women was one of life's most delightful. He had known dozens of women, slept with women since he was fourteen, most of them prostitutes or pretty slave girls. He had come to take for granted that his advances would be welcome, advances that meant one thing or another, depending on the woman and the situation involved, but Zaidee's tempers and moods were unlike any he had encountered before.

Impulsively, he pulled her into his arms and began to kiss her. Her lips were soft and warm and he had surprised her. She fitted into his embrace neatly and he savored it. How slim and round her body was. How soft her skin . . . He kissed her harder, stopping her resistance with experienced charm, bending her slightly backward, kissing her eagerly, hungrily, with a sort of healthy rapture, expecting success and pressing his advantage.

For half a moment she responded unthinkingly, giving in to the wisdom of her skin before she became frightened and could not bear it. Oh, no, she could not; he was too strong, too potent, too demanding.

A sob rose in her throat, part horror, part disgust, and she shuddered. He felt her panic and loosened his embrace.

"Oh, Zaidee . . ."

"Stop! Don't kiss me! Not like that!" Her voice was childishly petulant.

"What would you have me do?" he asked, honest curiosity gaining on honest desire.

But Zaidee could not answer that question. To say what it was she wanted demanded that she know, and she was far from the sort of self-understanding that would have permitted her to realize that she was looking for salvation, for an escape from the tedious domestic confinement that was wearing away at her spirit and her dreams. She had no idea at all of passion, or love, or even of her own body's capacities, and thus she could not respond to Rafael with anything but confusion.

"I don't know..." Zaidee answered, finally, exhausted by the tangle of her own feelings, unequal to the effort of facing them honestly. She could not speak frankly to Rafael or any man. Her education and training forbade it; her natural inclination to keep her own counsel supported that training. Zaidee's life was one of the unexamined sort; she did not know her own mind.

And so confused by her emotions, anger was the easiest one to express. "You have no right to ask such questions, sir!" she exploded.

Rafael smiled. "In that case, I ask your pardon!"

"But I do not grant it. Now let me go!"

Rafael dropped his hands and let them hang by his side. His horse, waiting on the road behind them, stamped and snorted.

"I shall let you go, Miss Zaidee, as you ask it."

"You do not respect me!"

"I admire you. I find you charming and beautiful."

She stared at him. If there was one thing that was sure, it was that he was a man she could not handle. He had already gone too far. She must get away from him at once and forget the feelings he had aroused in her. She shuddered although he now stood at arm's length.

"I never want to see you again!"

He shrugged. "If you change your mind, I shall be glad to hear of it," he said, and stood watching her walk along the road toward home.

He'll be back, Zaidee thought as she walked. Surely, he'll be back. . . . He'll come back begging.

# Chapter Eighteen

Within a week after Terrill Ruffin had visited the slave market, the circumstances of his life had changed considerably. He had moved from Carson's Hotel to a large, amply furnished house on the Santa Teresa Hill at the end of a new trolley line. The house's difficulty of access was compensated by its splendid view of the harbor, the white beach, and the green mountains on the other side.

In this house he had established the woman Estrella as housekeeper, with her own set of rooms at the back of the house overlooking the gardens, and full responsibility for buying food, preparing it, and keeping the house in order. Estrella, rapidly gaining vivacity and confidence, went to market every day, always with her daughter Marianna at her side. To Ruffin's relief and delight, Estrella proved to be a good cook, and after some months had passed, he invited James Barnes to his new house to sample his table.

"You have done very well," Barnes commented when he and Ruffin had finished a meal of *vermelho*, a reddish fish from the bay, accompanied by dishes of beans and rice, salads, and Estrella's version of corncake, a bread Ruffin missed and had taught her to prepare.

"I am satisfied," Ruffin admitted.

The two men rose from the table and walked to the

balcony at the front of the house. From the balcony they had a clear view of the city and the harbor.

"She is pretty enough, also," Barnes said, thinking how painfully he missed his wife.

Ruffin was embarrassed at the implication. "I did not notice that," he said, more coldly than he felt. In truth, he did appreciate Estrella's good looks, which increased daily with her improved health, although he had no intention of exploiting them for his own physical pleasure.

"Oh, come, Ruffin!" Barnes laughed. This American was more complicated than he had guessed at first, but he had not thought ice water would flow in his Yankee veins.

"She was abused by her master, in Pernambuco," Ruffin said gruffly. "He was the father of her child, as well as her own father. She was sent to the market by his wife, her mistress."

"Out of jealousy." Barnes's voice was resigned and suddenly serious.

"It's horrible, horrible! Abdominable!"

"Yes. I am sorry if I implied . . ."

"Never mind. Slavery begets evil."

"In both master and slave . . . and, I believe, the myriad evils of mixing the races disgraces humanity."

"Ah? You do?" Ruffin asked, feeling at once abysmally alone. In many ways, perhaps in all the important ones, he had more in common with Estrella and her child than with James Barnes. How was he different? Perhaps his own father, whom he knew nothing about, had been his mother's master, had owned her, had taken her without love or gentleness, perhaps even with violence. He did not know; he would never know what suffering, what blood and tears were his own lineage, or perhaps what joy, secret but no less powerful. He shook his head, suddenly aching with the dark weight of his thoughts.

"But the Brazilian Catholic church will forgive any evil, for a consideration!" Barnes said waspishly, and Ruffin realized that he had not been listening.

"The habits and customs of a people are not altered in one lifetime," he said, and to that Barnes nodded agreement.

"How is da Silva?" Ruffin asked.

"Fah! There is an example. He rots, poor man. It's worse daily. And his sons—I cannot trust them, either. Would you be willing, Ruffin, to go into the mines, in some months' time? I cannot rely on the reports sent by our managers."

"Of course, whatever is necessary," Ruffin said. "Let's discuss it over a glass of brandy."

"Gladly," Barnes said, slumping into a massive rosewood armchair and accepting a broad-bottomed glass of the heady French liquor.

Franklin Richler left the fields earlier than usual and walked through the peach orchard he had set out for his late wife on his way home to supper. As he approached, he heard Zaidee playing the new piano.

Daphne had ordered the piano from New Orleans soon after their arrival in Brazil. By the time it arrived, she was gone. The thought hurt him terribly, as did any recollections of his wife. The piano was German, a Bauer. It was an excellent piano and had arrived in a huge wooden crate, as big as a house. Richler had burned it. He would have burned the piano had it not seemed too eccentric.

Now, Zaidee had taken an interest in the piano.

She did not play very well, but she was improving with constant practice. Franklin Richler paused in the barnyard listening to her attempt at Chopin, remembering how Daphne had played through long Texas twilights in days gone by.

Quietly, he entered the house and went to the small bedroom where he now slept on a cot. (He could not bear to go into the back house where she had died and at this time of year he could not spare a man to build on another room.) His thoughts were distracted as he pulled out his wooden trunk and shook out his Confederate Army uniform. He had last worn it at Elinor's wedding, but he had been thinking about wearing it today in the fields, supervising the gang of ignorant Negroes who had never heard of Shiloh or Sharpsburg, or likely not even Texas or Tennessee. It should not matter. Why should laborers know anything of what was now just history? He did not expect it—or much of anything else from the foreign black men, although it was not true, as Zaidee suspected, that he could not manage them. He found it necessary to instruct them in everything—they were lazy and untrained—and he did so, but he did not enjoy it.

I guess I've gotten old, Richler thought. Although the crop was taking hold and looked promising, he did not rejoice in it, did not walk out in the evenings to admire the neat, green rows of sturdy young plants as he had done back home. But this afternoon, he had been seized by a desire to dress again in his uniform and walk by the river.

The air was full of Chopin as he washed his arms and face in a basin of water near the kitchen door. The Negress who cooked was out of sight, although he could smell fried pork. Zaidee called out a greeting and then went on playing. He did not smile as he put on his rumpled trousers and matching tunic with its rows of gold buttons. As he adjusted his sash in the mirror, he caught a glimpse of his face and was surprised to see how old he looked. During the war, his blond hair had grayed; now it was white. He was an old, white-haired man. At the last minute he buckled on his saber, and he smiled.

There is no harm in it, he thought. I do it for remembrance. His step became firmer and more energetic as he walked away from the house, the years and some of the sadness falling away as he crossed the barnyard and turned away from the sight of the little back house where his wife had died, and away from the cotton fields where he had spent the day. I want to walk by the river, he decided, just as Daphne and I did so often back home.

His daughters had survived well enough. They were young; seedlings could be transplanted without withering. The young do not look back. What have they to remember? Elinor was already well married and now Zaidee had a beau, a bold, self-possessed American who had recently arrived in the region, a man named Jesse Rall. Although he did not remember him, Rall came from the same part of Texas as the Richlers. Apparently, he had been in another Brazilian colony for some time, and he seemed to have some money. I don't believe he's a bad man, Franklin Richler decided, recalling Rall's dark beard, his rugged face and his great physical energy. Probably he drinks too much, but he is not a bad man, he thought hopefully and for no particular reason. He is much like men I knew in the army, and as Zaidee is so moody and impractical, perhaps she needs an older man to guide her.

To his surprise, he saw a young black boy cross the road ahead and duck into the rows of tall corn. He walked on. What was the boy doing? He did not hurry, he walked deliberately nearer, unafraid. By law, Brazilian slaves were forbidden to carry guns or knives; anyway, he expected no trouble.

At last he was near enough to see that the boy was a mulatto, and no ordinary-looking one. His kinky hair was combed tight, the shape of a turban, he wore light trousers, an open shirt and leather sandals, and he was cutting the corn with a razor, swinging agilely, slashing down the unripe corn, ear by ear, and pulling it in a basket.

Richler was amazed and then angry. Who was this thief? Not one of his own blacks. How bold he was! How vilely bold and how stupid. Didn't he know the corn was green? It was not fit to eat; he was cutting it too early! How stupid these Brazilians were!

"Stop, thief!" Richler yelled, running toward the boy. "You fool! The corn is green! It's green corn."

Perhaps Richler made a ridiculous figure, lurching along the dusty road with his white hair flying, his outlandish gold-trimmed uniform shining, his long parade saber bumping at his side. Perhaps he made a frightening figure, a figure of some exalted authority, dressed perhaps—in the eyes of the Negro boy—in the uniform of the Guarda Civil. Perhaps he seemed a man possessed, a devil dressed in gray and gold.

The boy drew erect, holding his glittering razor high, swinging it back behind his head. His eyes were blank with surprise.

"It's green, you ignorant thick-headed thief!" Richler yelled. He pulled out his saber and waved it threateningly.

Perhaps the boy felt cornered. He was frightened;

he was caught redhanded. The crazy old American still shouted at him, shouted foreign words. His heart leaped in fear; strength flooded his arms and legs. He felt as powerful as the tiger, as sharp and deadly as the fierce-taloned eagle wheeling above a foolish mouse. His stance was firm; his biceps rippled under his smooth brown skin. He swung the razor with all his strength, deflecting the useless gilt length of Richler's saber as if it were a stalk of corn and bringing the deadly blade down across the old man's skull.

The skull split like a pumpkin, exploding with dark blood. Bits of Richler's white hair clung to the blade like bloodied chicken feathers, and the old man fell to his knees.

At the sight, the boy screamed. Foam—yellow with fear—bubbled up at his lips. He gasped, choked and swung the blade again as he turned, this time cutting at Richler's back, cutting like a butcher through muscle, bone and tendon.

And then he ran.

No one saw him run, but when Jesse Rall and the slave woman Joana came on the body from different directions a few minutes later, Rall believed Joana had seen.

Joana knelt by the corpse, sobbing and screaming, covering her eyes. Rall rode up, the hooves of his horse dusting the pools of blood.

"Jesus Christ! Look at him!" Rall shrieked. "Where'd he go?"

Joana could not speak.

"I'll make you tell, damn it! Look at him, poor bastard!" Waves of pity and disgust swept over Rall. Christ, the old man was wearing his uniform. One more soldier dead. Why had it happened? All these people were killers—he immediately suspected a slave had done it, although not likely this woman. The cuts had been made with a knife or razor, by a strong man. He walked around the body.

"Stay with him," he ordered Joana, who still had not understood a word he said. He remounted and rode toward the Richler house where Miss Zaidee was expecting his visit.

Elinor had awakened alone in the white-washed adobe farmhouse where she and Tyler lived. The farm was set off from any neighbors by a few miles. At first she was surprised that Tyler was not beside her, and then she remembered that he had been called out late at night to attend the birth of Millicent Eaton's baby. The Eaton farm was about five miles to the north.

It had rained that night and the morning was cool and overcast. A wet wind blew briskly and the fields and low hills outlined to the east were gray and misty in the shadows of the clouds. For a while, Elinor lay alone in bed. She was content.

Finally, hearing the rustling of leaves in the wind and the lowing of the cow in the barnyard, she rose. As she stood up, she felt the sudden movement of the child in her womb, felt it with the mixture of amazement and apprehension she had experienced for two months now. In another two months the baby would be born, and then even when Tyler was gone, she would not be lonely. She would keep a part of him—his child—with her always.

Their servant, Maria Carlota, had kindled the kitchen fire and milked the cow by the time Elinor had dressed. She wandered out to the chicken coop to look for eggs, taking deep breaths of the fresh morning air and studying the bank of massed gray clouds.

"Will it rain?" she asked Maria Carlota in hesitant Portuguese. Maria Carlota was a free woman of mixed blood; Elinor and Tyler had agreed that they would never own slaves. Maria Carlota was slim and quick. Her eyes glittered like dark diamonds in her small, heart-shaped face, as she replied with a torrent of words that left Elinor smiling and shaking her head. Amid the flow of words she could distinguish and understand only a few. It was hard, so hard to learn Portuguese that sometimes she thought she would never succeed. Tyler had done better, perhaps because he knew some Latin, or else because he moved about in the world and had contact with more Brazilians.

"*Sim, sim,*" Elinor murmured, smiling at Maria Carlota as they scattered the hens and worked together to pile the day's eggs in a wicker basket. My child will learn Portuguese from Maria Carlota and her sisters, she thought, and of course, also English. We must never lose our English.

The sun had penetrated the bank of clouds and streaked them gold and silver when she heard the sound of a trotting horse and looked up to see Tyler approaching.

He is early, she thought. She handed the egg basket to Maria Carlota and walked to meet him.

At once she could see that something was wrong.

"The baby?" she asked.

Tyler slid out of the saddle and took Elinor into his arms. "No, the baby is fine. A healthy boy. But dear wife, I have some terrible news."

Elinor waited, bracing herself against the solid strength of Tyler's shoulder. She knew at once that it was very bad; the solemn sound of Tyler's voice, the shocked expression of his eyes told her. I must hear it bravely, she thought. I must take care for the baby.

"What is it?"

"There is no way I can make it sound better," he said. His voice caught, and he stammered, as he did when he was strained. "Your father . . . is dead. He was killed."

"Ohhh . . ."

"Elinor, dear one! Together, we can bear it. Come with me."

Tears rushed out of Elinor's eyes. Her poor father! He had been so lonely since her mother had died. He had not really cared to live . . . not the way he had cared before.

Side by side, they walked and cried together. Bit by bit, he told her all he knew of it, and Elinor came to understand, passing by turns through grief and pain and rage.

"I don't know," Tyler said. "We don't know. He was found dead on the road. Rall believes it was a local ruffian, he believes it was a thief cutting the corn, perhaps a slave . . ."

"Rall? Rall?" Elinor asked. The name sounded horribly familiar, yet as unexpected as the news itself.

"There is a man named Jesse Rall," Tyler explained. "Just recently settled here. I had not met him until this morning, at your father's . . . at your family's fazenda. He and the woman Joana found your father, already dead, on the access road." Nothing can make me tell her how he was killed, Tyler resolved. If I never forget the sight of it . . . his head smashed, his brains spilling out in a bath of blood . . . I will never tell her.

"Rall? Where is he from?" Elinor asked, seized

with a horrible certainty that it would be the same man who had corrupted Laray Holt, who had led Laray Holt to his death. How could it be? They were three thousand miles from Texas. And yet, how could it not be?

"Where is he from?" she demanded. "What is he doing at my father's house?"

Tyler saw Elinor's distress and felt her body stiffening, as if she had just now understood. He heard her sobs quicken, catch in her chest like breathless coughs. For the first time, he was afraid for her and the baby.

"Elinor! Shall we stop here? I think you should lie down."

"What is he doing here? Why was he at my father's house?"

"Rall?"

"Yes, Rall! Is he the same one? From Gonzales?"

"They say he is from Texas. Please, my dear, you must be more calm. Let me feel your pulse."

"Yes."

She sank heavily to the ground, settling herself and her full skirts on a patch of grass. Her breath came roughly, and she was overcome with memories of that night when she had seen and recognized Jesse Rall.

How was it possible that he was here? How was it possible that she would never escape those memories? It has been so long, she thought, confused and angry. So long . . . and we have come so far. It is not just that he has followed us here! We have turned our backs on the past, we have begun again fairly and we have worked hard. . . .

Her head was spinning and she felt she might be sick. She tried never to think of that night and had never told Tyler about it. Of course, she did think of it, sometimes . . . but less often lately and never since she had known herself to be with child, since she had grown accustomed to Tyler's loving touch. Her new life, their married life, had nearly banished those old guilts and memories and stilled the secret of her first dark experiment with love which had brought upon it, with what seemed in memory cause and effect, that awful unthinkable scene by the river when the Negroes had been tortured and Laray Holt had been killed. . . . She moaned.

"What *is* it, my dear? Please tell me."

"If he is the Rall who was in our county in Texas . . ."

"He may be. He is a big man, Elinor, florid and dark-haired."

She winced. Can I tell him, she asked herself, and decided that telling would cause more pain for both of them than keeping the secret. Someday, perhaps she would tell him, but today she must save her strength for the sufficient trouble at hand. "He was wild," she said simply. "He and my brother were . . . friends, before Laray Holt died."

"I am not inclined to like him," Tyler admitted, "but he has taken charge . . ."

"Why?" Elinor demanded, still not understanding a vital part. "What is he doing at my father's house?"

"He is courting your sister."

Elinor paled with astonishment. "My sister?"

"Yes."

"Oh, dear Lord." Putting her face in her hands, Elinor wept.

# Chapter Nineteen

Jesse Rall still believed that the slave woman, Joana, knew who had killed Franklin Richler, and he was determined to make her confess.

"She knows. She came right along, she must have seen him runnin'," Rall told the men gathered at the Richlers' house on the evening after the murder. It was dark and the smoking oil lamp on the center table cast a skein of light that yellowed the men's grim faces and barely touched the corner where Zaidee sat, silenced by grief and shock.

The men were neighbors. Kinch McCall was there, and Ernest Gregg, and others that the Richlers knew only slightly: Kinion Jones, who had come from Chocktaw County and was running a sawmill, Perry Webb, a soft-speaking man who was working on a Brazilian-owned fazenda near where Tyler and Elinor lived, and Coley Burgess, who had arrived with a good sum of money and had set up a cotton gin that the other Americans used. All of the men were Rall's drinking companions, all former Southerners who had passed through times of trouble and were determined to hang together and to survive.

"Waal, I say make her tell," Coley Burgess said.

How will they make her tell? Zaidee wondered. She had never been able to control Joana and some of the good habits her mother had trained her in had begun to slip. Joana was nothing at all like the familiar tractable Negroes she had known back home—she seemed to be from another race. She was nearly as tall as a man, and moody, and on her bad days her face set in such a fierce expression that she was frightening.

Zaidee slapped at a mosquito whining past her ear. The tension in the room was nearly unbearable, but she had pulled away from it. She sat on the sidelines; this was men's business. But she watched everything and listened to what each of the men said.

Joana was outside now. Rall had tied her and her husband Manuel back to back against a tree on the edge of the barnyard. Manuel was passive but Joana had surprised Rall with her strength and spirit. In fact, both Joana and Manuel had thrived in their months of working for the Richlers—they had arrived exhausted and gray-skinned, but Franklin Richler had fed them well, allowed them sufficient rest in their own tiny hut, and had not abused them. Richler was not the sort to mistreat Negroes. He had never been that sort and had always despised those who were.

"Back home, we had ways to make a nigger talk," Kinch McCall said.

"Sure we did. I say use the same ones," Coley Burgess said.

Zaidee felt numb. She was frightened, and so shocked by what had happened to her father that she could not think clearly. Who had done it? Why? Would she be next?

"Miss Zaidee, you'd best go into the bedroom," Jesse Rall said.

Zaidee looked at him as if he were a bug that had crawled onto her plate. How had he gotten to be in charge here? She disliked and feared Rall instinctively, but she did not trust her instincts. She was muddled. She was frightened. What kind of an awful violent place was this? What were these dark currents pulling people here and there, causing chaos, giving pain? She felt too weak to protest. She obeyed, rising and going into the back bedroom without a word.

What am I doing in this place? Zaidee wondered. I do not belong here—I will never feel at home in this violent land. I wish we had never left Texas. I wish I could go back. She thought of Rafael and wished she had not sent him away. He was the richest man she knew, and the handsomest. Perhaps she could learn to like his kisses. Perhaps he would take her away from here. This was no place for her. She would go to him and tell him so. He would save her...

Joana's first scream shocked her and she put her fingers in her ears. At the next one, she lay down on the bed and pulled the pillow over her head.

Outside, the men had clustered around the tree where the two Negroes were tied.

Since Perry Webb spoke the most Portuguese he tried to carry on an interrogation, using the simplest of words.

"You know who did it," he said. "Who was it?"

"*Não, não,*" Joana sobbed. She understood none of their words and she could not tell them what she did not know. She was innocent, but it would make no difference. Senhor Richler, the American master... he had been killed. Now must she die also? *Why* must she? She hated these Americans!

Rall hit her and she screamed. The whip's trail rose like a red crack across her outstretched arms.

"How 'bout him? He looks like he's holdin' back a secret," Ernest Gregg said.

Rall turned to Manuel. The black man looked terrified and guilty. Rall had no way of knowing that Manuel was half a man, that despite his powerful muscles and strong back he had a child's mind. Manuel sobbed when Rall struck him; he was confused and desperate. If he understood little, he understood this: he and Joana were innocent.

"*Não,* Joana, *não,* Manuel," he cried.

"Who then, you black bastard," Perry Webb demanded. "You understand me. Who did it?"

"Arigo, Arigo," Manuel said.

"Arigo?" Joana shrieked. She stared at him and questioned him in a quick Portuguese none of the Americans could follow, but Rall watched her face and was satisfied that Manuel had told the truth.

"We'll find this Arigo and if you're lying, you'll regret it," Webb said.

"Who is Arigo?" Rall asked Joana, striking her across the shoulders. Her large breasts quivered and he was excited by the suggested proximity of violence and sexuality. He felt a stirring in his vitals and knew that he would have this woman, at some point. When the time was right, he would take her. She writhed and moaned and he watched the long line of her neck twisting away from him. He looked down and saw that her legs, bared by the ropes that held her to the tree, were long and strong and shapely.

"Who is Arigo?" Perry Webb asked again.

"Arigo is just a boy. He lives at Barroso fazenda," Joana said and her eyes hardened. "I do not know! But that is Arigo."

"Let them go for now," Rall ordered. "Well, boys, what shall we do?"

"I say we go get this Arigo," Webb said.

"Let's handle it just like we would back home," Coley Burgess said. "No nigger murders a white man and lives. Let's make sure they know that."

"Got to know it right off!"

"Damn right!"

Nodding, the men looked to Rall. They drew together as he began to talk.

Amelia Ashby Scott found Rio beautiful and life there delightful. Like a caged bird set free, she savored every day, every fresh breeze from the wide harbor, every glimpse of the green mountains, every sunset. For years she had been restrained by mourning and sadness, but she had drunk her fill of gall and bitterness, she was ready to live.

Using her rudimentary Portuguese to find the way, she had taken a room at Mrs. Freligh's boardinghouse at number 69 Rua de San Pedro. The boardinghouse was a rendezvous for Southerners coming and going in Brazil, some of them seeking colonies and good land, some of them exhausted and discouraged, heading back to the United States as soon as they could. To all of them she extolled the virtues of the land and prospects for settlers in the region near Santa Barbara and a number of them set out for that locality as a result of her advice.

As soon as possible, Amelia rented a small house on a quiet street in Botafogo and set up housekeeping, but the main purpose of her life was the pursuit of her art. She enrolled for classes in the Royal Art Academy and her teacher, a Belgian named Eduard Rochelle, encouraged her to believe herself a very competent portraitist and set out to teach her all he knew about landscape and painting in oils.

For Amelia, all Rio was subject for painting. Once her household was settled and her daughter in the charge of a lively young nursemaid, she made a habit of walking the streets nearly every afternoon, sketching the street scenes and the people she saw, fascinated by the variety of costumes and racial types that passed along the Gloria Beach near her house. Gradually, her skill increased, as did her confidence, and through her art teachers, she began to meet others in the city who were involved in the arts, other painters, student musicians and those employed in the state orchestra, and some of the actors and actresses associated with Brazil's principal theaters.

In this society, Amelia felt very comfortable, more than she had in the inland colony or even at home in Alabama, but though she had long since ceased to mourn her departed husband, she took no interest in any of the gentlemen who would have paid attentions to her.

"I could not be happier if I were in Paris," she confided to Solange du Barry, the Brazilian actress who had become her dearest friend. "Indeed, I feel as if I have been given a wonderful gift of time in this lively city. I lack nothing, dear Solange."

"Save success, and love," Solange laughed, "and those two will come in time. I predict it."

As far as he could guess, about six months had passed since Darius Yates had been captured by the Indians. He had long since lost track of time. During those months he had passed from confused depression to a state of mind characterized by determination and resignation. He had survived loneliness that drove him half mad before he became accustomed to living in the nude and eating spit-roasted game and purees of strange root vegetables. He had even begun to understand the Indian language.

Perhaps he was mad. At any rate he was not the man he had been, neither the idealistic young aristocrat who had enlisted in the Confederate Army in '61 or the melancholy veteran who had set sail for Brazil. He was so unlike either of those men that others could scarcely have recognized him. In six months he had not shaved or cut his hair, had not seen a white man or heard or spoken a word of English.

As the months passed he lost his fear of imminent death and fell into the daily rhythm of the Indians. He learned to hunt and fish in their ways and enjoyed it as much as he had as a boy in Georgia. Although he could not be sure, he had begun to think that his captors liked him, for the restraints on his freedom were loosened gradually and his daily needs for food and shelter were met generously by the women of the tribe.

Still, he was closely watched, even while sleeping.

On a clear, starry night during the dry season, he was introduced to another element of Indian life. For ten days he had been given special foods, primarily white meat of the jungle partridge, roasted yucca, and a mushy liquid concoction of cooked and mashed bananas. He was also given a dark-green, bitter-tasting herbal drink that made him nauseous at first, then raised his temperature and accelerated his heartbeat.

After ten days he grew used to it and drank it easily as darkness fell. He found himself one of a group of ten men. The women of the tribe washed them, then painted designs in red on their cheeks and foreheads. With the others, he followed the chief into the jungle, all the others chanting softly as the rest of the villagers watched them go. They walked for half an hour and then arrived at a glade hidden on the bank of a small, swift-moving creek.

Yates was immediately awed by his surroundings. The glade was surrounded by giant trees as imposing as the pillars of a great vaulted cathedral. The earth was beaten smooth, vines cut away, and the nightjar gave its melancholy cry from the topmost branches like a soloist in a sky-high choir. He watched the men go silently about preparations for what he gathered to be a familiar rite. He waited, watching as they built a fire.

When it was ready the men sat around it and he took his place with them. They chanted as the chief ceremoniously placed leaves on the fire that released a white and pungent smoke. With a wide fan made of brilliant red and green feathers, the chief waved the smoke toward each of the men. Yates breathed it in deeply, following their lead, and felt himself slip into a euphoric, trancelike calm.

He sat very still, watching. After a few minutes the chief added more leaves and he breathed more smoke. Then the chief passed a decorated clay vessel and everyone drank the dark-green liquid. It tasted bland and Darius drank again, more deeply.

Soon he heard his own voice joining in the chanting. The words, which had been no more than sounds, seemed beautiful and a high, throbbing whine began to echo through his head, increasing in intensity until it left him bobbing and trembling.

He passed into a dreamlike state. His perceptions were varied and followed quickly upon each other:

intense erotic stimulation, ecstasy, and a chaos of intense and varied sense perceptions. He felt the jungle approach and then recede, saw every leaf on a tree, every vein in each leaf, was overwhelmed by the beauty of a butterfly. He saw fantastic animals and ghosts, met and spoke to his family members and fellow soldiers as if they still lived.

At one point, he jumped to his feet, exhilarated by the sensation of being able to fly. He laughed. He was minutely aware of the other men and suffused with love for them, then he slid into a more abstract sense of the world and lost control of the progression and forms of the visions.

Some hours later, he fell into a deep sleep and woke to a brilliant sunny day. Sitting among the naked, dark-skinned men, he felt completely at home and at ease.

Zaidee Richler watched the events of the days after her father's murder unfold with a sense of unnatural detachment, as if she were a spectator at a sensational melodrama with a plot both ominous and romantic. Rarely had so much happened to her so fast; rarely had she been at the center of so much scheming and mourning, but although she was at its center, she did not feel part of it.

She was alone at home most of the time, although Elinor visited daily. Elinor was in a delicate condition, and everyone agreed that she had better stay with the Ashbys until the funeral. Arrangements were being made for the funeral.

The coffin-maker arrived, then the minister. Neighbors came to pay respects and left covered dishes and loaves of bread. Jesse Rall and his friends were almost always around, ostensibly to protect Zaidee from any wild Negroes on the loose. Having so many visitors in the usually silent house gave it a busy and festive feeling quite out of keeping with the reason for their being there, and sometimes Zaidee forgot the reason.

Often, Zaidee ignored the visitors and played the piano. Some of the time she sat silently and listened to them talk. At the end of the second day everyone had left but Jesse Rall and she sat down to eat a simple supper with him, busy with her own thoughts, thoughts of escape and romantic speculations about Rafael Barroso. As soon as the funeral is over, she decided, I'll go to Rafael Barroso and tell him I'll marry him after all. And for our wedding trip we'll go to Europe.

Jesse Rall had sharply different plans for her future. He was taken with Zaidee, even apart from the fact that she was about to inherit a good-sized farm and would need a man to run it for her. In her he saw a lovely, unspoiled child—so fragile and blond, so dreamy-eyed that she stirred in him all the lust for innocence that Eva Bailey had stirred and then spoiled. Eva Bailey had not been genuinely innocent. He had found her out. Eva had turned out to be naughty and manipulative, but this one . . . why he was sure this one was a real Southern lady.

Rall was aware that the Richlers were a cut above him socially, that in Texas he never would have been sitting alone at a supper table with Miss Zaidee. But it merely increased his admiration to hear her play the piano and to see that her earbobs were pure gold. Instinct told him she was untouched and romantic, but if he was right in assessing her so, he failed to consider that innocence can mask immaturity, dreaminess an unreasonable self-satisfaction, and reserve a total lack of normal human affections.

When supper was finished, Zaidee lit the oil lamp. Out of the corner of her eye, she saw Kinch McCall and other men standing in the doorway.

"'Evenin', Jesse, ma'am," Kinch said. "The buryin's tomorrow." He had brought over a jug of the *pinga* he had distilled from sugarcane and the rest of the men, filing into the house with nods to Zaidee, sat down to drink.

*Pinga* was a clear, fiery liquor. No one knew how strong it was; it was never the same strength twice, but it was very powerful stuff, and McCall was doing well selling it to the Brazilians.

"Well, damn, then tonight's the night," Kinion Jones said. He was the only one of them who did not drink.

"So we're all in agreement," Jesse Rall said. "We'll do it together and official-like."

"Just like you said," Kinch McCall agreed. His face was dark red. "We'll be the law here, the American law."

"I reckon Manuel knows where to find Arigo," Perry Webb said.

"We'll take him along," Rall said. "There's not a whole lot more to say. We all know what to do."

"We all got guns," Coley Burgess said. He was the fifth man, and Ernest Gregg, with his yellow puppy, was the sixth. The six of them filled the Richlers' small parlor. Zaidee looked from one to the next. There was something mean-looking about Burgess. He was well-dressed and they said he had money, but his eyes were close together, like a rat's.

Zaidee watched all the men without saying a word.

They disgusted her, loud and red-faced from the *pinga* and smelling of it, too. Only Rall had retained his dignity. She had seen him take charge and organize the others. Of course he was not a real gentleman, not like the rich and refined gentlemen she admired, but he was powerful and he was decisive. She blinked from the depths of her withdrawal and studied him closely. He was dark and forceful, but his complexion was too red and his beard too unruly. He is common, she thought, but dependable. She was glad that he had undertaken to defend her.

"How 'bout a name?" Perry Webb asked.

"We got to have a name," Kinion Jones said. He grinned.

"We're the Knights of the Confederacy!" Rall said and stood up.

"The Knights!" Kinch McCall cheered.

All the men started for the door. Zaidee watched them. She had heard a lone rider approaching. She ran to the side window to see who it was.

It was Tyler Ashby.

"Dr. Ashby!" Rall said. "Well, howdy."

"Where are you all goin'?" Tyler asked. His voice was sober and disapproving.

"We're ridin' out to get the nigger who killed Mr. Richler," Rall said. Zaidee saw all the men nod and then she watched Tyler's face. She had never seen him look so stern and angry.

"You got no call to do that," he said. "The Brazilians have got policemen and they've got jails."

"To hell with the Brazilians," Coley Burgess said. "We got guns and horses and rope, too. No nigger's gone hack up a white man and live to stand trial."

"As I see it, it's our problem, and I say we'll handle it the American way," Rall said.

It sounded like a fine speech to Zaidee, leaning out the window to hear, but Tyler did not agree.

"Who're you goin' after?" Tyler asked.

"Shut up," Rall said, stepping in front of Coley Burgess. "We know what we're doin', Dr. Ashby. The question is, are you gone to ride out with us and avenge your wife's father's murder?"

"No, I am not," Tyler said.

"Waal, then, I don't reckon we have any further talkin' to do," Jesse Rall said. He pushed past Tyler and Tyler let him go. Tyler stood still and watched the men mount up. Perry Webb had run out to the barnyard to get Manuel.

Zaidee was astonished at Tyler Ashby. I have never seen a worse coward, she thought. Why, I pity Elinor, married to such a man.

"Get your things together," Tyler said brusquely to her. "I want to take you over to my parents' house. You shouldn't stay here alone."

Zaidee did what she was told, but she had lost her respect for Tyler. No woman could respect a coward. Why, next to him, Rall and his friends were real knights.

# Chapter Twenty

"You surprise me," James Barnes said to Terrill Ruffin.

"How so?" Ruffin asked.

Barnes and Ruffin had come together to a diplomatic reception held by the Emperor at the Palace of São Christovão to honor a retiring Minister of Finance and welcome his successor. Barnes had been to hundreds of such royal receptions and learned to tolerate them, the long and noisy conversations with white-bearded royal cousins, the sweet wines and the endless trays of cakes glistening with sugar, the lightly veiled tolerance the Brazilian Old Guard aristocrats had for foreigners, even foreigners like Barnes, who had lived in Brazil for over twenty years and had contributed enormously to the preservation of the status quo they felt he threatened.

But Ruffin appeared to enjoy the reception.

"You are more diplomatic than the other Americans," Barnes said.

Ruffin laughed. "It's no more than a game to me."

"A game you are winning. You charm them all."

"Sometimes it is all I can do to understand. Sometimes I feel I am half a beat behind."

"On the contrary, I think you have fallen into a particularly Brazilian tempo. For whatever reason, your step is graceful. Business has increased fivefold since you joined the house of Barnes and da Silva."

Ruffin felt proud. His Scottish employer did not give praise easily although he was a good friend and drinking companion.

"I have learned everything from you," Ruffin said.

"You are a fast learner," Barnes said. "For myself, I am tired tonight. I cannot stomach another coconut *dulce*. This room is airless, the Brazilians think night air will kill them. Let's seek a breeze on the balcony."

Side by side, the two men strode through the crowd of resplendent uniforms and white suits glittering with decorations and pushed through tall French doors to a marble-columned balcony overlooking a fragrant green park. The sky above was bright with stars and the long waves breaking on the beach below were green and foam-flecked, holding the last of the light slipping from the sky. Against the sea, the palm trees stood out like giant black feather dusters.

At one side of the balcony a beautiful young woman sat alone on a huge wooden settee. A leather-bound sketchbook was open in her lap and she was drawing with a charcoal pencil.

"*Por favor, senhora,*" Barnes said, surprised to see a woman alone and so industriously occupied.

As soon as she replied both men knew that her native language was English, and Ruffin knew that she was from the South of the United States.

"Ma'am?" he inquired, "are we interruptin' you?"

"Why, you speak English!" Amelia Scott exclaimed. Her clear green eyes lit up with interest. She looked at the two men. The elder was dignified and very tall. The younger was the handsomest man she had ever seen in her life. She appraised him. He was slim and fine-boned, his skin honeyed marble showing darker veins and sheathing well-defined muscles. His head was beautifully shaped, his dark eyes deep-set and expressive. She found his features fascinating.

I must paint him, she thought, and then, Why, I am a predator!

Ruffin smiled, and at that moment, Amelia Scott fell in love. It was a physical sensation and it overcame her, an immediate frantic passion that obliterated sight and hearing. Unless I get up and run away this minute, she thought, I am lost. She could not move. She blinked. What was he saying?

"Yes, of course," he said. "I am American. As you yourself must be."

"I am. I have come here from Alabama."

Barnes watched the two Americans, sensing the excitement that leapt between them like sparks from a fire. He felt amused, pleased for his colleague and friend, and ultimately, left out.

"Alabama . . ." Ruffin said, as if it were an exotic land he had heard wondrous stories about, drawling the final "a." They both laughed.

Barnes felt even more excluded. "Where is it? Where is Alabama?" he asked.

"It's one of the Southern states," Terrill Ruffin said quickly, and at the same time, Amelia spoke.

"It does not matter," she said.

Ruffin agreed. "We have left it far behind."

Amelia Scott introduced herself and the two men examined her sketch of the panoramic view.

"Very impressive, Senhora Scott," James Barnes said. "It has feeling as well as accuracy of detail."

Ruffin nodded. He was astonished at meeting this Southern woman—here of all places, and surprised at the excitement she aroused in him, more than he had felt for any other woman in Brazil, more than he had felt for any woman in a long time. It was unsettling; it opened doors he had thought shut forever. His eyes stole from the sketch to the artist. She was even lovelier, it seemed to him, than ten minutes ago. Her color had risen and her eyes danced. Watching her slim, pale fingers gesticulate fascinated him. He felt oddly shy.

". . . And Senhor Ruffin is working with me, in the firm of Barnes and da Silva . . ." he heard Barnes explaining. Amelia Scott listened attentively.

I must see her again. I must dance with her tonight, Ruffin thought, I must hold her in my arms, just to see what it is like. . . .

Such thoughts were mad. How could he be so drawn to a Southern white woman? What strange, half-buried fears and feelings might a friendship with her arouse? Perhaps it would even be dangerous. He need not try to know her, need not pursue the conversation a moment longer, but he could not stop himself; he was pulled toward her as a magnet to the pole.

And when she lifted her eyes to his, eyes fringed in dark lashes and shining with spirit and intelligence, he heard himself invite her to join him in a dance.

"Thank you, Mr. Ruffin, I should be delighted," she said, and placed her trembling hand on his arm.

Jesse Rall's confidence was strained when the Knights rode away from the Richlers' house. He had not liked the argument with Tyler Ashby. The look on Ashby's face had been superior and censorious. Rall believed he was doing right, but he had been in the community long enough to know that Ashby was rich and respected and he did not like to cross him.

Well, what the hell was wrong with Ashby? Was he just plain cowardly? Good Christ, this was no time for weakness. What good would it do to find the Brazilian authorities and try to explain that a nigger boy had hacked up an old American gentleman and run off? Who would ever listen?

"We got to do it," Rall yelled to Kinch McCall, beside him at the head of the little posse. I wish there were more of us, Rall thought. Back in Texas there were more of us, and it was better. It's black against white, he thought. That's what it comes down to in the end and we all know it. We've got to keep them in their place. Rall was drunk, and worried about the details of this night ride. How would they find this nigger boy Arigo? Damn it, they all looked alike, more like monkeys than men, and it wasn't like at home where you could spook them into a straight answer. All they had to go on was Manuel, although Manuel was too scared and too stupid to lie. . . .

"We got to look after our own," McCall said.

"Let's just get him and keep it quiet," Kinion Jones said. "That's the way."

Was Jones worried about losing business at his sawmill, Rall wondered. He didn't trust a man who wouldn't take a drink, even if he was a Georgia Methodist. It wasn't natural.

"I got my hound," Ernest Gregg said. Gregg was a quiet man who smiled too much and said little, but Rall trusted him. Gregg was reliable even if he treated his hound like a baby.

"If we let this one go, who'll be next?" Coley Burgess said. "The women cain't sleep nights."

"That's the way it is," Rall said. "Did I ever tell you about the man before me at Buck Wilson's place? The niggers hacked him up with an ax. We can't let them get away with this. They'll do it again."

Perry Webb, who had been talking to Manuel, rode up to Rall. "He says Arigo is one of the Barroso niggers."

"Can he take us to where he lives?" Rall asked. Barroso, he knew, was the biggest sugar planter in the region, a fat Brazilian as rich as a king. He'd seen him once, in the town of Santa Barbara on market day. But he was a white man, wasn't he, if it came to that. White was white and nigger was nigger.

"Better than that," Perry Webb reported. "He says Arigo got scared and started to run away."

"Yeah? He run away? Which way'd he run?"

"Only one way to run—west. Not even a nigger'd run east."

"Sure enough." Rall smiled. Things were falling into place. Arigo must be guilty if he was running away, and he'd be easy to get on the road. The road west led to the interior, to the fiercely fecund forest and the unbroken land. There was a full moon rising, bright enough to see by, and they had plenty of *pinga*.

Things were looking better. They'd get the damned nigger and then they'd raise the old hairy.

Rall gave a yell, an ear-splitting whoop and the others picked it up—it rose from their throats naturally, they had been together at Shiloh and Manassas and Gettysburg, if not together literally, they had all been there, or places less famous and just as ghastly. The yelling grew louder. It was like the howling of animals, it was red-hot fingers poking in their ears, and it inspired them with courage and a sense of who they were and the necessity and rightness of what they had to do.

The horses picked up speed and strength, too, and they raised dust and scattered pebbles, galloping along the unknown road west, lathering up in the service of hunting men.

About an hour west of town the road flattened out and the moon hung straight overhead. It was Ernest Gregg who saw Arigo first, at first only a shadow over the next rise.

"What's that?" Gregg yelled. He set down his young hound, carried across his saddle to spare him the hard run. Yelping, the hound ran ahead. The men caught up quickly.

Arigo was covered with dust and limped with exhaustion when they dragged him out of the underbrush. He was on foot and the angry men on horseback seemed to him as huge as giants. He fell to his knees, blubbering with fear, wailing for mercy, but his face was blank and inhuman, registering only his frightful anticipation of death.

He was dead, in a way, before they strung him up, for there was no fight left in him. His legs were weak and he could not stand alone. His body reeked of sweat and surrender as they threw the noose over it and the men were silent as two of them hauled the rope up over the branch of a tree by the side of the road and let the black boy swing.

Only Gregg's hound had not lost his enthusiasm. Barking frantically the puppy danced around Arigo's dusty toes, leaping at them and nipping long after they ceased to twitch.

# Chapter Twenty-one

Soon after Franklin Richler's funeral was over and his coffin had been covered with earth, Tyler Ashby found out that the young and seemingly inconsequential black boy Arigo, who had been, after all, a murderer, was not inconsequential, and would not be so easily forgotten.

The funeral had been a grueling experience for Tyler. It is too soon to be enduring this again, he thought, and realized how much more difficult it must be for Elinor. He reached out to steady her as they left the gravesite, and she took his arm gladly. Her pale cheeks were streaked with tears.

What was she thinking? He had no idea. His respect for Elinor had increased as their love deepened and sometimes it amounted to awe, but he knew he did not fully understand her. There was a part of her she held in reserve and he respected it. Perhaps it made him love her more. How lucky he was to have found her! She was beautiful, of course, and strong and serene. She was compassionate and yet undemanding—so unlike her sister. Zaidee's wailing during the funeral service had been wild and unrestrained and yet Tyler suspected it was somehow false—or was he misjudging a poor grief-stricken hysterical child? He felt a stab of guilt, and yet he could not stifle his suspicions.

There was something strange and troubled about Zaidee, he thought. She cared for nothing but playing her piano and riding in the country. Where on earth did she go, out riding alone? It was neither proper nor safe, as what had happened to her father proved, but she was stubborn. To forbid her riding might make her very angry. He wished she would marry, but she had told Elinor she could not abide any of the men considered eligible.

For the time being, Zaidee would stay at his parents' house. His mother had insisted that she wanted looking after during her first days of bereavement. His mother would see that she rested and ate.

When Tyler helped Elinor into his parents' carriage he saw that Zaidee and his sisters were already seated there, their pale faces strained and tight.

"I'll join you in an hour's time," he promised. Some medicines he had ordered from São Paulo were due at the railway depot and he intended to ride into town to pick them up.

It was not yet midday and as Tyler rode along the dirt road through open fields, down a long slope, he could see a half-mile into the distance. His first glimpse of trouble was a cloud of dust, raised by the pounding of a score of horsemen. His own horse whinnied nervously, spreading his nostrils.

"Whoa, easy, steady . . ." Tyler said.

When the riders were at a hundred yards' distance, he recognized them. They were Barroso's men, the same men who had barred their entrance to the Brazilian cemetery, Barroso's *jaguncos,* as he had heard them called, his hired ruffians. Riding among them was Senhor Barroso, himself, and his grown son, whom Tyler Ashby had seen only once before.

As soon as he had identified them, the horsemen surrounded Tyler. Scowls darkened their faces. All the men were armed with guns or long knives.

"*Bom dia,*" Tyler said. He struggled to control his horse. The animal was panicked at being pressed on all sides and danced skittishly.

"Senhor Ashby." Barroso's son spoke. Tyler turned to face the young man. He was distinctly handsome, a man with bold black eyes and curling black mustache, but his eyes were cold, and his mouth was set in a sneer.

"*Bom dia,* Senhor Barroso," Tyler Ashby said again. He did not know what else to say or which way to turn. The men surrounded him, pressing into his legs and the flanks and belly of his horse.

"We have found the boy Arigo," Rafael Barroso said in clear English. "He is dead. What do you know of his death?"

Tyler tasted bile. What could he say? He did not really know that Jesse Rall and the others had killed Arigo, because he had taken pains not to know. He had avoided Rall and the other men at the funeral, but still he could guess what had happened.

"Nothing," he said, "I know nothing about him."

"Then you do not know that Arigo was a favorite of my father's," Rafael Barroso said. Every word he said was like an oath. He spoke with a strong accent, pronouncing every word clearly, hurling it at Tyler, hissing.

"No, I know nothing," Tyler repeated. He was embarrassed and deeply shamed. He had opposed Rall's secret vigilante group, but it had brought trouble on all of them anyway. They would all be judged by this. And Rall had forced him to lie.

"Arigo was my father's bastard son," Rafael said clearly. Tyler felt sweat stream down his neck into his collar. Several of the *jaguncos* had pulled their knives and he had begun to fear that they would kill him.

The thought sped through his mind that it would be both horrible and ironic to die here in the dusty road, having survived so many encounters with death on the fields of war. Why had he come so far, fought so long to stay alive only to die for a cause he did not espouse, to die unarmed at the hands of ignorant ruffians?

"I am a doctor. I am a man of healing," Tyler said simply. He would not beg for mercy, but he would speak in his own defense.

"So they say," Rafael Barroso said. "Beware that you do not think yourself God, Senhor Ashby. Remember that you Americans are foreigners here. We Brazilians are not savages. We have our own laws and if you will live in our country you are obliged to keep them."

Tyler looked from Rafael Barroso to his father. The elder Barroso sat heavily in his saddle. He looked both angry and sad. "I am sorry," Tyler Ashby said. How different this meeting was from his first encounter with Barroso. The image of him lying in his hammock fondling the brown babies flashed through his mind, and then he felt the barrel of a gun in his back.

He twisted and his horse began to buck.

"*Não*, Damiao," Rafael Barroso said warningly and Tyler felt a surge of hope. The man called Damiao withdrew the gun.

"So you understand?" Barroso said. "It is clear? And you will tell the others?"

"Yes," Tyler Ashby said. "*Sim, sim*. I understand."

* * *

Although she would have preferred not to become involved or to risk stirring life into embers perhaps already cold, Elinor felt obliged to speak to Zaidee and warn her about Jesse Rall. The Richler sisters sat amid a bevy of Ashby women on the Ashbys' veranda in the late afternoon, two days after their father's funeral. The Ashbys had done all that they could to extend sympathy and hospitality to the Richlers, surrounding them with so much chatter and attention that neither of them had had a moment alone and scarcely time for a good cry.

All the same, both Elinor and Zaidee knew that there were things that must be talked about—things that were hard to face—and that their lives must be changed forever by the death of their father.

"Come walk with me," Elinor invited Zaidee in a soft voice. "There isn't a breath of air stirrin', and I declare I'll fall asleep if I sit here much longer."

"All right," Zaidee agreed. She felt suffocated by the Ashby clan. She had grown used to solitude and the ladies' constant chatter intruded on her dreams and fantasies. Only the thought that she would soon escape had sustained her during the long afternoon of determined and cheerful talk.

"Shall I accompany you, my dear?" Tyler Ashby called out the parlor window when he saw Zaidee and Elinor strolling toward the orchard.

"No, Tyler, we shall not be long," Elinor called back. Tyler was spending every spare moment in preparation for the official examination for his Brazilian medical license. To save Elinor worry, he had not told her about his frightening encounter with the Barrosos, but Elinor knew that something was wrong. She longed to leave the Ashbys' house and return to her own, but not until she had helped her sister come to a decision about her future.

Zaidee and Elinor walked in silence for a few minutes, passing the orchard of young peach trees and the empty barbeque pits, now nothing more than ash-dusted troughs, and followed the path along the row of sentinel bamboo trees at the edge of the cultivated fields. A kingfisher perched on an overhead limb, then reluctantly rose into the web of leaves.

"My goodness, it's still this evenin'," Elinor said.

"Yes'm..." Zaidee said dreamily, thinking that Elinor sounded like an old woman ever since she'd gotten married, always worrying about the weather and talking about nothing at all.

"Perhaps it will storm," Elinor said. "Are those rain clouds?"

"Very likely," Zaidee said. How infuriatingly smug Elinor was about her attentive husband and her happy life. Elinor had tacitly forgiven her for her malicious (so she had called it) gossip about Tyler Ashby's commitments when they had first met, but she doubted that Elinor had really forgiven her. Never mind, Zaidee thought, when I am married to Rafael Barroso and living in Rio, or perhaps Paris, I shall never see either of them again.

"Zaidee, dear, I've been thinking about you . . . and the fazenda, and what we should do," Elinor began, not at all sure how to proceed.

"Yes . . . well, I don't know, exactly . . ."

"Oh, who would have thought it would be so!" Elinor exclaimed, her voice taking on a note of pure grief. "Both Papa and Mama dead, and all of us so far away from home. Thank goodness we have Tyler and his family to help us."

Zaidee was silent. There was so much that Elinor did not know that she knew. They were no longer close. In fact, Zaidee thought, we are practically strangers. Elinor knew nothing about her romantic friendship with Rafael Barroso, about the Knights of the Confederacy. . . . For the first time in her life she felt more adult and more knowing than Elinor. Furthermore, she felt downright sorry for her, married to a man like Tyler Ashby.

"Brazilians are so different," Elinor went on. "Sometimes I'm sure I shall never understand them or their customs. Tyler knows quite a few of them, of course, and he agrees with me. We are two races quite unlike!"

You don't know a thing about Brazilians, Zaidee thought angrily. She felt her face flush with temper. If Elinor knew Rafael, so cultured and sophisticated, she would be amazed. But she did not speak, and the moment passed quickly and Elinor's next remark stopped her cold.

"Did you hear about the grand Brazilian wedding?" Elinor said, stretching to pick a *caju* from a heavy-laden tree. "Amanda Ann Ashby was just tellin' me. It seems the oldest son of the Barrosos is being married today, and who is he marryin'? Why, it's immoral! He's marryin' a little cousin of his who's only thirteen years old!"

Zaidee froze. She bit her lip. She was so shocked that she felt dizzy. Turning away from Elinor to hide her expression, she managed to choke out, "Are you sure? Is it true?"

"Apparently it is, although I can hardly believe it. Thirteen. Why, it's barbaric, isn't it, Zaidee? They say they've been betrothed since she was born. Those Brazilians!"

It can't be true, Zaidee thought wildly, or if it's true, then I have misunderstood everything. How could he be so flattering, so courtly, so charming to me if he . . . Rafael's handsome, mocking face came into her mind, as clearly as if he were next to her, and all of a sudden, in a hot flash, she understood that he had wanted her . . . sexually, and that was all. He had never promised her anything else. Zaidee writhed. All her untapped disgust at men's desires and sex itself rose and filled her with rage and hate.

"What a gossip you are, Elinor," she snapped. "Perhaps you are too narrow-minded to understand Brazilian ways!"

"Why, Zaidee!" Elinor was hurt, but she looked at Zaidee's face and saw that she was close to tears. Poor girl, she thought, she has endured so much, living way out there with Papa, often lonely and perhaps frightened.

"You're right," Elinor said soothingly. "I am wrong to speak of such irrelevant matters today. What I wanted to say . . . comin' out here . . . is that Tyler and I want you to come and live with us."

"Oh, no!"

"What, dear?"

"I can't! Why, Elinor, it would be too crowded. You'll be needin' the spare room for the baby soon. Besides, I want to stay in my own house. I'm accustomed to it."

"A woman can't live alone on a farm." Elinor's voice was confused. "How on earth could you manage?"

"I'd have Joana and Manuel, just as before, and the other laborers, I suppose."

"But, Zaidee, you know nothin' about directin' slaves."

Nor does Tyler Ashby, from what I have heard,

Zaidee thought spitefully. She took a deep breath and began to lie. If what she was about to say wasn't true yet, she would see that it became truth. "Elinor, I believe I shall marry soon. I have a beau, you know. Mr. Jesse Rall. You met him yesterday, I believe. Tyler knows him already and Papa would have approved. I feel sure . . ."

"Oh, I don't think so," Elinor said, plunging in despite her distaste for troubled waters. "I don't think Papa would have approved. I must talk to you about him, Zaidee. I don't think Mr. Rall is our sort."

Zaidee glared at Elinor. Her lips were set and Elinor realized for the first time that Zaidee was deeply angry at her, although still she did not know why.

"He may not be your sort of man, Elinor," Zaidee said, her eyes cold and blazing, "but you can't tell me that he's not my sort of man! We are not the same woman, Elinor. Not at all!"

Elinor was astonished at Zaidee's anger. She felt a rush of guilt and sympathy for her sister. "Oh, Zaidee, don't be angry! It's just that, believe me, I have reason to think Mr. Rall is a violent man. Oh, perhaps he has changed, perhaps he was driven to desperation at one point . . . when he was younger, but, Zaidee, Mr. Rall is the sort of man who takes the law into his own hands! He is not a gentleman, dear. He is too rough for you!"

"I prefer a man who's not a gentleman to a man who's a coward."

"Oh, there's no question of that," Elinor said. "Zaidee, I hesitate to say more, but I recall Jesse Rall from Texas . . ."

"And you look down on him? Because he is not a doctor? Because he is not wealthy?"

"No, that's not it."

"Don't forget, Elinor, this is a new country. We are outsiders here. To me, Mr. Rall is brave and heroic. I know him to be so. I respect him and admire him. To me he is a knight."

Elinor stared at Zaidee, as speechless as Zaidee had been a few minutes earlier. A knight? Was there no limit to Zaidee's romantic imagination? She might have laughed, had Zaidee not looked so serious.

"And besides, it's too late," Zaidee added. "He has asked me to marry him and I said that I would. No one can make me change my mind, and you and Tyler can't stop us!"

"I want you to be happy," Elinor said after a minute. "It's true I don't know him well, but I know you. You are very young, Zaidee. You are innocent, defenseless, alone . . ."

"I won't be alone. He will take care of me. . . . Elinor, don't you know that they have formed a secret society to defend us . . . a group of the men? To protect us from the niggers. Just like back home. And Jesse Rall is the leader. Didn't Tyler tell you, Elinor?"

Elinor paled and stumbled. Zaidee took her arm.

"No . . ."

"It's true." Zaidee's voice was proud.

"Not Tyler?" Elinor gasped.

"No, not yet," Zaidee said sympathetically.

A week had passed since Amelia Scott had met Terrill Ruffin at the royal reception, a strange week for Amelia. Nothing had actually changed: her house in Botafogo was still airy and pleasant, her domestic arrangements comfortable, her daughter Susan Jane a delight, and her art classes inspiring, but everything seemed changed. Oddly, the spice had gone out of her life. It seemed hollow; she felt alone.

In truth, Amelia had been alone for many years. Her wartime marriage to Huntington Beauregard Scott had been romantic and insubstantial. She had never really known Hunt; they had met at a regimental dance in Montgomery, fallen in love before the war, eloped impulsively, and had sustained only two passionate, tear-soaked reunions before he was killed at Antietam. Amelia did not regret her short, sad marriage. How could she, when its product was her own beloved daughter Susan Jane?

In her widowhood, Amelia had matured and developed strengths she would have been denied in maidenhood. According to Southern custom, a married woman was allowed a great deal more independence and liberty than her unmarried sisters. The widow of a general in wartime was in an even more favored position.

Amelia had not been devastated by the death of her husband, and she had grown accustomed to making her own decisions and to living alone, alone that was, in the bosom of her family, until she moved from them to her little house in Rio to pursue her career.

And here, she had been glad to shed the false reputation of position and political importance she had donned with her wedding ring and widow's weeds, to be again what she was, an artistically talented woman and a mother. She had been happier than ever before in her life.

Until she met Terrill Ruffin.

How foolish I am, Amelia told herself, knowing perfectly well what was wrong. I am as infatuated as a schoolgirl. I cannot think of another thing. But he . . . he has forgotten me. He does not write or call. She paced the floor in frustration. What could she do?

If only he weren't so handsome, she thought, I could put him out of my mind. But instead her heart beat faster, recalling the way Ruffin's eyes and mouth had been set in his fine-boned skull, and when a week had passed with no word from him, she succumbed to the urge to sketch it from memory, hoping to exorcise him from her thoughts.

She was so occupied on a sunny afternoon as Susan Jane napped in a nest of pillows and her friend Solange stopped in for tea.

"My dear! Who is that man?" Solange asked, seeing the sketch of Ruffin's head on the top of Amelia's drawing pad.

Amelia blushed and reached to close the drawing book.

"A secret, eh?"

"No, no, just a young American man I have met recently. I do not know him."

Solange laughed. "Not yet!" she guessed. "No matter, dear friend. Keep your romance a secret. I believe it has done you good already. You look five years younger when you smile so—whatever the cause!"

Amelia endured her friend's teasing without another word, but later, she put a few more lines into the sketch of Ruffin's head and impulsively wrote him a note, inviting him for tea.

# Chapter Twenty-two

Less than a week after Franklin Richler's funeral, Zaidee Richler and Jesse Rall were married and Jesse Rall moved into the Richler house, the little house that had seen so much trouble already. Because she and Elinor were so recently bereaved, Zaidee had said that she did not want a wedding party, and only Tyler and Elinor came to hear Reverend Henry read the service.

Zaidee, who had almost, if not quite, proposed to Jesse Rall, stood through her wedding ceremony in a dreamlike trance. This is not at all what I expected, not at all, she thought. When she turned to glimpse Jesse Rall's broad, florid face, she hardly recognized it. Only the facts that she would not have to live with Elinor and Tyler and that she would not be an old maid sustained her. Once she was a married woman, she could do what she wanted. Jesse Rall would learn to cater to her wishes, she expected. After all, it was her farm; he was only marrying into it.

Zaidee's wedding night was her first cold, hard, confrontation with reality. It was all she could do to keep from crying when Elinor and Tyler and the minister had left, the simple wedding supper and the cake Elinor had baked as a surprise had been eaten, and she was left alone with her husband.

"Honey, I reckon I'm a lucky man," Rall said. He

took another drink of *pinga*; he had been drinking all day and smelled of it, a strong sweet smell that Zaidee was to know very well.

Zaidee could think of no reply to that. Instead she shifted her gaze to the open window; outside it was dark and the nightjar had begun to call. How mournful his song is, she thought. I wonder why I never noticed it before.

"I guess you're the woman of my dreams," Rall said. He loosened his collar. Tyler and Elinor had noticed that Rall was well dressed for a man who seemed to have no money at all, but they would have been amazed to learn how he had acquired the clothes he wore, and who their last wearer had been.

Zaidee shrank into herself. She was more shocked than anyone realized by the violent death of her father, by the crushing news about Rafael Barroso, by the swiftness of her marriage. Now, she supposed, her husband would try to kiss her, and whatever else men did want. The details of it were unclear to her; she had never wanted to think of them and she did not want to now. She was so tired and bewildered. Why had she married this man she hardly knew?

Rall did not notice Zaidee's silence and lack of enthusiasm. "Come here, honey, and sit on my knee," he invited.

Stiffly, a dream-walker, Zaidee obeyed, thinking perhaps that he would hold her and comfort her. But he did not, he began at once to fondle and probe, to stroke and pinch and pull off her clothes. She bore it grudgingly until he opened his own shirt. Why, his chest was covered with black hair, just like an animal's . . . just like a black bear.

She recoiled in disgust. She, who had hated the

sight of the hairs on Ernest Gregg's wrist! Oh, what was she doing here? How would she ever escape?

"I can't," she said to Rall, even more alarmed as he fidgeted with the buttons of his trousers.

"Honey, I know all this is new to you, but you'll like it."

But Zaidee did not like it, not at all, and Rall's method of collecting on his marital dues left her more stunned and separated from reality than she had been before. Her shock and lack of response only convinced Rall that she was, as he hoped, a delicate and modest lady of the purest order. He satisfied himself as quickly as possible and went outside to smoke a cigar as she cried herself to sleep.

It so happened that on the afternoon Solange saw the sketch of Terrill Ruffin on Amelia's drawing pad, Ruffin met with James Barnes to plan his trip to the gold mines of Minas Gerais. It was his first trip to the mines, a long-anticipated one, essential for the completion of some business for Barnes and da Silva, and his opportunity to investigate the development of the mine in which he had invested personally.

When he returned home to prepare for the next day's departure, he found Amelia's invitation to tea in the basket where Estrella collected his mail. As he read it and held it in his hand, his heart beat faster, and he felt undeniably that the invitation was of greater importance than its simple wording.

Amelia Scott liked him, he felt certain, but of course it was for the wrong reasons. She thought him a fellow Southerner, a white Southerner. She felt comfortable with him, she trusted him to share her heritage and opinions, but she was wrong. Of course, he was not at all what she thought he was. How comfortable would she feel if she knew he was black? What would she think of him if she knew that he had come from the lowest rung of her society and that he had emigrated to Brazil on a mission of blood vengeance?

Still, he was tempted. She was very pretty; tall and willowy as a dancer, her hair the color of chestnuts. And how spirited she was! He admired a woman brave and free enough to live alone and follow an artistic career. In her way, she, too, was a person outside conventional society. He had liked her—yes, very much. She was appealing and sympathetic. Of course, in America they would never have met.

But this is not America, he thought. Brazil is different. Here I am judged for what I do and not the color of my skin. No one has ever asked me about my lineage. Barnes thinks me invaluable; I am the master of a large house; I am well on my way to becoming rich. He looked down at the color of his arm. Even in contrast to the starched snowy whiteness of his cuff, it was not dark, it was merely a golden tan.

She will never guess, he thought. We can become friends. Likely it will lead to nothing more. Life has played many tricks on me; now it's my turn to be the trickster.

Ruffin directed Estrella to do his packing, and left at once to meet Amelia for tea. He found her seated alone in a sunny flower-filled sitting room, very Brazilian with its heavy lacquered furniture and collection of wicker bird cages, yet somehow familiarly American with its crocheted lace pillows and pink and gold flowered carpet.

Amelia was sketching, just as she had been when he first met her. When her maid showed him into her sitting room, she rose and extended her hand in a friendly and very American way.

"I am so glad that you could come."

"Thank you for the invitation. Had it reached me one day later, I would have missed it. Tomorrow morning I go to Minas Gerais for some weeks."

"Ah." She opened her eyes very wide and spoke frankly; he was soon to learn that she always spoke frankly, unlike most other well-bred Southern women of her day. "And I would have missed you? And you would not have called or sent a note to inform me of your disappearance?"

"How rude I would have been!" Ruffin agreed, smiling. "But all that is in the realm of what did not happen. Fortunately, I am here."

"Fortunately." Amelia felt giddy and was absolutely happy in his presence. She found him even more handsome than she remembered. How amazing it was to have met a handsome, intelligent young American here in Rio; most American men here were dull and discouraged. She had seen many of them in Rio trying to secure passage back home. She had heard that two-thirds of the Southern emigrants were turning back, despite the unappealing prospects of Reconstruction and poverty. Only the day before she had seen a group of penniless, confused Americans waiting at the customs house. They had lost everything at the Juquia colony and after a year in Brazil they knew scarcely ten words of Portuguese.

This one, in contrast, seemed to have mastered Brazil. She watched Ruffin as he strode lithely around the room, examining her framed watercolors of Rio street scenes.

"My favorite is this white-bearded water-seller," he said. "You are accomplished."

She nodded. "I can paint," she said, "and I can brew tea. Would you like some?"

"Yes, please. May I sit here?"

"If you do I shall have to ask you a favor."

"What is it?"

"You must allow me to sketch your head. I am . . . fascinated by its proportions. I have tried to do it from memory, but something in its structure eludes me."

"How can I refuse a request so flattering and charming? May I drink tea and read the newspaper while you sketch?"

"Yes, of course."

Amelia hurried to pass him tea and shortbread and the *New York World*, an edition two months old but new to Brazil. Ruffin settled into a small armchair while she worked.

"What is happenin' in the States?" she asked.

"They are buildin' railroads and hangin' niggers," Ruffin said, tossing the paper to the floor.

"Oh dear!"

"Can Brazil be far behind?"

"Why yes, of course! Things are very different here!"

"I hope you are right."

"Now you have a completely different expression, Mr. Ruffin. Now you look quite gloomy. Don't spoil my sketch over what occurs three thousand miles away, I beg of you!"

"I am sorry."

"I think we must make our own happiness in this world, Mr. Ruffin. That is our only hope of securing it."

Ruffin smiled again. Of course, she is right, he thought. She is very right. "Can it be," he asked, "that you are wise as well as accomplished?"

"Perhaps. And you kind as well as handsome and successful?"

"I am. Are you good-tempered as well as hospitable and beautiful?"

"Yes, indeed. How marvelous we both are!"

And they both laughed, and Amelia fell a little more deeply in love. I have never felt this way, never, she thought. How extraordinary a feeling this is—I wish I could paint it. It is not really like falling . . . it is more like flying!

She is charming, Ruffin thought, and I am charmed. He jumped when the little gilt clock on the mantel struck six times.

"I have finished," she said, "at least for now. I have done my best, but I have not yet done justice to your jaw. Perhaps . . ."

"Another time? With pleasure, but no more tonight. As we have hardly had a chance to talk, it occurs to me that we might dine together. Is it possible that you're not engaged?"

Amelia felt a great sense of relief. She had tensed herself against the moment of their parting and felt reprieved. Her green eyes danced with happiness.

"Yes, it's possible and I should be delighted."

"Excellent. Shall I send a carriage for you? At eight?"

"I shall be waiting."

"Good. Miss Amelia? One favor?"

"Oh! Yes, sir? What is it?"

"Could you please leave your sketchbook behind?"

"Just this one time."

* * *

As the months passed, Darius Yates ceased to think of escape or to resist the Indians' desire to make him one of them. He grew used to it all, used to the drafts of hallucinatory potions and the profound visions they stirred, used to moves from one hidden clearing to the next, each lost in the vast, dense expanse of jungle. He learned to savor the odd-tasting meals prepared for him by the women, the ceremonies and hunting trips with the men. He learned the Indian language, learned their names for birds and plants and trees and insects, names he had never known in English for things he had never seen or heard of in his other life.

By trying never to think of the past at all or the present as a sentence in captivity, Yates was able to be moderately happy. He knew that the Indians valued him: he was strong and energetic and proved to be as good a hunter as he was a farmer. He lived as they did, from day to day, blotting out concerns for the future by concentrating on the present.

One day, the old chief pulled him aside. There was a young woman, he explained, whose husband had been killed a year ago. She needed a husband. He was young and needed a wife. The chief had dreamed about it and decided that they should be married.

Yates listened and nodded. Fleetingly, he considered the contrast between this marriage arrangement and the sort characteristic of his old culture. The difference was so marked as to be ridiculous. He thought of his beautiful, modest Georgia bride, of the intense romantic courtship that had preceded their wartime wedding. He thought of their wedding. There had been six bridesmaids who carried Confederate flags and wore flowers in their hair. Both he and his bride had been innocent of the facts of life. It seemed as long ago and far away as the Roman Empire. He thought of the Richler sisters; their charming flirtatious manners, their full, fashionable dresses, bright as flowers, their needlework and their eager, hopeful expectations of love and romance. Sometimes he wondered if Brazil had fulfilled their expectations.

The chief brought the eligible woman to his sleeping hut. She was short, dark-skinned, full-breasted, and very shy. Her teeth were as white as the bleached bones that pierced her ears. He had seen her before, but nothing distinguished her from the other Indian women.

"What is her name?" he asked.

"She is Xuma."

At the sound of her name, the woman smiled cautiously, and Yates felt closer to her. She was a woman, he was a man, that was all. Whatever the Indians considered marriage to be, it was based on that simple equation, just like marriage in the rest of the world.

"Your dream is a good one," he told the chief.

A few days later, the marriage ceremony took place. The women smoked partridges and fish and fermented fruit juice in earthenware jugs buried under ten inches of moss. Yates and his bride wore feather headdresses and stood in front of the chief, holding hands.

"You must sleep together and in every way be closer together than brother and sister," he told them. "You are a family." When they had both drunk some of the fermented liquor he prayed over them and then the celebration began.

The festivities involved feasting and drinking,

chanting and dancing and went on as long as the food and liquor held out. At the end of four days Yates was left alone with his bride for the first time. It was a chilly night and he was glad for the warmth of her body. Xuma was serene and submissive. He could not love her; she was as foreign to him as a howler monkey, but he valued her, and took pleasure in seeing her smile. She was a good woman and he accepted her as such. In some months her belly began to swell with his child.

# Chapter Twenty-three

I have never met a woman like her, Terrill Ruffin thought as he left Rio de Janeiro at the head of a train drawn by four fiery little mules and accompanied by twenty-eight bags of mail and supplies. He was excited to be going and completely exhausted. He had spent the evening and then the night with Amelia and it had been the most wonderful night of his life.

Perhaps it's because she's an artist, he thought. No, it's more than that. She is an artist and a woman, an American and a Brazilian. She is both wise and beautiful. Had I not come to Brazil, I never would have met her, and yet I feel as if my whole life was leading to this meeting.

Weariness nibbled at his mind, and he forced himself to sit straight in the saddle. The trip ahead of him would be long and rigorous. He would have ample time to reflect during the days ahead, days he already felt stretched on too long.

I miss her already, he admitted. At one point during the night he had asked her to come along with him—it had been a night when anything seemed possible. With regrets, she had declined, for her child's sake. "I can wait . . . barely," she had said.

He felt dizzy, remembering how beautiful she was. Her creamy skin was as soft as rose petals. Her brilliant eyes sparkled with wit and spirit. Her body was sleek and slim and she had given it to him so freely, so proudly, so willingly—giving him more than he had dreamed possible. I could not have loved Marie-Anne so, he admitted sadly. We were both too young and we loved with the blind luck of the young, without the depth and passion I feel now.

"Oh, Marie-Anne," he prayed, "angel above," addressing the image of her that appeared to his mind more powerfully than the low brown hills and green thickets beside the road, "I have not forgotten you, my darling, nor have I forgotten my promise to avenge your death."

He had changed, been changed by the passage of time and this strong subtle influence of his new life, and by Brazil itself, but he had not altered that intention. The desire for revenge that had driven him so far was still keen. It had not been slaked by success or diverted by his luck in meeting Amelia Scott.

I will not rest until I have found him and destroyed him, he promised Marie-Anne's spirit. He would ask at the mining camps; perhaps Rall would be there, or someone there would have heard of him. Rall was not in Rio, he felt certain, for all his inquiries had yielded no trace of him, but he could not give up the search.

Calling a halt to the mule train in front of a roadside shrine, a painted crucifix mounted in a wooden box and decorated with flowers by some faithful hand, he knelt to give thanks and to renew his vow to find Rall. No one knew the complexities of his heart, not even Amelia. He was weary of deception; he wanted to be what he seemed, and yet, he could not.

Not yet. Pray God there would be time.

When he rose to continue the ride, he felt intoxicated with hope and fear.

In good time, Elinor and Tyler's baby was born. Tyler was at hand to deliver his son, assisted by his sister Amanda Ann, and all went well with the delivery. The child, certain to be the first of many, was plump and vigorous, with bone-white hair and clear blue eyes that mirrored the sky whenever Maria Carlota hung his cradle from the lowest branch of a tree. Elinor and Tyler named the baby John Lamar, and he was praised and petted by all their families and neighbors.

Soon Elinor could not imagine life without John Lamar. His demands for food and attention, his long naps and midnight wakings gave her life a framework and structure that was both rigorous and delightful. Her arms felt oddly empty when he was with his nurse. She thought her baby astonishingly beautiful and was engulfed in good and optimistic feelings about every aspect of life. Her work raising money for an American church had begun with Colonel Ashby's generous contribution of four hundred milreis. She had even persuaded herself that Zaidee's impetuous marriage to Jesse Rall was for the best; Zaidee did not seem unhappy and Rall was busy managing the fazenda. Perhaps

Zaidee would have a child soon, a little cousin for John Lamar.

Surrounded as she was by such evidence that life was working out according to God's good plan, Elinor would have been perfectly happy except for her concern about Tyler. Tyler worked very hard both on their little farm and with his practice. Night after night he was called out to attend to a patient. All the Americans within riding distance depended on him for doctoring, and many of their Brazilian neighbors began to call for him as well.

Elinor knew that Tyler would never be rich through his medical practice, although he was now a full-fledged doctor as he had passed the examination for his Brazilian medical license. Often as not, his fees were paid in promises or in kind. One month all his fees happened to be paid in eggs. Again and again he had ridden home with boxes and baskets of eggs, until it became funny, until there were so many eggs that Maria Carlota had piled them into a pyramid in the corner of the pantry-shed.

All the same, Tyler took great satisfaction from his practice and it seemed inevitable that their finances would improve in time. When they were better established, the other Americans would be able to pay Tyler fairly, and meanwhile Tyler's family was willing to help out and their own garden and their spotted milk cow gave them plenty of vegetables and milk and butter for the table.

It was not money that worried Elinor. It was something less substantial and more ominous. Before the arrival of the Americans, the only medical practitioner in the region had been a free black, an African called Basilio. He practiced herbal cures, common-sense medicine and what seemed to be spirit remedies, and he had a large and loyal following. Of course he had no education.

Now Tyler's practice had aroused Basilio's opposition, and not only his, but that of the village priest. Somehow there was a strong bond between the Catholic church and the old African religions. They had existed side by side for so long they had become integrated.

Elinor found it impossible to understand why any white person would want to be treated by a black practitioner, but it was so. Many of the Brazilians did, and even resented Tyler's practice, as if it threatened Basilio's skills.

Most of Elinor's information about Basilio came from her servant. Maria Carlota came from a large family in town and she had known about Basilio all her life. He cured fevers with spells, she told Elinor. Sometimes he cured the coughing sickness with medicines rubbed on the soles of the feet. Some of his cures were just magic.

One market day Elinor saw Basilio. He was more than six feet tall, and very thin. His skin was the color of black coffee. Earrings made of seashells hung from his long earlobes and he was dressed in a white robe like an Oriental priest. Elinor stopped short and stared, despite herself, shocked and frightened.

All around her Elinor hear excited murmuring, "*Curandeiro, curandeiro* . . ." The crowd parted to let Basilio pass. An old woman threw herself at his huge bare feet, kissing them, her white head bobbing as she groped for his ankles. He stooped, his kinky hair falling forward like a horse's mane and lifted the old woman aside, sobbing and smiling, her toothless mouth wide, and then he walked on—straight toward Elinor.

A wave of fear and revulsion swept over her. She could feel his power. It shot through the crowd; it was dark and glowering. She met his eyes, wise and malicious and mad.

Stepping backward out of the crowd, Elinor turned and ran for the safety of her wagon. He is a devil, a dragon, she thought. He is evil and cunning. Of course he is a fraud, but he is horrible, horrible! How could any sick person go to him for help?

She decided not to tell Tyler that she had seen his rival.

Jesse Rall sat at a table in a tavern near the marketplace drinking *pinga* from a bottle the proprietor had marked with a candle. Absentmindedly, he scratched at the mark with a fingernail. Christ, what did it matter—the whole bottle cost less than half a dollar and he'd be sure to drink it all.

Rall was already drunk. He lit a cigar and put his boots up on the windowsill. Behind him, a roomful of men argued and shouted, laughed and sang and occasionally staggered to the back door to relieve themselves in the dust. He ignored them, content to be completely the outsider.

It was market day, and the streets of the village had been busy since dawn with farmers bringing produce to the markets. Rall scanned the street outside the tavern's open window. He waited. Sooner or later one of his cronies would come along. He was tired of drinking alone.

A mule train passed in a cloud of dust. A pair of black-shawled widows carrying wicker baskets of squawking chickens. A series of black porters with immense sacks of sugar or coffee beans balanced on their heads. And then, sauntering, Kinch McCall, wearing a straw hat and a red vest, looking more American than George Washington.

"Kinch!" Rall shouted and leaned out the open window.

"Waal, hello," Kinch drawled, removing his straw hat and coming into the tavern with an air of weariness.

"Have a drink?"

"Sure I will." He picked up the bottle, sniffed at it, and tipped it back.

"It's as good as your own," Rall said.

" 'Tis my own. I delivered here yesterday."

"Business is good?"

"Good enough. How are you, Jesse? How's your wife?"

Rall smiled, white teeth splitting his florid face above his thick black beard: white, red, black repeated in his clothes: white shirt with fine red stripes, black jacket. "Which one?" he joked.

Kinch roared. "Still runnin' the harem, eh?"

"You ought to git married, Kinch."

"Damned if there's any women left in town."

Rall laughed and puffed at his cigar. He was pleased with his domestic situation. Although he did not own the farm—it still belonged to the Richler sisters—he as good as owned it. He was in full charge of everything, and now that he was married to Miss Zaidee, he reckoned her share was legally his. Miss Zaidee was a good-looking woman, and if she wasn't easy to live with, Joana more than made up for it. Joana was hot-blooded and passionate; Zaidee was a fine-tuned Southern lady and the two of them together suited him fine.

"As the Brazilians say," Rall joked, "white woman for marriage, mulatto woman for fuck, Negro woman for work."

Kinch laughed. "You've adjusted better'n most," he said. "Sam Whitaker and the Wards are goin' back home, I hear."

"I'll never go back," Rall said. "Sure as a wheel's round, it must someday come to rest." He took a long swallow and slammed down the bottle. "But I don't change, neither! You might say I'm content. Seems to me we've got everythin' here we had back home, except Yankees."

"Waal, that's for sure," Kinch said. He found himself wondering if it was true that Rall had been run out of Texas.

"We'll have 'em all speakin' English yet," Rall predicted, his eyes as watery as the *pinga*. "Christ, they're lucky to have us here. The Anglo-Saxon civilization, which is the same thing as sayin' the Southern civilization, is the noblest the world has ever known! We were born to be masters. We got the true church. In time all the barbarians'll come over to it—how can they not? We got our own moral laws and we'll enforce 'em!"

"That's right," Kinch argued, but he wasn't as sure as Rall. Working with Brazilians as he did, he heard a lot of talk, and one thing he had heard was that some of the friends of Arigo had formed into a gang out to get Americans. It wasn't legal but the blacks had knives and razors which they strapped to their ankles. There was going to be trouble.

"Christ, let's git out of here," Rall said suddenly. "I feel like they're all starin' at us. Come along home with me, Kinch. We'll git a good dinner and you'll forget you was missin' Tennessee."

# Chapter Twenty-four

The shocks and griefs of the past few months had taken a toll on Zaidee's pride and spirit. It was more than a year since she had been married. And a year from now? Where would she be then?

None of the possibilities that came to her mind were in the least hopeful, and the worst of them was the likelihood that she would be right here.

Helplessly, she stamped her foot and felt her eyes burn with tears. She had never felt so lonely, so frustrated, or so left out. All around her, life was going on . . . time was passing—days, weeks, months—and she felt no connection with it. Every day in her life was the same and each was duller than the last.

Sometimes she raged at the fate that had brought her to Brazil and dreamed of going back to America. Letters she and Elinor had received from their cousins in Tennessee told of parties and barbecues and ice cream socials, of piano recitals and balls. Reading them, Zaidee felt sick. That was her heritage, that would have been her life, but it was three thousand miles away. It was gone forever.

Sometimes she dreamed of parties and people she had once known. She remembered them all, everything about them, as if it were yesterday. Oddly, Jesse knew none of the people she remembered, and he had no desire at all to go back to Texas.

Jesse was perfectly content with his life here. He worked hard and had increased the amount of land planted in cotton; he had his friends, the Knights of the Confederacy; and he came and went a good deal—on business, she expected, or else with the other Knights. Zaidee believed he was proud of her. He treated her courteously and she was vain enough to take emotional sustenance from his admiration.

And although she had not come to enjoy sexual relations with him, she tolerated them with a sense of noblesse oblige, shutting her eyes and gritting her teeth. Fortunately, he did not try to make love to her very often, less often as the months passed.

Zaidee was quite sure she would not become pregnant. There was something in her, she suspected, that was not made to bear a child. She had always thought so, and so far she had been right. She was not sorry; babies were a lot of trouble, and she had never understood the enthusiasm other women showed for them. Her sister Elinor was expecting another child already, and as a daily reminder of a pregnant woman's grotesque proportions, the mulatto slave-woman Joana was great with child.

Pregnancy had made Joana mean as well as clumsy and Zaidee had insisted that Jesse buy her another house servant. The girl he had brought home was named Pedra. She was as skinny as a broom and cross-eyed, but at least she was willing, so again Zaidee had some time to play the piano and reread old American newspapers waiting for Jesse to come home for supper.

It was an excruciatingly dull life, and seemed to

have no possibilities for change. Thinking of it, seeing Joana crossing the barnyard, Zaidee stamped her foot again, furiously, and when the stamping loosened the heel of one of her worn shoes—for what difference did it make when there was no one to see her?—she took off the shoe, spinning on her stocking foot, and hurled it across the room with all her pent-up strength.

There was a satisfying crash as it hit the face of her mother's heirloom clock and the shattered glass fell into splinters on the floor.

"What's wrong, missus?" Pedra asked, running in from the kitchen.

Zaidee laughed. In her own way, she had stopped time, and there was a perverse pleasure in destroying the past, since it was gone for her, gone forever.

As time passed, Darius Yates attained a position of leadership among the Indians. His child had been born and was healthy. He had learned the Indians' ways and had taught them more successful ways of planting. They practiced primitive agriculture, planting vegetables in plots cleared in the forest, then moving on to a new location when the soil became exhausted or the hunting poor.

Yates was at home in the forest and often went out from the cleared land with his wife, Xuma, or one or two others for several days at a time, gathering fruit or hunting.

One morning he and Xuma walked several miles to reach a certain fruit tree, a *caimito* tree that she remembered from some years past. As he swung along the shady path by her side, Yates did not stop to reflect or speculate, he had accepted the state of happiness, of savoring the day itself, that characterized the Indian existence.

All around them was the jungle, green and moist. The forest floor was thick and leafy; it swallowed sound, muffling the cries of the birds and animals announcing their approach.

The day was hot and calm and when they reached the *caimito* tree they found that the fruit was ripe. Yates climbed up into the lower branches and was tossing the glistening fruit to Xuma when he heard the totally unexpected whine of a bullet and saw it lodge in the tree trunk just above his shoulder.

Acting instinctively, he swung around the tree and slid to the ground. In a few seconds he heard another retort, saw green leaves trembling and saw that a bullet had found his wife.

Instead of fear or anger, Yates felt a tremendous sadness. He knelt beside Xuma and took her in his arms, but her breath failed and her eyelids fluttered and she stared blindly up into his face.

"Xuma . . . dear wife," he whispered, holding her as her eyes closed and her breathing stopped. Still he held her. He was stunned. In the years he had spent with the Indians he had seen death from sickness and from the attack of jaguars, from childbirth and from the Indians of another tribe, but he had forgotten the swift inexorable power of the white man's rifle, and for a moment he did not comprehend that it was the bullet that had killed her.

"Xuma . . . Xuma . . ." he said softly, calling to her spirit. Attuned as he was to the sounds of the forest, he heard danger in the unnatural silence. Whoever had fired was still nearby. Minutes passed, but there was no other shot, no noise that revealed the assailant's hiding place.

Yates's mind worked like an Indian's. I must take her back to the village for burial, he thought. She must be anointed and wrapped in bark. The body must be smoked and then there must be the chants and the fires and the grave. Gently, he picked up the still-warm body and carried it away from the tree, its dense weight straining his arms as tears ran down his cheeks.

Before he had gone ten feet he nearly collided with the end of a rifle. He blinked, and then his eyes opened wide. It was a white man, a man wearing a rough khaki suit and high black hunting boots, a man with tanned cheeks and light eyes, dark brown hair and beard, carrying a rifle Yates recognized as a Sharps .32.

The shock was mutual. Both men stared. Yates's mind raced. Would the man shoot him for an Indian? Would he be recognized as a white man? Could the world change completely in a minute's time? His lips worked, but he could not remember a single word of Portuguese and scarcely one of English. He bit his lip.

The hunter spoke rapidly, his voice high with excitement and surprise. Yates recognized his language as Portuguese, but he could go no further. He set down Xuma's body carefully, knelt, and put out his own hands, palms up.

For the first time in years he felt naked. He looked down at his body and then out at the strange man. There was so much to say, so much to explain, so much to ask and understand that for a moment he was overwhelmed and longed to escape back into the forest, but the moment passed and his embarrassment and confusion were overcome by a feeling of hope, ordinary hope for the future, something he had put behind him years ago and had never expected to feel again.

He felt no fear. What could he fear, he who had lived two lives already? Instead, he stepped forward, pronouncing his name again and again, and the white hunter took his hands in a firm grasp.

That same summer, Zaidee Richler Rall became so bored and lonely that she fell into the habit of confiding in the slave girl Pedra. Pedra was simple, Zaidee decided, but she was company. She was eager to learn English and had made some progress. Like many Brazilians, she was a devout believer in the spirit religion that combined the old African gods with the new Roman Catholic ones, and she was a follower of the witch doctor Basilio.

Zaidee had never heard of this religion before she began talking to Pedra, and at first she regarded it as just another Brazilian custom, quite as unsavory and bizarre as most. But when she heard that her brother-in-law Tyler Ashby had come into conflict with the native doctor, she was amused to think that Tyler, with his American education and all his pretensions, should be trusted less than a Negro faith healer.

"I want to know more about Basilio," she said to Pedra.

"A great man, great healer," Pedra informed her.

"Really? I should like to visit him."

"Oh, no, missus, not for white people. He's not for white people to know."

"What can he do for black people, Pedra?"

"Cure sickness, get love, or spoil it." And Pedra, seeing that she had a good audience, told of Basilio's miraculous powders and powerful prayers, how he could give old men potency and make barren women conceive. Pedra told Zaidee how she had once kept a live toad under her bed to hold a man's love, how she had fed it on cow's milk and had seen his affection for her rival wither.

"What happened then?" Zaidee asked. "Where is he now?"

Pedra frowned. "He dead," she said sulkily. "Never mind how. Macumba, that magic too strong for some people."

Zaidee listened, wide-eyed, half amused and half persuaded that Basilio's macumba was a way of controlling the frameworks of fate and human behavior.

Another day she questioned Pedra again. "Have you ever heard of a love potion that worked, Pedra?"

"Sure enough. I know a witch woman stole my man. With a potion."

"How did she do it?"

"She used the *bichos*, that witch woman. And then she take his shirt and cut holes in the heart of it and feed him *café mandingueiro*. For a time he resisted her, but such a love potion can't be resisted. She finally got him, missus. She made him crazy and wore him out."

Zaidee laughed, but she hung on every word and pressed Pedra with more questions until she understood. *Café mandingueiro* was coffee with a spell in it, served with much sugar and a few drops of the menstrual blood of the sorceress. Many of the ingredients of the spells Pedra knew about were nauseating and all of them strange, but Zaidee was prepared to believe that they worked.

To Zaidee, macumba seemed to be a way, an odd but very Brazilian way, of regaining control of her life. Perhaps she could get a love potion to make Rafael come for her after all, and a poison to punish Jesse Rall . . . or a poison to punish Rafael just a bit, to hurt him as he had hurt her . . . even a potion for Elinor, who had come around snooping again and criticized the haphazard style of housekeeping she and Pedra had settled into.

"I want to go to Basilio," she told Pedra.

"No, missus, not you."

"Well, then, you must go for me."

# Chapter Twenty-five

As soon as Joana went into labor, it was clear that she would have a hard time of it. On the morning of the second day, her screams were perfectly audible even in the house where Zaidee lived.

Zaidee woke and the sound upset and displeased her. "Can't you stop it?" she asked Pedra fretfully. "It makes my head ache."

Pedra stared at her mistress. She had just built the breakfast fire but the whole fazenda had been in an uproar for hours. The *practicar* who assisted all the slave women was helpless; Mr. Jesse, who had been in and out of Joana's cabin all night, was gruff and anxious; only Miss Zaidee did not seem to understand at all. She had misread all the trouble over Joana; she did not see that Mr. Jesse was wild in love with her, but as usual, related all his irregular comings and goings and his black moods to herself.

"Why don't you go get Basilio to help Joana?" Zaidee suggested.

"Could do that."

"Her screamin's like to drive me mad," Zaidee said. "Why do you think she's so long at it, Pedra? I never knew a nigger woman to take on so. Mostly they just drop babies like lambs."

"Just like anyone else," Pedra muttered. She had spent the night in Joana's cabin, holding her hand and wiping it with a cloth wrung out in root tea. The midwife had painted a white cross on the door and thrown herbs into the fire. Mr. Jesse had looked miserable; he could not bear to stay or to go.

"You do that," Zaidee said again. "Go for Basilio, Pedra. Bring him back here to help deliver that baby." Once he's here, perhaps he will help me, also, she thought.

Pedra dropped the skillet and ran along the creek path as fast as she could. Her bare feet made no sound on the soft, black earth, but her heart was pounding so hard that it echoed in her ears like the sound of drums, and who could blame her if she longed to keep on running. There would be trouble if Basilio agreed to come, and trouble if he did not. Poor Joana. Likely he would come. Although Pedra's own acquaintance with him was not as close as she had led Zaidee to believe, Basilio liked Joana. It was said that the sorcerer had fancied her, once, and although she had rebuffed him, she had done it carefully, with a great respect, so that he still spoke well of her.

While Pedra searched for Basilio, Jesse Rall took his horse and rode east, half drunk and as desperate as a man riding pillion with the devil, the sound of Joana's screams still fresh in his memory. Every hour with her had seemed worse; he could not bear her torment, he would do anything to stop it, even ask Tyler Ashby for help, and that was his intent.

It was still early morning, but the day's heat was rising, gathering at the horizon in thick, cotton-white clouds. Rall made his way to Tyler and Elinor's house and found Elinor in the barnyard, scattering corn for the chickens.

"Where's the doctor?" he demanded.

"Why, he's gone to town. What's wrong? Is someone ill? Zaidee?"

"No, not them. It's the woman Joana. She's having trouble with her baby."

Elinor had never seen Rall so disturbed. His beard was tousled; his usually florid face was brick-red and set in deep lines of worry. His sweat-soaked clothes were caked with red dust from the road and his red-rimmed eyes were tormented and wild. Looking at him she felt her hands begin to tremble and her stomach contract.

"What's wrong with Joana?"

"I don't know what's wrong! She's having a hard time, that's all I know. Where is the doctor?"

"He's gone to the clinic in town already," Elinor said, pitying any woman in travail. Inside the house her own baby cried out.

"Well, then." Rall turned to go.

"And how is my sister?" Elinor called out, for she had not seen Zaidee in some weeks. Even ten miles seemed a great distance to ride these days, since she was so busy at home and raising money for the American church. Seeing Rall like this reminded her, unwillingly, of that night by the riverbank in Texas and stirred up all her memories. Obviously, he did not remember. How could he have forgotten so much? She stared at him. He was the same, as darkly determined now as then, as forceful, blood-bent on accomplishing what it was he was after.

He is not like us; he is hard and free of the past. Why was he so upset over the childbearing of a slave? Why did he care?

Rall looked back at Elinor, sensing her distaste for him and struggling to remember something, as she stepped back to avoid his horse's hooves.

"Content, I expect," he said. "Miss Zaidee is content."

And Elinor had to be satisfied with that, although she suspected, knowing Zaidee, that it was likely very far from the truth. Zaidee had never been content.

Jesse Rall rode into town hoping to find Tyler Ashby in his office near the railroad station. Ashby held office hours and ran a small clinic there, making himself available to anyone who needed surgery or medical treatment, and dispensing medicines from a locked closet. In the same building, Charles Gannon, a dentist from Florida, had opened a practice and was kept busy treating Brazilians as well as Americans.

Just in the past few months, the Brazilians had started calling the district around the station Vila Americana, the American village, and the name had caught on. As it happened, a sign painter in the employ of the blacksmith near the clinic was perched on a tall ladder, adding the final "a" to a sign that read: *T. Matthews/ Blacksmith/Vila Americana*.

Rall scowled as he rode under the ladder. It would take more than a few signs to make this dogtrot settlement into an American town, he thought. Pigs and scrawny chickens ran loose in the mud streets and a pack of barefooted children gathered to stare at him as he tied his horse. He hurried into the clinic to look for Tyler Ashby.

But the railroad had made a difference. Salesmen had begun to come to Vila Americana, bringing dry goods and luxuries from São Paulo and Rio. A Georgian had opened a plow factory and the dentist's wife gave music lessons. Already the first two prostitutes had set up housekeeping at the far end of one of the two dusty main streets. The salesmen with their leather suitcases and linen suits ate in the tavern and slept upstairs but there was talk of a hotel opening. It was beginning to be a town.

Rall found Tyler Ashby holding a brown-skinned baby with a withered arm, but he closed the clinic quickly and followed Rall out to saddle his horse. Ashby was accustomed to being summoned to childbeds by distraught fathers. Unlike Elinor, he had no difficulty interpreting the panic in Rall's eyes.

"How long has she been in labor?" he asked.

"More than a day."

"Her first?"

"Yes, but it's not going well. She is in great pain."

So women must always suffer, Tyler Ashby thought. Why does he think this one should bear a child without suffering? He despised Rall, and even more so as the rumor about his keeping a slave mistress now appeared to be true, but there was no question that he would try to save the woman and the baby. He would do all he could to save any human life; it was his sworn life's purpose. Thank God his killing days were over. He could even begin to recall the war without the horror and despair he had felt for so long; Elinor had helped with that—her love had given him hope.

As they rode into the front yard at the Richler farm, both men smelled a strange and sickening smoke. It reminded Tyler of the charnel house at Fort Delaware prison. Will I never forget that smell? he wondered.

"Where is she?" he called out to Rall.

"Around back."

Ashby saw Zaidee in a window, saw her step back behind the curtains as they rode by. Poor Zaidee, he thought, I suppose she has chosen to ignore all this. What other choice has she? Trouble has come too often to visit this poor house.

Even expecting trouble, he was surprised to see Basilio looming in the doorway, a hulking specter in dingy white rags, his black hair wild as Spanish moss and his eyes glowing like dark coals.

There was a moment of silence, then a woman's scream from inside the hut. Without warning Jesse Rall leapt forward, attacking Basilio with his riding whip.

For a moment Tyler Ashby was too amazed to react.

"What are you doin' here, you black fool?" Rall screamed.

Basilio pulled back. He was four inches taller than either of the white men and fiercely imperious. The tip of Rall's whip cut red stripes across his shoulders and arms and he brandished a long curved knife.

"Don't come near me with that!" Rall shouted, carried past sense or reason by rage. "What did you do to her?"

Basilio ignored him. Squinting in the sunlight and smoke, he marched past the white men with a pharaoh's dignity as Rall barked, "Quack! Black bastard! Get out of here."

Tyler Ashby ducked through the narrow doorway. Joana lay on the floor, the midwife crouched at one side and Pedra at the other. They moved aside when he kneeled to examine Joana.

"What's wrong with her?" Rall demanded.

The man's out of his mind, Tyler Ashby thought.

"It's turned. It's upside down," he said. "I'm goin' to give her some opium and cut her. It's the only way."

"Do whatever you have to do," Rall said.

"Stop crying and go get some clean hot water," Ashby said to Pedra.

"What the hell was that black ape burnin' here?" Rall asked, kicking at the cookfire. The smell was sickening.

"Not me, yessir," Pedra said, crying. Pray God that Miss Zaidee did not tell the master that she had gone for Basilio, he would kill her sure.

Pedra and the midwife held Joana still while Ashby made a cut across her belly, removed the baby, and sewed it back up again. The baby was good-sized but very yellow. It was a boy and it was blue-eyed and light-skinned and Joana fell asleep when they put it in her arms. Pedra had never seen so much blood.

"She'll live," Tyler Ashby said when he was finished. The hut had been dark and hot and the blood had drawn hundreds of flies. Only then did he realize it was the same one where Daphne Richler had died.

"Take her out of there, get her some air," he ordered, going on toward the main house to see Miss Zaidee. The way Rall had treated Zaidee disgusted him. He felt sorry for her; she had already endured more than most women could bear. Perhaps it would be just as well if the child died.

He dreaded seeing Zaidee, but to his surprise she was calm and offered him tea. He did not notice that her luminous blue eyes were blank and he was relieved that she did not want to chat, but declined the tea and left as quickly as he could.

Later, when he told Elinor about it, it occurred to him that Zaidee had looked strange. Perhaps he should have stayed longer. But Zaidee had never confided in him and it was unlikely she would begin now.

Two weeks after his encounter with the hunter, Darius Yates sat in the stern of a wood-burning launch as it eased out into the current of the swift-flowing São Francisco River. The hiss of the steam whistle startled him, but he struggled to seem composed. He was not composed; he was tired and his nerves were on edge from the barrage of new experiences he had endured in the past two weeks.

Yates wore pants and a shirt, but the heavy leather boots he had put on that morning lay beside him in the bottom of the launch. The pants and shirt felt incredibly strange; the boots were intolerable. He had cut his hair and beard. Since his return to civilization he had lost weight—he could not stomach either liquor or spicy Brazilian food.

I have forgotten so much, he thought, more than just the little Portuguese I knew and the habits of civilization. Emotion choked him; he was prey to uncontrollable changes of mood and swung from euphoria to sadness in the space of a few heartbeats. I have forgotten pretense, worry, pride, despair, and I have forgotten how to tolerate the noise and busyness of the world. He looked out over the wide, silver-green river, fringed with the thick, leafy forest he had lived in for five years. He had been at home in the moist mysterious jungle, at one with nature, and he knew that he was leaving something he would never find again.

Slowly he was feeling less numb and less jarred by every sound and smell and sign of civilization. He looked across the launch and returned the smile of Joaquim Xavier, the man who had found him and had brought him here.

Xavier had been curious, but he had not been able to say much about his identity or experiences in the jungle, not only because of his difficulties with Portuguese, but from an instinct to defend and protect his captors and his life with them. Whoever the Indians were, they were not savages; he did not think of them so. He could not judge them; he only missed them. He had broken the habit of analysis. For years his sole concern had been survival.

Yates squinted at the brightness of the sun reflected off the river and wiped his forehead. Despite the heat he preferred the deck to the cabin. He craved light and air and nearness to the green trees, but his head ached from the ceaseless throbbing of the launch's engines.

The boat would take him to Aracaju, the port city—he had seen it on Xavier's maps. From there there were bigger boats. He could sail south to Salvador da Bahia or Rio, or he could—and the thought of it was preposterous and wonderful—go home. He smiled. If his luck held out, and he no longer believed in luck, only in fickle and cataclysmic fate, in three months he could be home in Georgia.

Jesse Rall was not altogether sorry when, after two weeks of life, Joana's blue-eyed, light-skinned son died.

There was no hope for it, nothing could be done for the child—he had failed slowly and died in his sleep, but it disturbed him to see Joana's sadness and to hear her cry.

To escape from the sight, he went into town. Had Joana been well, had she been herself, he would have gone to her and forgotten everything else, but tonight he could not.

It's best, he thought, to leave her alone to recover. Nigger women recover fast, fast as mules, they say. In a few weeks she would be ready for him again, and it was just as well the baby hadn't lived, although every slave was valuable. He grimaced. What if the little bastard had turned out to look like him? Even Miss Zaidee might not stand for that.

In the Vila Americana tavern he found Kinch McCall and Coley Burgess drinking together at a table by the door. The tavern was crowded and noisy. A haze of blue cigar smoke hung from the ceiling and one of the town's whores was crying in a corner.

"By Jesus, I'm tired of this stuff," Coley Burgess said, draining a glass of *pinga*. "No offense, Kinch, but what wouldn't you give for a glass of real whiskey?"

"Give everythin' I've got," Kinch admitted.

"So would I," Rall said.

"Sometimes I dream of Tennessee corn whiskey," Kinch said.

"By Jesus, look at that!" Coley Burgess shouted, jumping to his feet. It was twilight, and across the street and down the block they could just make out what looked like a small army of small dark-skinned men advancing on the railroad station.

The three men crowded to the open door to watch.

The usually busy street was deserted and it was oddly quiet behind them in the tavern.

"What's goin' on?" Kinch asked.

Rall looked out into the dim street. Twenty men were scurrying along the sides of the street like spies. They were barefoot . . . young . . . mulattoes. . . . Some of them looked familiar. . . .

All of a sudden he understood. They were members of the *capoiera* gang, the gang of knife-fighters out to get Americans, and he bet they were stalking Ashby's clinic. He reached for his pistol.

"Goddamn! Those black bastards are attackin' the doctor!"

There was the sound of breaking glass as Rall burst out of the tavern, the others close behind. McCall was too drunk to shoot straight and Burgess was unarmed, but in a few minutes Rall had put bullets into four backs, four men lay facedown in the street, and Coley Burgess had been cut.

When the shooting stopped the silence closed around them like walls. This is it, Rall thought, this is the beginning of war. Now there's no going back. And this was one war they were going to win. Excitement raced through him like fever.

"Jesus, help me! I'm dyin'," Coley Burgess moaned. A razor had opened up his arm between elbow and shoulder, severing the muscles and tendons. Blood spurted out.

"Take it easy, Burgess, don't move," Rall said. From the looks of the cut only his nearness to the clinic would save him, but Tyler Ashby had already opened up the door.

"Who were they? What's goin' on? Oh, dear Lord, bring him in here," Ashby said. He was shaken, but the sight of Burgess steadied him; he knew what to do with a knife wound. All at once he was cool and professional. "Put him here," he ordered. "Close the damn door." Deftly he fitted a tourniquet around Burgess's upper arm even before his head had hit the back of the examining bench.

"He'll live," Ashby pronounced grimly after a few minutes. "But who were they?"

The clinic's windows had been shattered and broken glass lay on the tile floor like icicles.

"Black bastards who don't like us, I reckon," Rall said.

Grimly, Tyler looked from one face to the next. Why did Rall sound so excited, so triumphant? He was glad to be fighting again, wasn't he? In his own way, each of them was still recovering from the war. Maybe they would never get over it.

"Are they Barroso's men?" Ashby asked.

"Some of them," Rall said.

"I heard a rumor around town that you killed some black baby," Kinch McCall blurted out.

"I? I killed a baby?" Ashby asked, incredulous.

"B-Basilio don't like you," McCall said.

"That baby died . . . out to my place," Rall explained.

"Surely people don't believe Basilio," Ashby said.

There was a silence and Coley Burgess moaned softly.

"They are nothing but a bunch of ignorant ruffians," Ashby said. It occurred to him that he had often said the same thing of the Knights.

Burgess moaned again.

"I'll git the one who cut you," Rall promised.

"Haven't you done enough already?" Ashby said. "Can't this madness stop, here and now?"

"Doubt it," Rall said. "It's only the start."

In the street outside they heard the slow hooves of the horse-drawn hearse driven by the town constable who had come to collect the bodies. Everyone knew the constable was one of Barroso's men and a cousin of Basilio.

# Chapter Twenty-six

Juliano Monteiro, Dom Pedro II's Minister of Immigration, was confused when he studied the complaint he received about the Americans in the Campo region from Dom Martim Barroso. It sounded like the Americans were lawbreakers, or was it just two unruly gangs fighting each other? He pondered the complaint. Dom Martim Barroso's son had formerly been in his employ. Dom Rafael was a level-headed man; if the matter could be easily settled, he would have settled it.

From the Minister's point of view, the American immigrants had been given every opportunity: they had been sold land at advantageous prices, they had been exempted from taxes for years to come. They had been supplied with transportation to their settlements and encouraged in every way. Yet, many of the colonies were not working out. The colony at Santarém had dissolved, that at Rio Doce was faltering, and now, from the largest settlement, the one they called Vila Americana, came disturbing reports of violence. The Americans seemed to consider themselves above Brazilian law; few of them had applied for full citizenship; it seemed they had lynched a witless bastard son of Dom Martim's, and now they had shot down four of his men in the streets of the town.

"It is not the Brazilian way," Juliano Monteiro said. "Our crimes are crimes of the heart. These incidents have nothing to do with passion! They seem to be concerned with race. I am confounded. What shall we do, sir?"

Dom Pedro frowned. Of all his immigration schemes, that of importing agricultural specialists from the American South was his favorite. He recalled meeting some of the Americans who had emigrated to the São Paulo province. The men had seemed hardworking and practical. Some of them were even educated and cultivated. He recalled one in particular, a man and his son called Ashby. It was impossible to believe they had caused this sort of trouble.

"There is an American gentleman living here in Rio whom I know rather well," Monteiro said. "He has been very successful in trade. He is in partnership with my old friend James Barnes and gets on well with Brazilians . . ."

"Yes? What do you suggest?"

"He speaks very decent Portuguese and is a strong and judicious man, although young. I was only about to suggest that we send him to the town, to visit the partisans, perhaps to mediate . . ."

"Very well," Dom Pedro agreed.

"The situation is apparently explosive."

"Do it at once, then."

"I will send him to see Barroso."

"Yes. And the family Ashby," Dom Pedro added.

* * *

Zaidee stood in the open doorway of her house. The house was dark behind her and the yard flashed with fireflies. She was alone, although it was well past midnight. She and Jesse had eaten an early supper together and after eating they had quarreled, as they did increasingly often. Their quarrel had been bitter and brief. Both of them were stubborn and their positions were worlds apart.

"Jesse, this won't do. I've got to get out of here," Zaidee had said. "I hate it here; there's nothing for me. At least let's move to Rio."

"And do what? I'm a farmer, Miss Zaidee. It's the beginnin' of the growin' season and I've put in forty acres of cotton. Now if you were a farmer's wife, 'stead of a princess, I'd have an easier time of it."

Zaidee glared at him. Sometimes she hated him so much she didn't see how her hatred could help but mark him. He was so ugly, so red-faced and coarse, so big and tousled. Her life was a prison and he was her jailor. Or was it a madhouse and he her keeper? Had he been put on earth to spoil her life, to hold her back from the pleasures that would otherwise have been hers?

"Well, I guess you'll just have to manage," she said coldly, none of the wild rage she felt breaking the surface. With effort, she kept in a state of icy calm that protected her from confrontations with everything she disliked. It was true that she did not care for the success of the fazenda. She took no interest in it. Pedra and one other slave woman did the washing and cleaning, the milking and churning and cooking and sweeping. Pedra hoed in the little garden; Joana weeded it occasionally. Zaidee ignored the tests and triumphs of this life around her, but at a terrible cost. The cost was being achingly lonely every day of her life, of suffering an incurable malaise of hopelessness and inertia. Never did she feel more alone than when she was quarreling with her husband.

Rall stared at Zaidee, and then shrugged. Anger at Zaidee was useless. Whatever he said to her, he could not alter her mind. Perhaps he did not care enough to be angry. Unspoken was his real complaint—"You are not a real wife," and hers—"It is my land, my house, not yours." Both of them knew she did not want the land or care for it; both knew theirs was not a loving marriage, but she did not know that Jesse was increasingly in love with his other wife.

Tonight he had left early, as he usually did. "I'll make do, I guess," he said. He stood, towering over her at the table with her nearly untouched plate of food. "I got business in town tonight, I reckon."

"I reckon you do," Zaidee said flatly, and watched him go. At the last minute she almost called out, "Don't go tonight" but she did not. He went out often, as often as he could, and whatever he did, he did not tell her about it.

He was going to meet with the Knights, she imagined. The Knights of the Confederacy were increasingly active; they had become known as a vigilante organization. In months past the gang of young troublemakers from Santa Barbara had opposed them on two occasions, occasions that had been outright pitched battles or so she had heard.

So far no Americans had been killed, but Coley Burgess had been hurt, and she had heard Jesse swear to find the nigger who had done it. The Knights' business was their own; Zaidee wanted no part of it, although sometimes she was afraid, staying here at night alone with only the slaves out there.

Sometimes, left alone, she heard rustlings, and hoofbeats, and worst of all, the dying screams of the frogs caught in the mouths of the frog-eating snakes in the stagnant pool at the end of the garden. On such nights, she fancied that she heard rustlings under her bed and when she lit a candle she saw snakes in every corner of the house.

But tonight Jesse had gone, without another word. Zaidee was left alone, again, to amuse herself as she liked and to go to bed alone. But tonight she could not sleep. She was kept awake, perhaps by all the things she had not said, or else by the hot pulsing of the blood in her veins.

At midnight, she was still awake, and, standing in the open doorway, she first heard and then saw Jesse's horse coming very slowly down the road. The moon was orange and nearly full, and she could see him clearly as soon as he came around the bend.

She paused, watching, and she did not call out. Jesse passed the house, passed the doorway without seeing her, seeing the house was dark. Now I suppose he will come to my bed, she thought, and the thought made the blood rise to the surface of her skin and pound in her temples. She did not want him . . . actually, but she needed him, needed the midnight wrestling that sometimes left her feeling more peaceful. She waited, intensely conscious of her own body, soft and white and clean under the white cotton and lace nightdress she wore.

She waited, but he did not come.

He has gone to put the horse in his stable, she thought. Then he will come. But when enough time had passed and then twice enough, she lost patience. Perhaps he is so drunk he has fallen asleep in the stable, she thought. How like him!

Barefoot, trying not to think of snakes and whatever else might be hiding in the grass, she ran out of the house and across the barnyard. He was not in the stables, but when she stood beside it she could see lights in Joana's little house at the edge of the quarters.

Perhaps he is there, she thought innocently. Perhaps Joana is causing some other trouble. Never have I known a more worthless, more ungrateful nigger woman. Perhaps she is sick and Jesse will finally agree to sell her.

Closer to Joana's hut, Zaidee could see that both her cookfire and her lantern were still burning. When she heard Jesse's voice, it slowed her steps, and she moved stealthily, approaching the side of the house, where there was an open window, a square of yellow light.

From ten feet away she could see perfectly well into the hut, but she could not stop, she was drawn in closer by surprise and baffled incomprehension changing quickly to understanding. All at once it became clear.

Joana lay naked in her white-string hammock, her brown and voluptuous body extended and relaxed, and Jesse knelt beside her. He knelt! Zaidee could not believe it. He knelt, himself naked, and as she watched, he stroked Joana slowly and lovingly as if she were a pet cat, his red hands passing up and down her flanks and over her rounded belly, reaching up to fondle her large breasts. It was a scene of ease and familiarity, of sensual delight, and it wounded Zaidee past the point of pain.

She stepped back into the shadows, staring, still.

Joana's hands wandered to Jesse's head and she brushed a lock of his black hair off his brow as he leaned over her and began to kiss her.

It was early morning when Terrill Ruffin approached Rio de Janeiro after his journey to the gold fields in Minas Gerais. The city was bathed in golden sunlight, the rounded mountains glittering green and capped with mist. The great bay was a perfect, brilliant blue in the distance and he entered the outskirts along the shore road, a road which brought his mule train past white-washed peasant huts set in orange groves that scented the air with sweet, pungent perfume.

Ruffin was delighted to be approaching the city he now called home, and he was positively eager to see Amelia Scott. Although he had much to report and discuss with his partner, he went first to Amelia's house in Rua Benedictus in Botafogo and sent word to her that he was home.

Within minutes she was in his arms: cool and fragrant in a dressing gown of white silk, impossibly familiar and strange at the same time, lovelier than he remembered, her green eyes glinting with gold.

"How I have missed you!" he murmured.

"And I you. I have expected you every day for a week."

He laughed, kissing her. "I would have come sooner, could I have flown."

She laughed. "How wonderful you look."

"Where is your sketch pad? And you, you are as beautiful as an angel!"

"Come. Stay for breakfast."

"I am sorry, but I cannot. I have left everything waiting at the offices. Barnes will be anxious to see me, but I will return as soon as I can. We can dine together, can we not?"

"I shall cook for you myself," she promised.

"I have a present for you. A Brazilian relic in its natural form." He dug into his waistcoat pocket and drew out something wrapped in a handkerchief.

"It's an egg!" she guessed and then forgot it as he kissed her goodbye with a fervor that left her breathless.

When he had gone she unwrapped the egg-shaped nugget of gold, one of many, for as Ruffin explained to Barnes within the hour, he had been present at a fabulous gold strike in their mines at Sabara that would double and perhaps triple their profits for the year.

"It's quite extraordinary," Ruffin explained, "in fifty years this vein had been overlooked. The new steam pumps make it possible to delve one hundred fathoms below the surface. I saw everything. The miners are well treated and I must admit the manager to be an honest man. I have so much to tell you . . . you look well, sir . . . and I am so glad to be home!"

The tall Scotsman smiled. "I can understand that. Alas, I predict that you will be disappointed by the Emperor's request."

"Request? The Emperor?"

"So it would seem." Barnes smiled, passing Ruffin the letter from his friend the Minister of Immigration that had been waiting for Ruffin's return.

Ruffin read it silently and with mounting amazement. Himself? . . . a diplomatic mission? . . . an intermediary? . . . reports of racial violence, gang warfare between Americans and *capolagim*?

"I admit I would prefer not to go," he said finally, thinking that it was the last thing on earth he wanted to do. He had never felt more estranged from his fellow

Americans . . . except Amelia. He had no sympathy for their difficulties in adapting to Brazilian ways. His temper stirred and he felt his pulse race. The recalcitrant colonists in Vila Americana were his natural enemies; they were the people he had fled; they were the people who had left America because they could not face legislated racial freedom, let alone give up their past, let alone deal with the future!

"And I would prefer not to spare you," Barnes said. "But a request from the Emperor . . ."

Amelia's family lives in Vila Americana, Ruffin thought. "Yes," he said.

Four days later he left Rio again, this time sailing south to Santos from where he would take the new railroad straight to Vila Americana. Minister Monteiro had explained everything he knew about the Barroso complaint and Ruffin had been surprised to recognize the name. Could this Barroso be the same man he had met in New Orleans? The possibility gave him an odd feeling that his life was coming full circle.

# Chapter Twenty-seven

When she saw Jesse Rall with Joana, Zaidee thought that her life would end, or at least change completely and forevermore, but it had not.

Something had saved her, or else damned her, at the precise moment of understanding, that clear moment before she was engulfed by humiliation, anger and hatred. At that moment, when she might have burst into Joana's house like one of the Furies, might have slipped forever into active madness, screaming out all her disappointments and betrayals and confronting them, at that moment her murderous impulses had stopped her and she had become cunning.

She became cunning, no less angry, no less humiliated, but sly. She became more withdrawn and more dangerous.

At the time she had turned away from the house and the scene clearly framed in the window and burned forever on her memory. She had stumbled home, half blind, and had seated herself in front of the piano. And in the dark, she had begun to play, softly at first and then louder and faster, pounding the piano keys with some of the high fury that her body needed to express while her brain was busy with its own scales and crescendos, sliding from thoughts of murder—killing him, her, separately, together—to thoughts of escape, leaping from one to the next.

And finally, the sound of her playing brought him into the house. She did not hear him coming until he stood directly behind her and then she did not hear at first but smelled and sensed him.

"What's wrong? Why aren't you sleepin'?" he asked calmly.

"From now on, it's none of your business. I shall do what I like," she said, and she brushed past him, trembling. Without looking back, she went into their bedroom and locked the door.

So he knew that she knew, or at least that she had crossed some barrier into another place of even more severe isolation and unhappiness, but he accepted it, perhaps thinking that it was only temporary, and slept on the floor downstairs.

But Zaidee was too brittle to bend, and too crazed to survive the battering blow to her self-esteem and her pride. In a perverse way, she became fascinated with Joana and stood for hours, sometimes, by day and night, half hidden in the feathery boughs of a huge willow, watching her house, watching her come and go, occupied with her housekeeping chores and gardening. She thought about it all.

How could Jesse have taken up with a nigger woman? It proved he was no better than a beast himself. She saw it clearly with increasing anger: his frequent absences, his concern over the birth of Joana's baby. He protected Joana, he let her live as she wished. He had fathered her child.

It was so humiliating! Tyler had delivered the baby, so he must know. Elinor must know, and all the other women of the American community, and all of their husbands! She was a laughingstock. She writhed, feeling the insult to her sexual reputation, all the more because she hated sex.

How did he dare? She despised him for it, and at the same time she respected him, for he had turned out to be a worthy opponent. He had beaten her at having his own way. He had taken what he wanted. But perhaps his victory was only a temporary one, perhaps she should still triumph in the end.

I shall kill him yet, she vowed—him and her. And because pride was all she had left, she was careful to dress in her best clothes, to arrange her beautiful hair very neatly, and to take care to avoid the sun.

Like a doomed butterfly flying toward a candle, she moved closer to action, plotting how she might do it, how she should destroy everyone who laughed at her, and how she should escape them all.

Tyler and Elinor's second child was born later that spring, a healthy girl christened Maribelle who promised to resemble her mother in every way. Both the Ashbys were delighted with the child; their home life was a safe nest that seemed even more precious as the trouble between the Knights of the Confederacy and the *capoeira* gang increased.

It is all based on a misunderstanding, Tyler Ashby thought as he rode from his farm into his clinic in town, dressed, as always, in a carefully pressed white linen suit with a rosebud pinned to his lapel. We all came here seeking peace, he thought. What went wrong? From the first misunderstanding over the burying ground, the trouble had spread like a grassfire, and Jesse Rall's Knights seemed to thrive on it, as eager for bloodshed as raw recruits.

It has come to the point, Tyler admitted, approaching the dusty town of Vila Americana, that I expect real trouble. He peered down the quiet street toward his clinic, but today the street was empty save for a brood of striped chickens and a sleeping dog. He rode slowly down its length, calling back "*Bom dia!*" to a woman who shook her dustrag out a window.

There are signs of our influence everywhere, Tyler thought, in the bales of cotton from American-owned farms heaped on the station platform, in the new blacksmithy, in the pile of rattlesnake-striped watermelons filling a slat-sided wagon. Soon we will have an American church near the American cemetery and a proper elementary school.

There is much to be proud of. I am only one man,

working alone, but I have treated many patients with success, delivered many healthy babies and improved the health of older children and mothers. I have brought in new medicines from Rio and São Paulo. Of course there is much I do not know, much I have yet to learn, and many people still have more confidence in Basilio than in me . . . including the Barrosos and their priests.

But in time, in good time, we will prevail, Tyler thought. We will be remembered for our plows and picnics when the Knights are forgotten. Or so I hope.

Opening the door to the waiting room of the clinic, he saw a man lying on the floor with an arm swollen to the size of a ten-gallon barrel and as black as coal.

"Take that boot off him," he ordered the man's weeping wife. With one swift motion he rolled up his sleeves and reached into his medicine bag for his scalpel.

When he stepped off the train at the Vila Americana station, Terrill Ruffin had the odd and not altogether pleasant feeling that he had disembarked at a station in the lower South. Perhaps he would not have felt it if he hadn't known the Southern states, but there was a distinctly American flavor about the platform—crowded with bales of cotton being hauled and shifted onto freight cars by burly black porters—the stationhouse—yes, he heard a conversation in English already—and the street he walked along in the bustle of a market-day morning.

The signs: *T. Matthews/Blacksmith* and *Wilson's Market*. The American-style buckboards hitched to the rails in front of the smithy. The surprising sight of a fair young lady with hoopskirts and a leghorn hat with a wide, flopping brim.

He smiled at her and she smiled back. "Pardon me, ma'am, but do you speak English?" he asked her on an impulse.

"Why, yes, I do."

Georgia, Ruffin guessed, or possibly Alabama. "Can you direct me to Dr. Ashby's clinic, ma'am?" he asked.

"Of course I can, sir. Everyone knows Dr. Ashby! Are you a newcomer, sir? Have you bought land yet? Have you a family? Where have you come from? Oh, I'm sorry, I don't mean to seem curious, but we're all friends here, you see. We're quite a community. Well, we have to stick together."

She showed him the building and Ruffin took a seat in Ashby's waiting room next to a tiny, dark-haired Brazilian woman holding a sleeping baby. He looked around. The calendar on the wall was from the First National Bank of Mobile. A copy of Henry Gray's *Anatomy, Descriptive and Surgical*, stood on a small shelf. The windows were curtained in white gauze in the American fashion and he could have sworn that the flowered carpet had come from New Orleans. It gave him a peculiar feeling.

He rose when the door from the inner office opened. So this was Amelia's brother. Ashby was tall and handsome—he could see the resemblance to Amelia—but he looked tired. His white linen suit was immaculate but rumpled, and Ruffin felt immediately that he was a gentle and reasonable man.

Both men hesitated when their eyes met, and then Ruffin took the lead, speaking in English. "Dr. Ashby, I have come on business, but I am not ill. I am sure I can wait until you help this woman."

And when Tyler Ashley emerged from consultation, Ruffin found him sympathetic and concerned.

Ruffin presented his letter of introduction. Ashby explained all that he knew of the situation and agreed to go with Ruffin to talk with the Barrosos as soon as it could be arranged.

# Chapter Twenty-eight

Silently, sullenly, Zaidee lived alone in the hell of jealousy and vindictiveness her marriage had become. She scarcely spoke to her husband and could not bear the sight of Joana. She longed to see Jesse dead, she wanted it more than she had ever wanted anything else. The craving poisoned her and gnawed at her strength.

Elinor, when she came to visit, proudly showing off her baby daughter, was so alarmed by Zaidee's pale, pinched face and haunted eyes that she sent Tyler around to examine her. Tyler suspected Zaidee's sufferings were spiritually induced, but when she complained of sleeplessness and pains in her "inner organs," he gave her chloral in an alcohol solution.

The drafts of chloral enabled Zaidee to sleep, sometimes so soundly that the sun was high overhead before she woke to find Jesse gone and Pedra, the only slave she could bear to have in her house, eating the cold remains of breakfast.

"I want to go to Basilio," Zaidee said with odd urgency one morning when she had finally dressed herself and sat with idle hands watching Pedra pound manioc into flour. Zaidee had dreamed of traveling on a train with Rafael Barroso, and in the dream she had been wearing widow's weeds. She smiled, remembering. I guess that's a prophetic dream, she thought. I guess it's up to me to make it come true.

Pedra looked startled. "What do you want with Basilio?"

"Never mind what. Where is he?"

But Pedra would not tell; she was afraid to tell her mistress more about Basilio or his magic. She knew—everyone knew—that Basilio hated the Americans. She was sorry she had ever tried to amuse her mistress with stories about magic; the mistress had fastened on them like a snake on a frog, and there was enough trouble already.

"I know you are hidin' something, Pedra," Zaidee whined, slapping Pedra's arm. "Damn it, I give up on you!"

Pedra watched her mistress go into the house. She understood the depths of Zaidee's sufferings better than anyone else. Miss Zaidee was clever, as the mad often are; sometimes she seemed to know more than she was told. Did she know there would be a bonfire and ceremony tonight? Was that why she was asking? How could she know? Pedra puzzled over it. At any rate, she planned to go. Nothing could stop her from going; she would set out as soon as she had finished her work.

Zaidee was on edge all day; Jesse had taken some cotton to Coley Burgess's gin and did not return for supper. After eating, she dismissed Pedra and sat alone, looking at an old copy of the *New York World* in the fading light.

The ear-splitting cry of a jaguar startled her, and

she jumped to her feet. The jaguar was not far away. How did Jesse Rall dare leave her alone in this isolated farm on the edge of the forest? Outrage stiffened her courage and she ran to the door to look out. In the purplish twilight, she saw Pedra crossing the back pasture toward the river path.

She is going to Basilio, Zaidee guessed. I knew she was hiding something! I am sure she is going to Basilio!

Impulsively, Zaidee threw down the newspaper and ran out the door. It had been close and airless in the small house, but as soon as she felt the fresh air, she felt exhilarated and her ears were filled with the haunting cries of nightbirds and a million insects. The sun had just set, as it does in the tropics, early and suddenly, and the greenness of the forest, always encroaching on the cultivated land, gulped at the last of the light.

Purpose gave her courage as she ran along the river path, following Pedra. When she caught sight of her she followed with all the speed she could manage, lurching, sometimes stumbling over roots and rocks, her heart thundering in her ears.

She saw the lights of the bonfire as soon as she heard the drums. At once it was clear that something special was happening. The fire was massive and red-orange in the blackness. There was a crowd of forty or fifty men and women around it and more of them coming into the clearing from every direction, slipping out of the shadows, their voices buzzing and keening, rising like the wind.

At the sight of Zaidee, the white-skinned intruder, her dress disheveled, her glittering copper-gold hair in a wild tangle over her shoulders and back, some of the Negroes pulled back in fright.

None of them were as frightened and surprised as

Zaidee. She had never expected this! The strange dark faces terrified her. Where was Pedra?

In the first split-second she could only stare without understanding. Her eyes took in the half-naked dancers, the fire and rising white smoke, found the figure in the center of the crowd—it was Basilio—sitting cross-legged on a red mat. She heard the drums beating faster and faster, heard the unintelligible chanting rising higher. She inhaled smoke and *pinga* and incense.

And still they came, emerging from the darkness at the fringes of the clearing as the bonfire leaped and crackled and sparks shot upward toward the dark-blue sky now faintly studded with stars. They were fierce, foreign, barefoot. Some of them had manes of twisted hair and others had wound bands of yellow cloth around their throats.

Zaidee went cold with fear. She stumbled but she could not fall, there were so many bodies pressing in on her, carrying her along toward the fire. Brown hands pushed and jostled her, slapped and pinched her. She felt her breath snag somewhere deep in her lungs, too deep to catch, and her mind scrambled, threatened by an airless panic as the crowd pressed in on her like a man-headed monster.

"Pedra! Help!" she gasped, even as she was carried into the dance with a group of women, swaying and stepping in time with the drums and the darkness and heat. Most of the dancers were wide-eyed and drunk, either from drink or from the smoke, and they were separating into two masses, the men facing the women.

Across the fire, the men were stamping and howling and moving their bare legs and thighs in the rhythm of sex. All around her the women mimicked their dance and Zaidee was locked in with them, forced into step and soon breathing so hard that she was grateful when the gourd was passed to her.

The gourd held a thin, sweetish liquor that burned her throat. Heat raced through her veins and leapt to the surface of her skin. Her ears buzzed and her vision blurred. She was hot, so hot that she lifted her long skirts and when she felt hands pulling at her dress she let it fall aside and continued dancing in her camisole and petticoat.

And then the progress of the dance thrust her directly in front of Basilio. He stood apart, swaying on his red mat. Zaidee had one clear glimpse of him before he seized her—she saw a skeletal black body, a face painted with white, mad, reddened eyes, a wide full-lipped scowl, a mane of kinky hair—and then she was locked in his grasp, feeling herself pressed to his chest and loins as he thrust himself at her, roughly, terribly, in time with the beating drums, a crazed white bird in the grip of a dragon.

Zaidee thought she was dead, or wished she were. It was unbearable. His mouth touched hers! His body touched hers! The smell of him filled her nostrils; her head snapped back and a prayer for death exploded in her head. She was answered with blackness—dragged into a state throbbing and incomprehensible, intolerable and real.

Fierce with terror, she squirmed and beat at him, she screamed insanely and somehow . . . after how long? . . . she broke free and took flight, again birdlike, flying from his grasp and those dark hands that caught at her as she wriggled through them and beat her way out of the crowd.

Revulsion, shame and rage battled to dominate Zaidee's state of mind as she made her way home along the river path. She had never imagined such horrors existed or that she could endure them. She was exhausted; each step was an agony to her muscles and the way seemed twice as long coming back. She wanted nothing but to be safely alone at home, to collapse in her bed and cry forever.

It had been a nightmare. Basilio had touched her, toyed with her, defiled her hideously. He was a savage! She retched, remembering his painful grip, his rank odor, the white grimace of his mouth on hers.

Sobbing weakly, she dragged herself across the barnyard and into her house. At first she did not realize that she was not alone.

Jesse sat in the dim kitchen drinking with his friends. One, two . . . she could not see how many. Damn those Knights. Oh, how she wanted to be alone! Jesse jumped up when he saw her. He was so tall, so massive she jerked in fear.

"Zaidee! Good Christ! What's happened?"

She barely recognized him. Jesse? Yes, with all his terrible friends. It was Jesse. She clutched at her ripped camisole, covering her breasts with her hands. She could not speak.

"Cover yourself, for Christ's sake! Where have you been?" he demanded, reaching out to catch her, but she could not bear any man's hands. They were all alike. Her eyes were swimming. She struggled away from him, shamed again.

"Who did this to you?"

The familiar brusqueness of his voice rekindled her anger. You, you did it, she thought obsessively, you and Rafael and all men! You and all the men like you who don't respect me and take care of me. Her strength was gone, and with it her sense. I wish he were dead, she thought—I wish they were all dead. If it had not been for them she would not have gone to Basilio, she would not be here, she would not have suffered any of it.

"Tell me who did this to you. Tell me. Tell me who it was," he ordered. He seized her, held her at arm's length, shaking her like a kitten caught in the buttery, holding her out for all the others to see.

She could not admit that she had gone to Basilio, and she would not. She'd get rid of them—another way.

Her eyes narrowed. He had no right. He had lost his rights. She would stop him. She would get rid of them all. "A black man . . ." she hissed. "Yes, a very dark man . . . you know him. . . ."

The silence was explosive.

"Who?"

"He carried me off . . . I hate him! . . . he abused me!" Her voice grew stronger in the lie.

"Who was it, Zaidee? Goddamn it, I'll kill him!"

She whispered, "Rafael . . . Barroso."

If Jesse Rall had any doubts that Zaidee was telling the truth, he could not reveal them in front of the other men. All the Knights were there, hanging back in the shadows, aghast and embarrassed, then angry.

"Goddamn, Jesse, let's go git 'im!" Kinch McCall exploded.

"They've always bin after our women," Ernest Gregg said.

"You better git her to bed," Coley Burgess said.

"Are you hurt, Miss Zaidee? Can you stay alone?" Ernest Gregg asked. Zaidee ignored him. She could not look at him or any of them. She seized a crocheted shawl to cover herself. Her arms were scratched and bruised.

"Are you sure it was Barroso?" Jesse Rall asked. He

was the only one to ask, following Zaidee into the bedroom.

Zaidee gave him a sidelong glance of pure hate. "What do you mean?" she asked. "Don't you believe me?"

"Do you want someone to stay with you?" Rall asked.

"No," Zaidee said, with the first terrible intimation of the consequences. "I want you to leave me alone."

Rall turned at the door. "What did he do to you?" he asked.

"What do you think?" she said. "What do you think he did?" Her face was taut and pale. "Get out of here!" When he was gone she threw herself face down on the bed.

Rall went back out to the kitchen. The other men had already left and the bottle of *pinga* standing on the table had two inches of liquor left in it. Rall drained it, thinking . . . Rafael Barroso was the son of the richest and most powerful man in town and had what amounted to a private army to defend him. The Barrosos were proud and rich. . . . Probably Barroso had been after Zaidee for a long time. He was an arrogant bastard . . . thought he was better than others. Well, he was wrong. He was wrong if he thought he could mess with an American woman.

Rall stood alone in the darkness, still wishing it had never happened. He could hear the other Knights moving around outside, hear their horses snorting and stamping. We'll ride straight to the Barroso fazenda, he decided. In the dark we'll have a fair chance. The boys'll help me and I'll call out the bastard. I have to. I'll kill him. I have to.

Still, he had a sense of doom that was like the

feeling of riding into battle at Shiloh Churchyard on the second day.

The sense of déjà vu that had possessed Terrill Ruffin when he first arrived in Vila Americana had strengthened during the day.

Ashby had closed up his clinic and the two men were riding together in Ashby's small carriage, on their way to meet the Barrosos with Juliano Monteiro's letter of introduction in hand. Their departure had been postponed by the arrival of a man whose foot had been run over by a wagon; Ruffin had watched Tyler Ashby set the bones and was more convinced than before that Amelia's brother was a fine doctor.

"The Barrosos' property begins here," Ashby said as they crossed a little creek and passed the Brazilian cemetery.

Ruffin looked around. He could smell sugar in the air and was reminded of the big sugar plantations near New Orleans. The sight of the rambling manor house and the speechless black serving girl who ran to announce them did nothing to dispel the impression.

"I have been here only once before," Tyler Ashby admitted. He remembered the day well; on that occasion he had anticipated forming a friendship with his neighbors; how differently it had worked out. He could not recall the day the Barrosos had confronted him on horseback, without shuddering. Since then, every time he had seen Rafael Barroso in town, the man had cut him completely. Nonetheless, he thought, I shall be able to introduce Ruffin to Rafael Barroso and his father.

But when Rafael Barroso appeared at the door and

saw Ashby and Ruffin standing there, it was Ruffin he recognized, much to Ashby's amazement.

"Saints preserve us!" Barroso exclaimed, "I cannot believe my eyes! Is it you, monsieur? I cannot believe it! So we meet again!"

"So we meet again," Ruffin repeated, as Barroso wrapped him in the embrace he had come to expect from Brazilian men.

"It is incredible!" Barroso exclaimed again. "But I was right, was I not? You have done very well in Brazil, eh? You have come with the best of credentials, eh? Come to mediate among the hot-tempered provincials, eh?" He laughed and Ruffin laughed, too. After a time and a volley of jokes in French and Portuguese, they remembered Tyler Ashby.

"We have met before," Ruffin explained. "We met in New Orleans when Senhor Barroso was serving his government in the foreign service, you might say. I recognized his name, of course, but I did not dare to believe that I would meet the same Barroso here."

"Here!" Rafael laughed. "This is my home. A far different place from the city of New Orleans, eh?"

"I prefer Rio de Janeiro," Ruffin said.

"Ah, Rio is the most beautiful city in the world," Barroso agreed. "But I must stay here with my father... for the present time. He is not well, senhores, and I convey his apologies that he cannot come to meet you."

"Barroso is responsible for my comin' to Brazil," Ruffin explained, and again the two of them laughed like conspirators.

I have never seen Brazilians in such high spirits, Tyler Ashby thought, feeling that he was being introduced to something quite new as he followed Ruffin and

Barroso out to the shaded terrace on the west side of the house. There, in cushioned chairs and hammocks shaded by grapevines trained over trellises, the three men passed the twilight hours, drinking coffee and then cashew wine, returning there after a very late, Brazilian-style dinner to drink more coffee and some aged French brandy the likes of which Ashby had not tasted in years.

"It is good to talk to you, very good," Rafael Barroso admitted to Ashby, when so much had been drunk and discussed that they seemed good friends, friends whose differences could always be resolved reasonably. "You understand what an outlaw this man Rall seems to us. A savage! And you see how we cannot violate the traditions of the church."

Rall, Ruffin wondered. Could it be the same Rall? He was tired and pleasantly drunk. It did not seem likely. Barroso and Ashby were getting on so well he had relaxed and was only half listening. He heard a nightingale and thought of Amelia. Soon he would be back in Rio with her. He had resolved to ask her to marry him. In this atmosphere of peace and well-being he felt confident that she would say yes.

"I do not condone Rall's activities," Ashby said fervently. "Not all the Americans are in favor of the Knights! But what do you think of the witch-doctor Basilio?"

"The people have their customs," Barroso said. "They are simple people close to the seasons and the soil. They have their old beliefs. We maintain order by allowing them their old gods and old traditions. It is not the same way you are used to, but it is the Brazilian way."

"Perhaps the passions the old gods stir might become too volatile to contain," Ashby suggested.

"We have passions to match," Barroso said, snapping his fingers for a serving girl to bring more brandy. "We Brazilians are a passionate people." It was dark and none of the men was aware how late it had become, but the brilliant night sky was studded with stars and the moon was full. There was the faint light of cookfires in the slave quarters behind the big house, and then all of a sudden there was a rattle of gunshots from the same direction and the sound of horses approaching at a great speed.

"What is it? What is wrong?" Ruffin demanded, brought to the present with a start, immediately alerted to trouble. "Where are your guards?"

"Most are away tonight," Barroso said. He looked slightly embarrassed. "There's a religious ceremony. But who is it?"

There was a scream from the front of the house, and another gunshot. And then it all happened so fast.

"Stand back!" Ruffin warned. He heard the riders coming—incredibly—crashing straight through the house, heard horses' hooves in the tiled corridors and the open courtyard.

Tyler Ashby was speechless. He jumped to his feet and stood beside Rafael Barroso as Jesse Rall and six of his friends rode out onto the terrace.

"Goddamn it, Rall! What are you doin' here?" he yelled.

Rall looked wild and scared. The Barrosos' slaves were approaching from every direction. "Keep them back," he called to his men, "and cover me while I get him."

Kinch McCall fired into the air and Coley Burgess put a bullet through the throat of a fat mulatto woman who had run out from the kitchen, waving her red petticoat. "The rest of you niggers stand back!" he shouted, barely heard above the women's screams.

Jesse Rall, looming over Rafael Barroso from his saddle, backed him off to a corner of the terrace.

"I know what you did to my wife," he said, "and I'm gone kill you for it."

"You are mistaken or you are insane," Barroso said.

"Stop, Jesse! Stop!" Tyler Ashby begged.

"You're the worst coward I ever heard of," Ernest Gregg said. He smashed an oil lamp with his pistol and the flames ran out along the spilled oil.

Ruffin stared at Jesse Rall with disbelief changing to a wild excitement. He had vowed that he would never forget his face and he had not. Rall had changed; he was fatter and his beard had grown so that it covered his cheeks but the sight of his face quickened rage and pain that he had thought dead.

Inspired by a keen and razor-sharp impulse of hate, he seized the half-empty bottle of brandy and jumped onto Rall's horse, landing just behind the saddle like an Indian, spooking the horse and startling Rall so that he fell forward and Ruffin was able to grab the bridle and head the horse away from the terrace.

Ruffin kicked with all his strength, kicked desperately as he clung to the horse with his knees and ducked the bullet Kinch McCall aimed at him. Rall's horse sidestepped and danced and bucked until there were some twenty feet of darkness between the terrace and the two riders. Rall's gun fell to the ground.

Ruffin wound the reins around Rall's arms and chest and pulled his head back so that they were facing each other.

Alone, the sounds of scuffling on the terrace seemed far away.

"Do you remember me?" Ruffin demanded in a low, fierce voice.

Rall struggled. Ruffin splashed brandy in his face. "Remember me," he commanded, "for just one minute before I kill you—for what you did to my wife."

"Who are you?" Rall gasped.

"Terrill Ruffin! Ruffin! Ruffin!"

Rall's eyes bugged with fear and pain and perhaps recognition as, in the space of a few seconds, the horse bucked again, Ruffin smashed the brandy bottle on the stirrup and slashed at Rall's neck as he pitched off. When Ruffin looked down, Rall's body was dragging at the end of the reins and his head lay in a pool of dark blood like the yoke of a monster's grotesque egg.

# Chapter Twenty-nine

"You were mistaken, you must have been mistaken," Elinor said to her sister.

Zaidee lay in bed and Elinor had come to Zaidee's house to take care of her newly widowed sister. Zaidee did not answer at first. Her arms were bruised and lay limply across the embroidered counterpane. She stared at the blue and purple butterflies her mother had worked into the ribbed cotton but she would not lift her eyes to meet Elinor's.

The remains of Jesse Rall's body had been quietly buried in the American cemetery. Kinch McCall had been locked in jail for murdering Barroso's cook. Pedra had run off, it seemed, and so had Joana.

"Zaidee, it could not have been Rafael Barroso, for Tyler was with him all evenin'," Elinor said persistently.

Zaidee sniffed. Her nose was bruised and a bruise under her eye had swollen so that she could not open it. "Water," she said, finally, "I want to drink, Elinor."

Elinor held the cup while Zaidee struggled to a sitting position. She was angry at Zaidee, and confused. How much was she to blame for what had happened? It was inconceivable to her that Zaidee would have deliberately sent her husband after the wrong man, yet that was what seemed to be true. Either she had been mistaken or she had lied. Elinor was increasingly sure she had lied. She felt uneasy and out of her depth with Zaidee, sensing that she was very disturbed and not sure how to deal with her. How long ago it seemed that they had been little girls together. How Zaidee had changed, if that was what had happened.

"I know you are very sad about Jesse, dear," Elinor said gently. "I know you are terribly shocked."

"I am glad," Zaidee said. Her eyes were cold and alert. She lay back on the pillows Elinor had arranged for her.

"You don't know what you're sayin'," Elinor said in a quavering voice.

"I do know. I hated him."

"Oh, Zaidee!"

"I hated him, Elinor. He insulted me. He made me a laughingstock. He kept that nigger woman and he cared more for her than for me!"

Elinor recoiled at the anger and madness in Zaidee's voice. "I am sure he did not," she said as soothingly as she could manage.

"What do you know of it? You have avoided him—and me—as much as you could. I could not bear it, Elinor. You have no idea what it was like—marriage to him!"

I am sure I don't, Elinor thought miserably. Her own husband, with his kindness, his honest gentility and his brooding charm, was as different from Rall as rain from gunpowder. Perhaps she should have prevented Zaidee's marriage. She alone had known of his history in Texas. Perhaps it was partly her fault.

"Poor Zaidee!" she sighed. "But what can be done now, dear? He is dead. What can I do to comfort you? What would make you happy?"

"There's only one thing I want," Zaidee said.

"What is it?"

"I want to go home to America."

"Why, Zaidee, I expect you could." Elinor tried to suppress the idea that it would be, after all, a relief to be free of worry over Zaidee. "If that is what you really want."

"It is. That's all I want," Zaidee said.

It was raining when Ruffin returned to Rio. The rain had been falling for two weeks, a dense drizzle alternating with violent thunderstorms and downpours that swelled leaves and smashed flowers to the earth in a fragrant pulp. The weather's frenzied intensity seemed fitting. Ruffin's state of mind had been equally stormy.

Ruffin had stayed on at the Barrosos' fazenda for more than a week after the Knights' attack, painful days of mourning, of coming to terms with what had happened, what his own part in it had been, of who he really was and what the explosion of violence had meant. His personal vendetta was settled; he had sought

Rall and found him; he had seized the opportunity and killed him. He had repaid one act of violence with another—and found himself honored for it. To the witnesses, he had killed Rall in self-defense, to save the life of Rafael Barroso and perhaps others; only he knew that he had done it for himself and for Marie-Anne.

"You saved my life. You are my brother," Rafael Barroso had said to him. "As far as I am concerned, this Rall was a common murderer."

But Ruffin had been humbled by his own act. No life was common. He had cut off a human life, a life quickened by God, in a moment of vengeful wrath. The horror of the moment would haunt him forever—along with those other moments of horror he had come so far to escape. He could not feel sorry that Rall was dead, and he did not, but he felt sorry that he had killed, and the relief at having ended his quest for revenge only partly soothed that regret. He knew now that revenge changed little and could not in itself bring relief from pain. In the end, only forgetting could do that.

"God's will be done," he had whispered in the minutes that had followed the act. "His will be done on earth as it is in Heaven." Rall lay dead, the earth soaked with his blood. Rall's horse had danced in the darkness, Ruffin astride him choked and silenced by the easy enormity of death . . . and life . . . and then he had gone back into the fray, back to the terrace where Barroso's men had gotten hold of Kinch McCall.

During the week that followed, the week when Ruffin acted the role of mediator he had been sent to Vila Americana to perform, he had focused his strength on defending Kinch McCall from the same swift punishment he had given Jesse Rall. The Brazilians had wanted to lynch McCall on the spot. He had killed

Barroso's favorite cook, an old and well-loved servant. He had tried to kill Rafael Barroso and had shot at Ruffin, too.

"He must be tried. The chain of unlawful executions must be broken," Ruffin had argued with Rafael Barroso.

"Violence breeds violence," Barroso said.

"It can also extinguish it, like the consuming explosion of two fires," Ruffin had insisted. "With your support, Barroso, we can have the wretch sent to Rio for trial." Privately, Ruffin worried and wondered if there was something about the American character that ignited trouble even when exported three thousand miles. Finally Barroso had pledged his support to Ruffin and peace had been made.

And now Ruffin hoped to make another peace, one more important to his future. He shook rain off his oilcloth coat as he mounted the steps to Amelia Scott's door, took a deep breath of the dense, humid air scented with the blossoms of the climbing orchid that hung down over the pilasters, and knocked.

His hand was shaking. During the past two weeks he had weathered such storms, such tempests of will and passion, that he felt changed forever. Rall was dead, and with him had died, absolutely, a part of the past, but it had taken with it part of his own soul. Newborn, he faced his future, a future he hoped would center on a life with Amelia.

But only if she would have him as he really was. He knew that he must tell her his story, tell her the truth, and he was deathly afraid it would make her cease to love him.

"Miss Amelia?" he said to the servant who opened

the door. His body felt weightless, as if it had been drained of all blood.

"*Bom tardes,* senhor! *Sim, sim.*"

He followed the servant into the sitting room where he had first taken tea with Amelia, and there she was—as beautiful, her tall, willowy figure draped in white, her wide, green eyes shining with love and welcome.

"Darling one!" she whispered, taking him into her arms, but he stiffened, pulling away.

"Amelia, I must tell you the truth about myself."

"Why do you look so grim?"

"I have misrepresented . . . my lineage."

She pulled at his hands. "Your hands are cold, Terrill! I don't give a fig for your lineage, I assure you."

"But you don't understand. This is important, Amelia. I must be honest with you. The fact is . . . the fact is . . . my mother was a Negro. I am of mixed blood, Amelia."

Ruffin paused. So much of his strength had gone into the telling that he felt dizzy. He felt her arms go out to him.

"Darling, don't you think I always knew? I don't care, Terrill, believe me, who your parents were. The past is dead. Brazil is a new land and you are the man I love."

She waited. He filled his lungs with air and the courage to go on. "And I love you. With all my heart, darling. I love you and I want to marry you."

"You shall have your way," she said and began to kiss him.

In the first light of dawn, a brand-new steam-powered ocean liner slipped out of the wide blue bay of

Guanabara. The boat's whistle was a lament, a hollow cry that pierced the fading pink and purple haze that hung over the harbor and the city. A slim crescent moon dangled over the hump of Corcovado, pointing northeast.

Darius Yates stood alone at the ship's railing, looking back over Rio. He found the city beautiful but forbidding. He was glad to see the rooflines shrink in the distance; no city could please him; he longed for a sanctuary framed by nature, a green and silent retreat.

Out of Yates's sight, on the windowed observation platform built above the paddlewheel, Zaidee Rall also watched the city's green mountains and curving shoreline fade past recognition. She shivered. The morning was cool and the air thick with moisture. She had been ill constantly throughout the journey from Vila Americana, and yet she feared that she had gained weight.

Below decks, the ship's big engines rumbled. Their vibrations hummed through the wooden decks and the iron railing shook in Darius Yates's hands. A seagull swooped low over his head and he heard a woman crying in Portuguese, "*Até a vista, até a vista,*" farewell, farewell, although she could not possibly be heard ashore.

"Goodbye to Brazil," Yates said, smiling as he turned away from the railing. The salt air had quickened his appetite, and he was in the mood for a good breakfast. He set off for the dining room below.

Tea, Zaidee thought, perhaps I could stomach some tea. She was tired to death of thick, powerful Brazilian coffee. How wonderful it would be never to face it again, never to see her sister Elinor again, never again to work like a slave on an isolated farm, never again be forced to speak Portuguese. She smiled despite her malaise and lifted the full skirt of her new traveling dress to navigate the slippery iron stairs.

The large dining room below was crowded with passengers taking breakfast and the air was blue with the smoke of dozens of Brazilian cigars. Both Zaidee and Darius Yates coughed, entering the room from opposite ends, and both headed for a small table set under an open window.

There they met.

Yates spoke first. "Can it be possible, ma'am? If I am not mistaken . . . don't we know each other?"

Zaidee stared. He looked familiar. By his accent he was an American gentleman, yet there was something odd about him. She studied his face and suddenly realized that it was Darius Yates.

"How very surprising!"

"So it is you, Miss Richler!"

I don't believe I shall tell him I've been married, Zaidee decided.

"Yes, it is me," she said. "Dear Lord, let us sit down to marvel at this coincidence, I beg of you. I feel quite unwell this morning."

"No doubt it's the vibrations of the motor, Miss Richler. Here, let me help you."

Settled in her armchair, Zaidee put a napkin to her lips and looked closely at Yates. He was thinner than ever, but he looked stronger. His hair was badly cut, but his ordinary black suit defined a firm, muscular body and all of his gestures had an indefinable and elegant sureness.

"I am so sorry you are . . ." Yates struggled to recall the word gentlemen used to use with ladies. He caught it. ". . . indisposed, Miss Richler."

Zaidee sniffed. "You look well, sir. Not a day older

and yet, you have changed, I can sense that. Five years have passed, sir, more than five years."

It seems three times that long to me, Yates thought. He beckoned to a waiter and ordered himself breakfast and Zaidee a pot of tea.

"Thank you," Zaidee said. "Are you traveling to New York, Mr. Yates? Of course, you must be. I see you, too, have decided to entrust your life to one of the new ships. I'm sure you agree that nothing could be less appealing than the thought of a voyage like the last one we shared."

"Quite so," Yates said. He felt distinctly ill at ease. He had forgotten the conventions appropriate for dealing with a young American lady although in the months that had passed since his return from the jungle he had come to tolerate, if not enjoy, the clamor of civilization. Meeting Miss Richler here unsettled him, as it did her. He smiled, trying to seem kind, even if he felt disassociated.

"Let us speak frankly," Zaidee suggested. She felt too ill and too world-weary to pretend. "I cannot bear to tell you all that has happened to me in the past five years. I . . . we . . . my family has passed through a siege of fire and emerged utterly changed."

"We are all changed," Yates said. "The world we must someday leave is utterly different from the world into which we were born. But isn't that always the case?"

"Perhaps." Zaidee trembled. For the first time in her life she was alone, an unmarried woman of modest means with a good part of her life yet to spend. What shall I do? she wondered, whatever shall I do? She felt poised a footfall away from a precipice of unknown proportion. A wave of nausea swept her and for the first time she allowed herself to frame the thought she had suppressed for two months. Perhaps she was pregnant. Was it possible?

"Our generation has been tested on the largest scale, I believe," Yates said. He smiled. "And see? We have survived bitter days and desperate years."

Some of us have, Zaidee thought. Tears spilled from her eyes and she felt the entire dining room begin to pitch and toss. She leaned over the table and grasped Yates's wrists with a strength that surprised him.

"Take courage, dear Miss Richler," he said. "I respect your wish not to speak of your time in Brazil, but I suspect that you, like me, have been strengthened by it. We must go forward now, honoring what was best in the past and leaving behind those memories which bring only suffering. We sought a new world in Brazil, but we shall find it in America."

Zaidee clung to him. How well spoken he was, how courtly and heroic. An incredible hope came into her mind. Perhaps this man was to be her savior . . . had not Providence brought them together again?

"Please," she whispered, "will you escort me to my cabin, sir? We must speak about this more later."

"Of course," Yates said kindly. "I am at your service, Miss Richler."

## ABOUT THE AUTHOR

CYNTHIA VAN HAZINGA, a native of Hillsboro, New Hampshire, lives there in a 200-year old house, and in New York City with her husband. She graduated from Wellesley College in 1965 and is an avid student of American history, particularly of the Civil War era. She has published four other novels about the American South, and has traveled there, as well as in Brazil and in Europe.